"*Asher's Eye* is the thrilling story of a young man struggling with his faith (and his family) during the Babylonian exile of the Jews. A timeless tale of a boy growing to manhood and coming to terms with the beliefs of his people, the novel offers a historically detailed and believable rendering of ancient Babylonia. Asher is an endearing and inspiring character who will live in the imaginations of his readers long after the novel is finished."

—CAREN J. TOWN
Georgia Southern University

"Dudley weaves an enchanting midrashic narrative of the struggles of life in exile, where longing for home and a sense of divine abandonment are woven into every moment. All who read this novel will be touched by the universal themes of belonging, family, and one's calling in life. Set in the Babylonian exile, *Asher's Eye* has a particular currency, where hope finds its truest form in the midst of fear, violence, and otherness. This is a story for all ages!"

—HEMCHAND GOSSAI
Northern Virginia Community College

"Following the rich Solomonic world portrayed in *Joel and the Egyptian Cat*, David Dudley takes us closer in time and farther afield to the Babylonian Empire and the captives living within it after the fall of Jerusalem. The stirring story told is one of intrigue and desperation, where questions of loyalty, identity, and strange visions confront a young man faced with weighty decisions. A captivating read."

—DANIEL PIOSKE
Georgia Southern University

"Dudley has created a masterpiece of biblical mystery: How does one become a prophet? And what marks a prophet and sets him or her apart from the world? Dudley is a talented storyteller. He not only mines the world of Israel and Babylonia but fashions an allegorical, even magical, answer to the question 'What makes a prophet?' In so doing, he transforms the biblical story into a modern mystery. I recommend this marvelous story."

—RICHARD LISCHER

Author of *Our Hearts Are Restless: The Art of Spiritual Memoir*

Asher's Eye

Asher's Eye

by
DAVID L. DUDLEY

RESOURCE *Publications* • Eugene, Oregon

ASHER'S EYE

Resource Publications
An Imprint of Wipf and Stock Publishers
199 W. 8th Ave., Suite 3
Eugene, OR 97401

www.wipfandstock.com

PAPERBACK ISBN: 978-1-6667-3712-7
HARDCOVER ISBN: 978-1-6667-9622-3
EBOOK ISBN: 978-1-6667-9623-0

VERSION NUMBER 050222

For Dan Pioske
My colleague, my teacher, my friend

Chapter One

Asher hated his life.

He hated the overcrowded, dusty village where he existed.

Hated the Babylonians for forcing his family out of Jerusalem and dragging them here to a strange land.

Hated the soldiers who raped and killed his mother on the way.

Hated how his father never laughed now, no longer promised that one day they would return to Jerusalem and start living again.

Hated his brother, Azarel, for being four years older and free to come and go as he pleased, even spending nights out getting drunk and visiting prostitutes, or so he claimed.

Hated that his older sister, Tirzah, had never learned how to cook a decent meal.

He hated himself, born with one brown eye, like everyone else's, but the right one blue as the sky over Jerusalem. People stared. Pointed. Wondered out loud what sins his parents had committed that YAH had created their son a freak.

Asher the freak.

Most of all, he hated YAH, the god of Israel, who was strong enough to curse him but not powerful enough to defeat Marduk, the high god of Babylon.

Asher wanted to hurt something—or someone. Inflict pain to make up for his own.

This evening, like most, Asher nursed these hatreds as he sat on the cramped rooftop terrace of his family's mud-brick house. Asher's father, Benaiah, was silent, gazing toward the west. Somewhere in the desert, he had buried his wife and his parents. Now he never spoke their names. Asher had learned not to mention them either, ever since he'd complained about his sister's awful cooking and wished that his mother were still alive to prepare lentils and onions the way he liked.

"That's all you can think about, your belly?" Benaiah had snapped. "Your mother—was she just someone to cook your meals and wash your clothes? Did I raise you to be so selfish?"

Asher apologized, but after that he never spoke of the dead unless his father did first. Even then, he would not share how his heart longed to hear his grandmother's funny stories about her girlhood or feel his mother's hand on his forehead, soothing him to sleep when he was sick.

At the far corner of the terrace, Asher's brother and sister were engaged in fierce competition: every evening before dark they played the Game of Twenty Squares as if the fate of kingdoms depended on the outcome. Tirzah usually won, much to Azarel's disgust. She seemed to be winning again now, judging by his complaints and accusations that his sister was a cheat. Tirzah laughed; she remarked that she had no need to cheat when it was so easy to beat him.

Smothering boredom made Asher want to shout, fight, jump off the roof and run somewhere, anywhere. He yearned to be out with friends, but Korah, the closest of them, had been sick a long time with fever and was only now recovering. His father insisted that Asher remain at home so he wouldn't catch it, too. Fever was common in the summers, and many died. No one knew what brought it, but the Babylonians offered countless sacrifices to remove the plague. Marduk must hear their prayers, but for reasons of his own, often chose not to act. Maybe he was punishing his people for not bringing him enough offerings. All gods, Asher decided, were careless and cruel. Some just had more power than others.

Korah's sickness was the excuse Benaiah needed to imprison Asher at home. When he dared complain, the answer was always the same: "Boys your age find ways of getting into trouble. You're a good lad, Asher, but even obedient sons can forget their training when temptation comes along. I don't want you to end up robbed, beaten, or tossed into the canal to drown. You're safer here at home. One day, you'll understand."

Asher did *not* understand. He wasn't a child; he was sixteen, not a "lad," but a young man who'd been working ever since he could remember. Tomorrow, he would start a new job—the first true one of his life. Laboring beside his father and brother didn't count. He despised everything about being a potter. Azarel was right to say a monkey had better skill with clay than Asher did. That comment had led to a brawl and earned him a black eye, but his brother was right. As a potter, Asher was an utter failure.

The Game of Twenty Squares was nearly finished.

"Let me play the winner," Asher asked.

"You mean 'let me play Tirzah!'" Azarel growled. "Be my guest, if you have the stomach for losing to a girl."

"To a woman, you mean," Tirzah corrected. She threw the dice. "And I win!"

Azarel stood up so quickly he nearly upset the game. "As usual," he grumbled. "From now on, find someone else to humiliate."

"I said I'll play," Asher put in.

"No more for me," Tirzah told him. "I'll just enjoy my victory."

"I'm going out," Azarel declared.

That got his father's attention. "Not too late," he said. "And be careful."

Benaiah said that every night. Some nights Azarel obeyed; many others, he didn't.

"Let me go too, Father," Asher begged.

"What did I tell you? Don't ask me to change my mind once I've given you my decision."

"I'm gone," Azarel said. As he went down the stairs, he threw Asher a big smile. Just because he was nineteen, he thought he was master of the neighborhood, free to come and go as he wished. Benaiah didn't approve, but he admitted that Azarel was a man who could do as he pleased—and pay for his mistakes.

Asher's angry thoughts were interrupted by the sound of two people laughing downstairs. The deep, bellowing laughter was that of Asher's uncle, Ezekiel, Benaiah's younger brother. The other, high and light, like the tinkling of bells, was Asher's aunt, Elisheva. The sounds grew louder as they climbed the steps to the terrace. Uncle Ezekiel appeared first. As usual, he was grinning with happiness. His curly black hair was tied back with a piece of scarlet cord, and the neckline of his tunic was embroidered in an intricate pattern—his wife's handiwork.

"Come up, my darling," he called down the steps. He extended his hand, and a slim, pale one grasped it. In a moment, Aunt Elisheva appeared, beaming.

Like all married Israelite women, Elisheva covered her head. But unlike most others, she wore a scarf of brilliant mixed colors: blue for the sky, gold for the morning sun, scarlet for the ripe pomegranate, green for the fronds of the date palm. Elisheva was as lovely as Uncle Ezekiel was handsome; together, they caused people to turn and gaze when they walked through the village hand-in-hand.

"Good evening!" Ezekiel exclaimed. "See what we brought." From behind his back, he produced a water lily blossom. "For my lovely niece," he declared, offering it to Tirzah as if he were presenting a casket of jewels to a princess.

"What about me?" Asher asked.

"Give him his treat," Uncle Ezekiel told Aunt Elisheva. "As if we could forget him!"

"Here," she said, producing a small cluster of dates.

"In honor of my nephew's new job!" Ezekiel exclaimed. He tousled Asher's hair. "Tomorrow you'll learn there's much more to dates than just gobbling them like a Nile crocodile chomping fish!"

Uncle Ezekiel was right: Asher had a job in the largest date palm plantation on the west side of Babylon. He was lucky to get it, for Babylonian boys were almost always hired before Israelites. His uncle, who made friends with everyone he met, knew a manager and had gotten him the place. That was a piece of luck, one fortunate thing in the middle of so much family gloom.

There were enough dates for everyone, and as they enjoyed them, the setting sun shone directly on Babylon. The golden light glinted off the glazed bricks decorating the city's walls. It struck the ziggurat, a mountain of bricks honoring the gods, whose shrine stood at its top. Beyond it rose another tower, its terraces rich with fruit trees and flowering shrubbery. The master builders of Babylon had discovered a way to raise water all the way to the top and let it flow downward, nourishing the gardens at every level. It was said that King Nebuchadrezzar had built the tower to please his queen, who came from a mountainous land far to the north.

Tirzah gazed at the city, too. Asher knew how she dreamed of escaping their village and living where the shops were full of strange and beautiful goods—and having plenty of money to buy whatever she wanted. But because she was a girl, Benaiah, ever the protective father, wouldn't allow her into the city on her own. Tirzah would end up married to one of the boring village boys and be sentenced to a lifetime of never-ending drudgery.

The light faded, and Benaiah announced he was going to bed.

"We'll stay up a little longer," Uncle Ezekiel told them.

"To watch the stars come out," Aunt Elisheva added.

Asher had to smile. "To watch the stars come out" were his aunt and uncle's words for hugging and kissing, their chance to enjoy a bit of privacy. Yes, they had their own room, but the rooms had no doors, and married people, Asher knew, needed time for themselves—alone.

Asher and Tirzah said goodnight, and he was soon on his bed, a mattress stuffed with straw on a wood frame. He had a light blanket, but it was so warm he didn't need it.

Thinking about the next day made him nervous. He wanted to do well so he'd never return to his family's pottery shop, but working in a new place meant another round of stares and whispers--even of people making gestures to ward off the evil eye.

Asher the freak. Sometimes people laughed at him; sometimes they turned away in disgust. Sometimes in pity.

Why couldn't strangers just pretend he was like everyone else?

A scratching sound on the wall behind him disturbed his thoughts. A lizard? Then a mosquito began buzzing in his ear. He swatted at it, but one never managed to kill such a pest. Despite the annoyance, he felt sleep coming over him.

As Asher drifted off, he knew he should pray, as he had been taught.

But to which god?

YAH?

Or Marduk?

Chapter Two

"Asher, wake up." Uncle Ezekiel knuckle-rubbed the top of his head.

Nearby, Azarel sprawled on his mattress. He hadn't undressed, and his hair was a tangle. And—he was snoring.

Ezekiel shook Azarel's shoulder. "On your side," he told him. "We've heard quite enough of your grunting."

Azarel groaned, did as he was told, and pulled his thin blanket over his head. "You'll have to be up soon," Ezekiel warned.

No answer, just muffled animal noises.

"You have fun all night and pay for it the next day," Ezekiel declared. "Get into your clothes," he told Asher. "Your meal is ready."

Ezekiel shook his head at his brother, scrunched under his cover, snoring again. "Does he come home like this a lot?"

"I don't think so," Asher lied.

Ezekiel sighed. "Brotherly loyalty. How much does he pay you to cover for him?"

He began to answer, but his uncle shushed him. "We can talk about it later."

Asher presented himself for the morning meal, the combined effort of his uncle and sister. Elisheva, who should be helping Tirzah—after all, cooking was women's work—was most likely still asleep. Ezekiel doted on her and did all he could to spare her from household chores. Tirzah resented it, and sometimes complained—when he was not around.

Asher picked at his meal-- barley mush, a round of flat bread, and a plum. Tirzah had packed him a jar of millet porridge, more bread, a cucumber, and an apple. He would carry a skin filled with water.

Asher and his uncle said goodbye and made their way to the canal, which separated their village from the walls of Babylon. Fellow Israelites greeted them warmly, for Ezekiel was highly respected as an expert in the laws of YAH and how to interpret them. Back in Jerusalem, people often consulted him for his wise counsel, but since they were brought to Babylon, he often kept to himself and firmly refused to offer his opinions about matters having to do with YAH. He seldom joined the other men for prayers, and some people got to whispering that he'd gone a bit soft in the head. But he was so friendly and kind that everyone loved him.

This morning, Ezekiel was in fine spirits and spoke warmly to all who greeted them. He enjoyed walking by the water, for there one might see cranes searching for frogs, or a rat, or a mottled water snake. Some people swore that crocodiles lurked in the reeds, waiting to devour disobedient children. That's what the old people claimed.

Just then, a reed boat loaded with baskets approached, paddled by two men. Even though they were Babylonians, Ezekiel called out to them, asking them how they were doing this splendid morning. They shouted back and prayed the blessing of Marduk upon Ezekiel and his son.

"So, you're my son," Uncle Ezekiel teased. "That's news to me."

"Me too."

"You do look like me, you lucky fellow. You're well named, Asher ben-Benaiah."

Asher did like his name, which meant "blessed." That's not how he felt this morning, though.

They came to a grove of trees, in front of which stood a shrine to the Babylonian goddess Ishtar. Her statue was fixed atop a pillar so that the goddess's eyes were about the same height as the eyes of the passerby. She was facing forward, an elaborate crown on her head, a many-pointed star behind her, and two lions beneath her feet.

She was completely naked. Asher couldn't help but stare.

He felt his uncle's hand on his shoulder. "Yes, take a good look. The whore-goddess beloved of these foolish Babylonians. She is filthy, and yet . . ."

"What?"

Ezekiel sighed. "Beautiful. Dangerous. Do you understand?"

Asher did. After all, he was sixteen, old enough to be interested in girls, in what marriage meant. "I do," he said quietly.

"Be careful. Temptation is powerful because it wears a beautiful face. It's no mistake that these idolaters present their goddess as young and desirable, rather than old and wrinkled." Ezekiel glanced around the grove. "Is anyone coming?"

"Nobody."

"Then let's worship this prostitute the way she deserves." With that, he walked to the pillar, pulled up his tunic, and urinated.

Asher had to laugh, but he wondered if the goddess would swoop down from the heavens and strike his uncle dead for his blasphemy. But she could do that only if . . .

If she were real.

Nothing happened. Maybe Ishtar wasn't paying attention.

Ezekiel finished. He was grinning. "You want a turn?" he asked.

Asher shook his head.

"You sure? I won't look at you."

"That's not it. I just . . ." He didn't say, "I half-way believe in her and don't want her to get mad and punish me." He was silent.

"I understand," his uncle told him, even though he could not suspect what Asher was thinking. "Come on. We don't want you to be late your first day."

They came to the gate of the plantation. Brick walls taller than the tallest man extended on both sides. Beyond it stood row after row of date palms, bursts of deep green fronds atop rough brown trunks. To the right of the gate stood another shrine, also to Ishtar, again without clothes.

"They worship her as the goddess of fertility," Ezekiel muttered. "They believe that if they honor her, she will ensure a good harvest. Pure nonsense."

Asher wondered why his father would allow him to work in such a hive of idolatry. He had to ask.

"Because you need a job," his uncle reminded him. "If you work for Babylonians, you'll be working for fools who believe their businesses are blessed by their gods. You can't escape it."

"Then maybe I should find a job in our village."

"There aren't any there. You know that."

"It's okay, then, for me to work here?"

"You're old enough to know right from wrong. And strong enough to resist temptation. Just remind yourself that these gods are nothing. If Ishtar were real, would she have put up with a son of Israel relieving himself on her shrine? I could have done worse, and nothing would have happened. Nothing could."

Maybe not . . .

A slave boy standing watch at the gate asked their business. "I am Ezekiel ben-Buzi, and this is my nephew, Asher ben-Benaiah. He starts work here today. I arranged it with your overseer."

The slave boy glanced at Asher, and he grimaced. Asher had had years to get used to that startled expression, but it still hurt.

"You are expected. I will inform him."

On both sides stood flat-roofed brick buildings. A plaza opened before them, and beyond that, the date groves. The plaza was crammed with carts, some loaded with palm fronds, ropes, and machetes. Others bore baskets, shovels, spades, water jars, and bulging sacks. Workers, both free and slave—men, women, girls, boys, even children-- bustled about. It all felt crowded and confusing.

In a moment a man, somewhat older than Ezekiel, came toward them. "How are you?" he asked. "This must be your nephew." He looked closely at Asher, but his face betrayed no surprise.

"Naram-Sin, my friend! This is Asher. Thank you for hiring him."

"I'll show you where you'll be working," Naram-Sin told Asher. "Ezekiel, are you joining us?"

He said no, for he had things to do back in his village. He would come by in the evening, though, and walk home with Asher. "YAH keep you this day," he whispered. "Naram's okay—even if he is a Babylonian!"

Chapter Three

At the far end of the plaza stood another gate, and beyond it, the forest of date palms. This gate was kept not by a slave boy, but by an old woman perched on a chair, wrapped in colored robes and draped in beads.

Naram-Sin approached her and bowed. "Good morning, My Lady. May Ishtar bless you."

"Who's this?" she asked, gesturing toward Asher.

"An Israelite."

"Why is he here?"

"He needs a job, and you told me we could give him a chance."

"Yes, of course. I remember. Come here, you." The woman beckoned to Asher. He didn't like being ordered around, but he stepped forward, keeping his eyes down, postponing for a few seconds, at least, what he guessed was coming next.

"Look at me," the woman commanded. She sat forward and fixed her eyes on his. She didn't look repulsed, but rather--fascinated.

"How are you called?"

"Asher, My Lady."

"Such strange names you people have," she muttered. "Does it have a meaning?"

"In Hebrew, it means 'blessed.'"

"I see. And are you blessed?"

"I think so."

"Why?"

"I have the honor of working for you and will use my wages to help my family." Asher wondered if his words sounded as insincere to her as they did to him.

She nodded. "A pretty speech. Are you telling me the truth?"

"Yes. I do want to be here."

"You look as weak as a lamb. What makes you think you can do a real man's work?"

"My people have always labored hard. I won't let them down."

"Don't worry about 'your people.' *I'm* the one you need to worry about. I'll be paying you."

"Yes, My Lady."

"What happened to your eye?"

How tired Asher was of being asked that question!

"Nothing. I was born this way."

"No one put a curse on your mother while she was carrying you?"

"Not that I know of."

"You weren't born with two normal eyes and then the one turned color?"

"No, My Lady."

"No one put the evil eye on you?"

He was getting tired of her nosiness.

"No."

"Come closer."

He did.

"Look at me."

He obeyed.

"What's your name, again?"

"Asher."

"Are you gifted with second sight?"

"What's that?"

"Do you see things other people don't?"

"I don't understand."

"Evil spirits? Demons? Messengers from the gods?"

"I don't think so."

"Can you—see into the future, tell what's going to happen before it does?"

"No."

She seemed disappointed. "An Israelite with one blue eye," she muttered. "But handsome. Well made. Perhaps . . ."

"We need to go," Naram-Sin told her.

"Yes, of course." She dismissed Asher with a wave of her hand.

"Lady Iltani takes great interest in portents and dreams," the overseer explained. "She consults diviners and those who claim the power of reading the future."

"What does that have to do with me?"

He shrugged. "Something about your eyes."

"I figured that. There's nothing else special about me."

"Maybe there's more to you than meets the eye."

Asher got the joke. "The blue one, you mean?"

"Yes. Do you see well?"

"There's nothing wrong with my eyes!"

"I believe you. Work hard, and in a few minutes, the others will get over their surprise and accept you for what you can do, not how you look."

Asher wished that were true. In his memory were stored times when his eye had caused him trouble—lots of it. Maybe he'd be better off if he were blind in that eye and could wear a patch. At least then he could invent an exciting story about how he lost it, perhaps defending his family against robbers.

Now they stood beneath a canopy of trees whose fronds grew so densely that they kept sunlight from reaching the ground. All was shaded, and the air felt a bit cooler. High above, a boy no older than Asher clung to a tree trunk with one hand while he used the other to pluck dates and let them drop to the ground.

"What's he doing?" Asher asked.

"Thinning the dates. The trees produce so many that if we allow all of them to ripen, none will be as large as we want. He knows which ones to throw away and which ones to leave."

"But that wastes many."

"No, it doesn't. Others come along and pick up the green ones. Then they're ground for animal feed. Nothing is lost."

They came to an open area, in the middle of which grew the largest date palm Asher had ever seen. Before it stood another pillar topped with a carved image--a stern, bearded figure with massively muscled arms, wearing a decorated tunic and long skirt. Two pairs of wings grew from his back, one pointing upward and the other down. In each hand, the god held a weapon, a double trident, with three threatening prongs at either end.

"Marduk," Naram-Sin declared. "The High God of Babylon. The tree is named after him. It's the first one ever planted here."

They soon stopped by a field of trees about twice as tall as Asher. Three huge carts, far too heavy for men to pull, stood at the field's edge. Six oxen huddled in the shade, a watering trough nearby.

Something smelled bad, like a latrine in hot weather. No wonder: the carts were loaded to overflowing with animal dung. Men were shoveling it into wicker baskets large enough to require two to heft them. These they carried in among the trees and dumped them around their bases. Other workers used hoes to dig the droppings into the soil. The work looked exhausting, and the awful smell made Asher's stomach quiver.

"Here's where you'll be working," Naram-Sin informed him. "Be sure to drink a lot of water. Tomorrow, find something to cover your head. At mid-day, you can rest. Eat any dates you find on the ground, but don't pick them from the trees. Those caught doing that are dismissed. You'll work until evening. The foreman will let you know when you can stop. Understand?"

Everything in Asher wanted to shout how unfair it all was. He'd been hoping for work no harder than in the pottery shop, but here he was, facing labor ten times as horrible.

"Will this always be my job?"

"What's wrong? Don't you like it?"

"It's not that, but--"

"You think it's beneath you?"

"No—"

"Then what's the problem?"

"I just thought that--"

"Let me tell you something. Everyone who works here begins by shoveling shit."

Asher startled.

"That word offends you? You'll hear a lot of bad words and dirty stories here. Don't worry; you'll get used to them."

"And it's forever?"

"It doesn't have to be. The harder you work, the quicker you might get chosen for something else. You can advance here, Asher. We have Israelite foremen. What you become is up to you."

That sounded fair enough.

"Do you have any more questions?"

He shook his head.

With that, Naram-Sin grabbed a shovel and showed him where to work. "A foreman will check on you. But don't wait for him. He might have his eye on you even now. Watch what others do, and then try to do better."

Asher put his lunch pouch in the shade and drank from his water skin. He tried to focus on what the overseer had told him about making something of himself.

But there was still a cartload of—shit—standing there, waiting. No one was going to move it for him.

Chapter Four

Asher noticed a fellow his age filling a basket with dung, but its sides kept collapsing, slowing him down. A scarf wrapped around his head kept off the sun; the workers wore similar things. He looked harmless enough, all spindly arms and skinny legs and no sign of a beard. Asher approached him. "Can I work with you?"

The guy looked at him but showed no surprise at what he saw. "Sure. My usual partner didn't show up."

"Your accent sounds like mine. Are you an Israelite?"

"Yes. You?"

"Asher, from Jerusalem. And you?"

"Josiah, from Bethlehem."

"Were you brought here when . . ." Asher stopped. It was bad luck to mention how the Babylonians conquered Jerusalem and forced its leaders here to serve them. Also, it was a stupid question. Would any Israelite *choose* to live in Babylon?

Josiah nodded. "We've been here four years. Your family?"

"The same. Do you stay in the village on the west side of the city?"

"We used to. Now we live on the east side. Come on," Josiah urged. "We can talk while we work."

In a short while, they were filling baskets and handing them off to older and stronger men. Asher was soaked with sweat; his tunic clung to his body, and perspiration ran into his eyes. The effort was too great. He'd collapse and they'd drag him out of the way--another weakling, another failure.

Josiah came to his rescue. "Get some water. I'll find you a hat."

Asher grabbed his waterskin and stood in line at the well. In a moment, Josiah returned with a head-covering of woven palm fronds. It looked odd, but it kept the sun off his face and out of his eyes.

"Thanks. Where'd you get it?"

"One of the girls weaves them every morning, then sells them to people who've forgotten their own headcloths."

"She can make them that quickly?"

"In just a few minutes."

"Are other things for sale?"

Josiah nodded. "Whatever you want: food, scarves, sandals, tunics, palm wine, medicine, amulets, and-- other things."

"You mean sex?"

"Uh huh. Don't be surprised if you're approached—by men as well as women. All the new fellows are, sooner or later. Around here, someone's always trying to sell you something—or buy it from you-- even what they call 'love.'"

Asher didn't know what to say.

"Are you surprised?" Josiah asked. "You look shocked."

"Not shocked," Asher lied. "I just never thought about it."

"You'll get used to it—if you last. Some guys make it for a few days, then they've had it. You'll find out soon enough."

"It's that bad?"

"Let's get back to work," Josiah told him. "The first few days are the worst. I'll help you as much as I can."

"How long have you been doing this?" Asher asked. "Shoveling manure, I mean."

"Ever since I started here. Ten months ago."

"Naram-Sin told me that all workers begin with this job, but they can move on to other things."

Josiah grimaced. "He gives that speech to everyone. I bet he also said that no one would bother you. Tell that to the guys who get picked on!"

"You mean yourself?"

Josiah shrugged. "Sometimes."

"You *can't* be promoted?"

"You can, but there's no guarantee. They put you where they need you. I do my best, but I'm not strong and everyone wants to work somewhere else. Other guys are always chosen over me, so here I am. I'm honest and work hard, so I'm not in danger of losing my job. It's better than nothing."

"What would you be if you could?"

"Back home, I was training to be a priest, but in Babylon, we have more priests than we need. My father told me I had to earn some money. This job stinks"—he paused to let Asher get his joke—"but it's all I could find."

"My grandfather was a priest. He died on the march from Jerusalem."

"Your father?"

"No. He never wanted it, and Grandfather said he asked too many hard questions."

"I don't like questions much. Besides, YAH has already answered the most important ones."

Like why he let us end up here? Asher wanted to ask.

"Do you still want to be a priest?"

"Sure. And one day I will, with YAH's blessing."

"Why not try and find something better than this in the meantime?"

"I think about it, but when is there time? Besides, YAH will free us soon. They say that our king, Jehoiachin—the one they call Jeconiah--and his family enjoy great favor at court. If they promise loyalty to King Nebuchadrezzar, he'll allow us all to go home." He smiled like a child. "That'll be a happy day!"

"Yes," Asher agreed. "Yes, I guess it will. But when is 'soon'? It's been years already."

"It won't be much longer now. Many of the priests say so. The prophet Jeremiah was wicked to write us exiles that letter. He said we should settle down in Babylon, plant gardens, get married, have children. No, Asher! We might have to live here for a short time more, but we must never become Babylonians. If we're faithful to YAH and his laws, he'll find us worthy to go home again."

Josiah's eyes gleamed.

Asher wanted to believe him. But who was right--Jeremiah, or all the priests who kept promising that YAH would overthrow Babylon and free his people, just as he did back in the days when Moses went up against the wicked Pharaoh?

Maybe they were *all* wrong. If YAH had been beaten by Marduk, then YAH had no power left to do anything. Maybe the people of Israel were doomed to stay in Babylon forever.

Or, as Jeremiah wrote, at least for many more years.

* * *

At last, the morning ended.

Asher and Josiah found a place in shade. Josiah gobbled his bread and stew, then announced he was going to nap. All around them, workers were already asleep. "You have to rest," Josiah explained. "If you don't, you won't make it this afternoon." With that, he lay on his side, curled up, pulled his turban over his eyes, and was silent.

Asher doubted *he* could ever sleep like this, surrounded by men and boys breathing loudly, snoring, farting, some murmuring in their dreams. Even in the shade, the heat was terrible; no breezes stirred, and the air was filled with mixed odors of sweating bodies, dung, and rancid food.

So this was the job Uncle Ezekiel had gotten him through his so-called friendship with a Babylonian!

Asher lay in the dust, pitying himself, wishing he were home.

All too soon the horn sounded, and they returned to work. Heat bounced from the iron-hard clay. Overhead, the sky was a dull, dirty gray, the sun hidden behind a haze of dust. There were hours of hard labor ahead, but Asher had made it through the first half of his first day, and he felt satisfied with himself.

He and Josiah continued shoveling manure, but Josiah seemed in no mood to talk. Instead, he began quietly chanting the Pilgrim Songs of Zion. After a while, Josiah seemed unaware of his surroundings. He worked without ceasing, and from time to time, a faraway smile flickered over his face.

Asher glanced at Josiah and wondered if he were wise or stupid. Then he decided: Josiah was free to leave the plantation and find other work. If he decided to stay and survive by daydreaming, that was his choice. Asher vowed he wouldn't make same the same dumb mistake.

At last, as the sun began to hang low in the western sky, the horns sounded. Workmen crowded toward the gates, laughing and chatting, boasting about how much palm wine they would drink, how much food they would eat, and how many women they would bed.

For their part, the women clustered in their own groups, talking about the evening's cooking, wondering how the children at home were doing, complaining about the men's stink and the mountains of washing waiting to be done.

Asher walked with Josiah. They came to the first gate, and there was Lady Iltani, still on her perch, calling out to certain workers, waving, laughing at things people told her, enjoying herself. Asher caught her attention, and when she beckoned him, he went over.

"Good evening, My Lady," he began. "I hope your day has been good."

"It has. How did you like yours?"

"Very well," he lied. "I learned much and am thankful for the chance to earn good money."

"A fine start," she agreed. "Go rest. Tomorrow always comes earlier than we expect. May the gods bless you," she added.

The two young men went on their way.

"Why did you do that?" Josiah asked.

"Naram-Sin introduced me this morning."

"So?"

"It doesn't hurt to be polite."

"She cares nothing for you," Josiah declared.

"And I don't care for her, but my uncle taught me to make friends wherever I can."

"Even with the Babylonians?"

"Especially with them."

"Why?"

"Because they have power."

"And see how they use it!" Josiah sounded bitter.

"You're right, but they can also use that power to help us. After all, they're paying us to work. Without jobs, we'd starve."

"You sound like a Babylonian."

"Thanks a lot."

"I'm not trying to pick a fight. Just think about it before you go getting too friendly with any of them. They can't be trusted."

Asher looked at the palms of his hands, covered with blisters. His back and shoulders ached, and he knew he was sunburned. Whose fault was that? Marduk's?

YAH's?

He didn't know, and maybe it didn't matter. His raw hands and sore back didn't care because the answer didn't change anything. At this moment, they knew only one thing: they hurt.

Chapter Five

At the main gate, vendors were hawking fruit, cheese, flat bread, palm wine. Indecently dressed women lounged about, flirting with potential customers. Asher scanned the crowd, looking for his uncle.

"You sore?" Josiah asked.

"What do you think? Every single muscle, including some I never knew I had."

"I remember that feeling. You'll be all right. I've got bigger muscles now than I did when I started, and that was only a few months ago. Act like you're about to die, and your mother will feel sorry for you and pamper you. It worked for me."

"My mother's dead. She was murdered on the journey from Jerusalem. My grandparent both died, too."

"I'm sorry. Every family's lost someone."

"I know of people who lived through the march and then died once they got here. That's not fair."

"Yes, but even worse, some have gone over to the Babylonian side. They've turned against our laws, our customs, YAH himself. You must know people who've done that."

"My father's mentioned it."

"It will go hard for them when YAH delivers us."

"I suppose so."

Asher spotted his uncle in animated conversation with two men of Babylon. One looked annoyed, the other amused, judging from his grinning face. "Here's my nephew," Ezekiel exclaimed. "Just done with his first day. How was it?"

"Terrible. And dirty. And smelly."

"No kidding! You reek."

"This is Josiah. He lives on the other side of the city."

"Shalom, Josiah."

"And to you, sir."

"Just call me Ezekiel. Everyone does."

"You're Ezekiel the teacher?" Josiah sounded impressed.

"I suppose you could call me that."

"My father and grandfather talk about you sometimes! They remember your words and repeat them to other priests. You're famous!"

"I don't know about that," Ezekiel said modestly.

"I have to go," the grumpy-looking Babylonian broke in. "Be careful of how you talk about our gods, my famous friend. The temple priests don't like blasphemers."

"The temple priests don't like the truth. It threatens their money pouches."

"I warn you—as a friend," the man said. "Think about it." He walked into the crowd and was lost to sight.

"He's right," the other Babylonian said. "You'd best be careful. Would you appreciate hearing us mock *your* god, accusing him of not existing?"

Ezekiel looked thoughtful. "I have no need to defend the God of Israel. He's quite capable of looking after his people and his own honor."

"All evidence to the contrary?"

"Why do I waste my time with you, Nasaar? You don't believe in your gods, but you're very touchy if anyone tells the truth about them."

"I like you, Ezekiel," Nasaar replied. "Otherwise, I wouldn't put up with your nonsense. Still, it's fun to talk. Your ideas are so—how shall I put it?—*unusual*."

Ezekiel beamed, apparently pleased with what he took as a compliment. "Until we run into each other next time, then. Meanwhile, sacrifice to Marduk to atone for not believing in him."

Nasaar chuckled and produced a seed cake from a pocket. "For the young fellows. They look famished." Then he went on his way.

They broke the cake in three pieces and ate as they moved through the crowd.

"Some Babylonians are wise enough not to believe in their own gods," Ezekiel remarked. "Take Nasaar. He makes fun of them but when I tell him about YAH, the one true god, he laughs at me. He wants to know how I can be so sure my god exists and all the others don't."

"He'll find out," Josiah said. "When YAH frees us."

"So you're a believer?" Ezekiel asked.

"Of course! I'm going to be a priest, like my father and grandfather."

"Good for you."

"Asher, why don't you study and become a priest?" Josiah asked.

This was not a question Asher felt like answering. He might say, *Because I don't know if I believe in YAH anymore,* but that would lead to the biggest fight of his life, with his uncle, whom he loved.

Instead, he lied: "YAH hasn't called me to it. He's never called my father, either. The priests say you have to feel YAH speaking to your soul, the way he did to Samuel. If he doesn't, you can't ever be a true priest." Asher hoped that sounded convincing.

"What about you, Josiah?" Ezekiel asked. "Has YAH spoken to your soul?"

"Yes, sir. I mean, yes, Ezekiel. When I was ten. Ever since then, I've known."

"Where do you study?"

"At home, with my father and grandfather, Eliezer and Simeon. They invite others to the house in the evenings, too."

"I've met your grandfather. He's a wise man. I sometimes saw him in the temple."

In a moment, Ezekiel and Josiah were talking about the plight of the Israelites in Babylon and the news from Jerusalem, where the Babylonians had put a man named Zedekiah on the throne of David.

"YAH must favor us highly," Ezekiel declared. "He's given us *two* kings now: Jehoiachin here in Babylon, and Zedekiah back in Jerusalem. What other nation has two kings at the same time?"

Asher could tell he wasn't serious, but Josiah didn't see anything funny in his words. "Which one will be king when we all return home? We don't want to fight among ourselves."

"Perhaps they'll draw lots . . ." Ezekiel was joking when Asher stopped listening.

He was sick to death of conversations like this one: why had YAH allowed the Babylonians to take Jerusalem? Which prophets were speaking the truth—Jeremiah, who predicted a long exile, or the two kings' prophets, who predicted a speedy and happy return to Judah? Always the same boring questions, the same arguments, the same inability to agree on anything except to disagree.

The two men seemed to forget that he, Asher, was walking with them, and he felt annoyed at being ignored. Josiah's excitement irritated him, but Asher grudgingly admired his conviction that YAH was going to prove Jeremiah wrong and free his people, just as he had freed them from Egypt, so many years ago.

What had happened to his own faith in YAH?

He knew the answer: it had died and been buried along with his grandparents and his mother on the endless road between Jerusalem and Babylon.

Chapter Six

At home, they wanted to hear about his day, but Elisheva made Asher wash and change first. When he was presentable, he joined his family in the courtyard, where the women prepared the evening meal. Azarel was missing—gone fishing with friends.

Benaiah knew about Josiah and his family. As priests from Bethlehem, they prided themselves on being descendants of King David's family. He also knew that the family had been torn apart because of what Prophet Jeremiah had written. Some of them agreed with his advice to settle down in Babylon for a long stay, while others looked to YAH to save them immediately.

"That's why you've never met Josiah," Benaiah explained. "After a huge fight, his part of the family left our neighborhood and moved to the other side of the city. They wanted nothing to do with those who've stayed around here—"

"And assimilated," Ezekiel broke in. "They've disgraced themselves. From the start, they were happy to forget Israel. A son of theirs married a Babylonian girl—with his parents' blessing! The girl gave birth to a boy two weeks ago, and word is that the child has not be circumcised."

Elisheva gasped.

"That's according to Joseph, down the street. The boy's father presented himself at the house where his son is living and insisted that his grandson be circumcised. He wasn't even permitted to enter. Turned away--at the door."

"I hadn't heard that," Elisheva said, "but Miriam told me one of the men in that family has become a banker, lending money not only to Babylonians, but to Israelites, too. Lending money at interest!"

"Which Moses strictly forbids in the Book of the Law," Ezekiel added. "It's only a matter of time until these so-called Israelites forget who they are and declare themselves loyal children of Marduk."

"People do what they have to do in order to survive," Benaiah remarked.

"And sell their souls as part of the bargain?" Ezekiel retorted. "That might be all right for some, but not for me. Never for me."

Benaiah looked weary. "We shouldn't be judging our neighbors."

"I don't judge them."

"But that means it's still all right to gossip? You shall not bear false witness, brother."

"This isn't false witness, and we're not in a court of law. This is the truth about Israelites who have abandoned their faith and are living as pagans."

"Many in Jerusalem were doing the same," Benaiah reminded them.

Please don't let them quarrel this evening, Asher thought. *Their fights ruin too many meals.*

Elisheva must have felt the same way. "You men go wash up," she broke in. "I think we've had enough talk for now."

Asher had no appetite. The conversation before the meal had unnerved him. Now he knew what his uncle would think of him if he suspected his doubts about YAH.

"Doesn't your stew taste good?" Elisheva asked him.

"It's delicious," Asher assured her. "I'm just so tired I could fall asleep right now."

"Sleep after you eat," she advised. "You need your strength for tomorrow."

When the meal was done, his father suggested Asher go to bed. It was not even dark yet, but he didn't fight it. His body was exhausted and his thoughts gloomy.

He stared at the ceiling. Why couldn't he have the certain faith that Josiah and his uncle had? And what about his father? He was hard to figure out.

Just a few hours earlier, Asher had decided that Josiah was a fool. If that were true, so was his uncle.

Faithful fools.

Chapter Seven

Asher groaned when Ezekiel roused him next morning. His arms and shoulders ached, and his mouth was dry as dust.

"Lemme be!" he complained, turning his face toward the wall.

"None of that! You made it yesterday, and you'll do better today."

"Yesterday I hadn't already been through a day of torture!"

"Poor Asher! So persecuted."

"Don't joke! I mean it. I'm in no condition to work."

"Shall I have your father come in and persuade you to get up?"

"No! Just let me stretch for a moment."

"Your brother's not here."

"Where is he?"

Ezekiel shrugged. "You tell me. 'Fishing' is what he said. I'll bet that's not the truth. Sleeping off a drunk someplace he shouldn't be, more likely. You've got to the count of ten to have your feet on the floor."

Asher pulled the cover over his head. Maybe this was all a bad dream. It wasn't. Soon, he and his uncle were on their way to the plantation. Ezekiel was unusually quiet. They walked past some other villagers on their way to their work, and he scarcely noticed them. Usually, he greeted everyone, Israelite or Babylonian.

"Are you all right?" Asher asked.

Ezekiel rubbed his eyes. "Everything looks blurry, and my feet aren't steady. Don't worry. I'll feel better in a minute."

They rested, then walked on, but it was obvious he was *not* better. When they came to Ishtar's statue, Ezekiel collapsed against a tree. "I think I'm going to faint, and my eyes have gone funny. Around their edges, everything is pulsing, like I'm looking at the sun through branches. Light breaks through and blinds me. And I have terrible headache."

"Sit down," Asher urged him. "Drink some water. You'll be all right." He tried to sound confident, but Asher was alarmed. He'd never seen his uncle anything but healthy. He *needed* him to be well. The family couldn't take much more . . .

Ezekiel dropped down at the base of the tree, eyes closed, breathing rapidly.

"Shall I get help?" Asher asked.

Ezekiel shook his head. "No. Let me have more water." He drank deeply from the skin bag. Then he fell asleep, instantly. Asher stood by him, uncertain of what to do. Should he speak to the next person who came by, say that his uncle was ill? No one appeared, and Ezekiel slept.

But not long. Soon, he woke, stood up, and said he was all right.

Coming out of the grove, they had an open view of the sky. Although it was early morning, in front of them, to the north, the sky was turning dark. A huge storm seemed to be approaching—fast.

"We should find cover," Asher told his uncle. "Back in the trees."

Ezekiel didn't hear him. He stood fixed like pillar, staring at the sky.

"Uncle!" Asher cried. He tugged on his sleeve. No response. "Come on! It's going to storm hard. Maybe lightning. We have to get somewhere safe."

No answer, no motion.

Now Asher gazed into the darkness. But oddly, at its center, he saw a dazzling radiance, and around its edges, sparks and flashes of lightning. Suddenly, the din of a roaring wind smashed him like a fist to the chest. Asher dropped to his knees and covered his face with his hands, trying to protect himself from some overwhelming, crushing power. He peered through his fingers and saw his uncle knocked off his feet backwards. He crumpled on his side and lay motionless.

He's dead, Asher thought. *And soon, I will be, too.* The roaring continued. Wind whipped around him; flying sand slashed his skin and he felt grit between his teeth. Asher expected the storm to break directly overhead, but there was no rain. Lightning crackled above them, and thunder boomed so loudly it hurt his ears.

Then Asher saw them.

Faces. Faces floating in the air only a few cubits away from him. Faces shining like gold, yet transparent as water.

An ox. A lion. An eagle. A human.

And wheels. Four, or eight, one wheel inside another. Wheels covered with eyes, open eyes that bored into him.

Knew him.

Panicked, Asher fell to his side, drew up his knees, and tucked his head to his chest. He couldn't move; power from the burning light kept pushing him into the earth, as if he were wet clay being mashed onto a potter's wheel by gigantic hands.

The whole city is being destroyed, Asher thought.

There was nothing to do but cower where he was and wait for death.

Later, Asher could not remember how long he lay in the dust, gasping, crying out, wetting himself. Then, it ended. Simply ceased, faster than it had arrived, leaving no trace.

The crushing weight gone, Asher was able to sit up. The storm of darkness and light had disappeared, and the morning was calm and sunny. Or was it still morning? How much time had passed? He glanced at the sun, which had not moved. It hadn't rained. The tearing wind hadn't brought down any tree branches, let alone trees themselves. He felt his face and arms and found no trace of sand. His loincloth, however, was damp with his own urine.

The only thing unusual was the figure of his uncle, still sprawled on the ground as if he'd been struck by an invisible axe.

Asher tried to stand, but his legs wouldn't support him. He crawled to his uncle and rolled him onto his back. He was certainly dead, and Asher could only wonder why he himself was not. But Ezekiel was alive. His eyes were open, and he gasped for breath. Asher choked back a grateful sob, but tears of joy changed to a cry of dismay when he saw his uncle's face.

His right eye had turned blue.

But that was not the most terrifying thing. He recognized his uncle's expression, for he'd seen it on his father's face three times: first, when Benaiah's mother collapsed and perished on the road from Jerusalem. Second, when Benaiah cradled his father, who died just a few days later. Last, as he keened over his dead wife, raped and murdered by drunken Babylonian soldiers.

"Uncle?" Asher whispered. "It's Asher. Please, tell me you can hear me."

Ezekiel looked at him and did not recognize him. He touched Asher's cheek; his arm was shaking.

"Can you get up?"

He tried to move but had no strength. Asher put his arms around him and pulled him to a sitting position. The dreadful expression of boundless grief struck Asher again. Something terrible had happened, something beyond his power to explain.

"Uncle?" Asher asked. "Talk to me. We're all right now. We're alive. Tell me what happened."

But his attention was again seized by his uncle's eyes. "Your right eye's turned blue," he told him gently. "Like mine. Look." He pointed to his own blue eye, then put his finger lightly on his uncle's face. "Blue! They're both blue."

Asher looked around, praying someone would come along to help. "We can't stay here," he explained. He got his feet. At first, he felt woozy, but the sensation passed. He extended both hands, and his uncle took them. Asher pulled him up, and immediately Ezekiel's knees gave way. Asher caught him before he fell. He tried again, and this time the man was steadier.

From somewhere, the sweet smell of burning incense came to Asher's nostrils.

"Let's go home," he urged. "We'll take care of you."

Ezekiel simply stood there.

"Come on," Asher said. He took his uncle's hand in his own, and they started home.

Now they met people, both Israelites and Babylonians. Most people didn't notice them, but others looked puzzled to see a grown man holding the hand of a "lad" who was obviously guiding him. Ezekiel moved slowly, and he kept touching his forehead and his eyes, as if trying to clear his sight.

Here came their neighbor, Joseph, a load of dry sticks on his back. He stopped when he noticed them picking their way along.

"Shalom, Ezekiel, Asher," Joseph greeted.

"Shalom," Asher replied. "My uncle is ill. Something's happened to him. He was walking with me to the date plantation when . . ." He had no words.

"Does he have fever? His eye!"

Asher nodded. "I know. We were walking and we thought a storm was coming up—"

"A storm? The day is perfectly clear."

Asher nodded. "From the north. It got dark, and a strong wind, and a sound—"

"There was no storm," Joseph corrected him. "Look! The sun is shining. Did you dream it?"

"No! At least I don't think so. I fell down and so did my uncle, and when it was over, he was the way you see him now."

Joseph shook his head, trying to make sense of things. "Ezekiel?" he asked. "Can you hear me? It's your neighbor, Joseph. Tell me you know me."

There was no sign of recognition.

"See, he's ill," Asher said. "I have to get him home."

"I'll help," Joseph offered. "You take one side, and I'll take the other. That way, we can catch him if he stumbles."

It took a long time to get home, where Elisheva had been working at her loom. She cried out when she saw her husband. Joseph said he had to be on his way and would look in later. Asher could see the man was relieved to be going.

Asher tried to explain, but once again, he couldn't find words.

"It doesn't matter," Elisheva told him. "Help me get him onto the bed." Then she bathed his face and hands. Ezekiel was awake, but he didn't try to speak, just lay open-eyed and staring while his wife tended him.

"His eye," Elisheva whispered. "How did it happen?"

"I don't know! A storm came over us—darkness, wind, lightning. It flattened us both. I thought he was dead. When he looked at me, his eye had turned color. I don't know how it happened!"

She touched his arm. "A storm? It didn't storm here. Let me," she told him, wiping his face with the wet cloth, which felt cool and comforting against his hot skin. "It's all right. Whatever happened, you're both here now, and I'll take care of you."

She put her arms around him, and Asher let her hold him a moment. Then he went to the pottery shop with the news.

He found his father at his wheel, his hands and forearms brown with wet clay. Azarel was tending the kiln. Tirzah was there, too, painting a pattern on a pitcher soon to be glazed and fired.

Asher told them a bit about what had happened, and they closed the shop and hurried home. There they found Ezekiel deeply asleep, Elisheva beside him, holding his hand.

"He hasn't moved," she told them. Her voice quivered.

Benaiah leaned over his brother and spoke softly. "Ezekiel, it's Benaiah. You're home. You're safe. If you can hear me, speak."

Silence.

"What shall we do?" Elisheva asked.

"I'll get the physician," Azarel volunteered. "Asher, come with me."

Their father looked grateful. "Yes, go. Tell him he must come immediately. Thank you, Azarel, for thinking of it."

The moment they were out of the house, Azarel began an interrogation, demanding that Asher tell him everything. He explained as best he could, but he could see that his brother wasn't satisfied.

"You're not making sense!" Azarel accused. "There was no storm. It's been clear and calm all morning. Tell me the truth!"

"I am! I swear it."

Azarel pushed him against a mudbrick wall. "Confess," he demanded. "You two went to Eliab's place to enjoy one of his potions."

"I don't know what you mean!"

"Don't play innocent with me! Eliab sells his stuff to lots of men. You have a drink, then everything looks different. You see things—nice things, like beautiful women willing to do whatever you want. You're a bull in rut. You think you're free. You're flying."

"We've never done anything like that," Asher protested. "Why make up a lie?"

"Our uncle plays like he's such a virtuous fellow! All his talk about keeping the laws of Moses. I never guessed he was into Eliab's stuff, or that he'd get you hooked, too."

Asher broke away from his brother's grasp. "I've told you what happened! I don't understand it, either. I'm worried, and you should be, too. What if he's sick and can't get better? What if he . . ."

"Dies?" Azarel said. His tone was flat. "All right. I'm sorry. You know I don't want anything like that to happen."

"Okay. Let's get to the physician. He'll know what to do."

The physician poked and prodded, peered into his patient's eyes, checked for broken bones, asked a lot of questions. Then he admitted he was puzzled. There was nothing wrong as far as he could tell. All they could do was wait and watch, praying that Ezekiel would awaken and be his normal self. He offered Elisheva a draught to help her rest, but she refused it. Then he took his leave, promising to return in the evening.

That left the family standing silently around the sleeping man's bed. Asher felt helpless and frightened.

"I want you to tell us everything that happened, from the beginning," his father said. "Then you should go to your work."

"I don't want to go there! I should be here, with you."

"I understand. But the physician says all we can do is wait. When your uncle wakes up, we'll be here. You can't afford to lose your job on the second day."

Then Asher described the darkness, the bright light, the wind, the power.

But he said nothing about faces or the wheels whose rims were covered with all-seeing eyes. If he did, the family would think he was a liar or a madman.

When he'd told everything he was willing to share, he made his way to work, relieved to get out of the house.

Chapter Eight

Lady Iltani was just leaving the plantation when Asher arrived. Her litter stood by her chair, two burly bearers at attention, ready to carry her home.

"You're late!" she cried. "But I'm not surprised. Do you think you can show up when it suits you and find your job waiting for you?"

"I'm sorry, My Lady! I left the house on time. My uncle walked with me. On our way, he became ill. He fell down, unconscious, and I had a hard time waking him. When he came to, he was confused. He didn't recognize me! I had to lead him back to our village."

"That's the truth?"

"Yes."

Her expression softened. "Where is your uncle now?"

"Asleep at home. The physician came, but he couldn't find anything wrong. He said all we can do is wait."

"Who's looking after him? He has a wife?"

"Yes. And my father, sister, and brother."

"Your mother?"

"She died on our journey here. So did my grandparents."

The Lady Iltani looked toward to sky. "That's what happens when your god is weak. What did your people do to make him abandon them?"

"One of our prophets, Jeremiah, says we angered YAH by worshiping idols."

"You mean the gods of Babylon?"

"No. Even before we were brought here. The gods of Canaan. Baal. Ashteroth. Moloch. The gods of Assyria."

"Ah! And *your* family? Which gods do they worship?"

"My family has stayed true to the worship of YAH."

"And this is how he repays you," she scoffed. "Exile, death! No wonder you blame this YAH, or whatever you call him."

He couldn't remember saying he blamed YAH, but he knew it was true.

"I blame Babylon," he whispered. "Your soldiers killed my mother for no reason. I will always hate them." The second the words were out, Asher wished he could call them back, but it was too late. "I'm sorry," he said. "I should not have said that."

"Why not? We might be better off if more people spoke their thoughts. You think I'm an ugly old hag. Tell me the truth!"

"My Lady—"

"And a meddling busybody."

He couldn't speak.

"And cold-hearted."

"Please, I—"

"Don't worry, my young fellow. You're the first person in a long time with courage enough to tell me what he really thinks. You'd be a fool *not* to blame your god--or those soldiers. If Marduk left Babylon to its enemies, I would curse him. The gods might have power, but they owe us their protection in return for our sacrifices. Otherwise, what good are they?"

"My Lady—"

"Stop that! I'm not your lady. I'm your employer. What do you want from me?"

"To go to my work."

"When you should be home with your sick uncle?"

"There's nothing to do except sit there and worry. I'd rather be earning something. My family needs it."

"Such a loyal son of Israel." She felt inside a pouch tied at her waist and came up with a tiny clay figurine—a dog. "Here," she offered. "Dogs are sacred to the goddess Gula, she who guides physicians and heals the sick. Bury this by the door of your house where others won't notice it. Like the dogs of Nimrud, it will guard the threshold and keep sickness and death away."

What should he do? Accept the gift--an image dedicated to a goddess of Babylon? That was idolatry. YAH would not like it. But where was YAH?

He hadn't protected Asher's family, saved his mother from a slashed throat. He was powerless. A nothing.

And Gula? What was she?

He accepted the image.

"May Our Lady Gula heal your uncle," Iltani said. "Let me know what happens. I am sorry for your uncle's sickness."

Asher thanked her and went his way. He turned back once and saw her still looking at him. The woman puzzled him. He feared her, yet he felt grateful for her kind words. And what of the little dog? YAH permitted no idols, but here he was, accepting one as a gift and agreeing to bring it into his father's house.

He knew he should smash it, grind the pieces into dust. But what if the lady asked about it, wanted it returned? He could say that he'd lost it. Or he could do as she suggested. The gods of Babylon were powerful; that much was certain. And his uncle was terribly sick, maybe dying. Wouldn't it be best to do everything possible to help him? If Gula were nothing, then no harm done. Just superstition. But if she were real . . .

He found Josiah where they'd been working the day before. No one was helping him.

"You came back!" Josiah exclaimed. "I'm glad. Now I'll have someone to talk to. Where's your water skin? And your food? And a hat?"

Asher felt foolish. "I forgot them. I was late and hurried to get here."

"Did you oversleep?"

"No. My uncle and I left the house on time, but on the way, something I can't explain happened to us. We both passed out, I think; I don't know for sure. When I came to, he was still unconscious. When he finally woke up, his right eye had turned blue, like mine! I kept talking to him, but he didn't recognize me. I had to lead him home. He's asleep now. The physician came and couldn't find anything wrong. He said all we can do is wait."

"It sounds like he had a stroke."

"The physician said nothing about that."

"What about you? You look awful."

"I'm all right."

"You should be home with your family."

"My father said I needed to come to work. We can't afford for me to lose this job, especially if my uncle doesn't recover."

"You're not telling me everything, Asher."

"How do you know?"

Josiah shrugged. "Not sure. Grab a shovel. While we work, you can talk, if you want."

So Asher told about the black darkness, then the dazzling light, the tearing wind, the crushing power that held him to the spot, unable to move.

But not a word about the terrifying images he had seen: the monstrous faces, the searching eyes.

Josiah listened intently. "Don't you realize what's happened?" he said after a long moment.

"No. What?"

Josiah's eyes gleamed. "It was a vision!"

"What are you talking about?"

"From YAH."

"That's crazy. YAH doesn't do things like that."

"He used to. Moses saw him face to face. He spoke to the prophet Samuel when Samuel was just a child. Elijah heard him—"

"That was all a long time ago! Things are different now."

"Are they? How do you explain your uncle's eye? He's a seer, and I'll bet you are, too."

"No, I'm not. I've never had a vision."

"But YAH showed you *something* this morning. Next time, he might even speak to you!"

"Not if I can help it!"

"You must be someone important to YAH, to bless you the way he did."

"It didn't feel like a blessing. It—scared me."

"I get it. I'd have been afraid, too."

"Can we not discuss this anymore?'

Josiah put his hand of Asher's shoulder. "Of course, brother. We can talk later."

Asher couldn't imagine wanting to do that.

"You two, back to work!" shouted a man coming up the row of date palms. "Jabber on your own time."

They got down to it. Josiah retreated into his own world of murmured prayer and chanted psalms, which suited Asher just fine. The work was just as hot, hard, and smelly as the day before, but he welcomed it. As long as he could focus his attention on the next shovel-full of manure, he could keep from thinking about what had happened to him.

But that proved impossible.

* * *

As they were leaving the plantation that evening, Iltani called to Asher. He told Josiah to go ahead without him, but he said he'd wait.

"You survived your second day," the woman observed. She was holding a cup that Asher guessed held palm wine.

"Yes. I did all right."

"Come closer," she told him. He did, but she held up her hand. "Not too close. I've smelled enough buffalo droppings to last me a lifetime."

Asher smiled, for his sandals were caked with damp manure, and his legs and arms were smeared with it.

She gave him an appraising look.

Asher lowered his eyes. "Yes?"

"How would you like to work for me, in my house?"

Had he heard correctly? "I don't understand."

"I need a houseboy. My last one joined the army. Didn't even ask my permission! Told me he had to do his part to defend our empire, as if there's any power on earth strong enough to challenge us. What about *me*? I need a strong young man to help me at home, not just some silly slave girls. What do you say?"

He liked being called "a strong young man," when only yesterday she'd declared he looked weak as a lamb. "I don't know. What does a houseboy do?"

"Serves me. Brings me food, drink when I want it. Delivers messages. Goes about the city with his eyes and ears open and then comes back and lets me know what he's learned. Tells me the gossip. Amuses me. Whatever I need done—whatever suits my fancy."

"I don't know about any of that. You need a Babylonian for that kind of work."

"I'm sick to death of Babylonians! I want something different. Someone I can talk to. Someone who will speak his mind."

"But I'm just a—"

"An Israelite?"

He shrugged. "I can't deny it."

"A man?"

"If you say so."

"You tell *me*."

His heart was pounding. He wished he escape, but something held him. "A man," he said at last.

The lady nodded. "That's the right answer."

"I have to ask my father."

"Tell him that your wages will be triple what the manure shovelers earn. And you'll have decent clothes and good food. You'd be a fool to refuse me. You know that?"

He did, but he still wasn't sure. Her offer was so unexpected that he couldn't quite grasp it. The whole day had been like that. "I'll talk to my father tonight," he promised.

"If you agree, come dressed tomorrow in your best clothes. Then I'll know your decision. If you decide not to, we won't discuss the matter again."

"I understand."

"Think carefully! Chances like this one don't come around often, certainly not to captives."

Asher found Josiah waiting for him. He explained Iltani's offer, and Josiah laughed. "What so funny?" Asher asked.

"That's she blind enough to make you an offer like that. Can't she see we want nothing to do with people like her?"

"I don't know what she thinks, but the pay's good."

"Asher, you're crazy to think about accepting her. No true Israelite would willingly work in the house of a pagan. YAH's laws warn us against associating with those who aren't children of Abraham."

"We *do*, though. We have to. If you believe what you're saying, why are you working at the plantation? There are shrines and idols everywhere."

"You're right. I shouldn't be here, but my family needs the money."

"So does mine. What if my uncle doesn't wake up? We depend on money he earns doing odd jobs. Does YAH want us starve because we're too proud to work for Babylonians? I don't think so."

"But to go *willingly* into their houses and serve them like slaves?"

"What do you think *you* are? A slave who earns just enough so that no one can call him that. Look at yourself. Look at me! You know something? I'll bet the shit we're shoveling all day isn't just from oxen. It's from pigs, too. And we're supposed to have nothing to do with swine! But here we are. If we're true Israelites, we won't come back to work tomorrow. Better to die of hunger that defile ourselves with pork."

"You're not being fair! YAH understands that sometimes we can't obey all his laws."

"Since when? I'll bet that's not what your family would say. I've heard the story of why you don't talk to half of them. Who decides when it's okay not to keep every law?"

"Our priests. That's their job."

"We have to ask them what to do all the time?"

"Not about everything--"

"I wonder if YAH actually cares about my working in a Babylonian house."

Josiah sighed. "You're going to do it, aren't you? You've already decided."

"I have to ask my father, but he won't care. Since my mother was killed, he doesn't care about anything."

"We won't be seeing each other, then," Josiah told him. "You'll be busy pouring wine for that Babylonian hag while I'll be shoveling manure. You won't want anything to do with me."

"That's not true! I'll still be myself."

"I hope so."

"Don't you trust me?"

"I don't know you that well. I guess I'll find out."

Josiah's cautiousness was irritating. Would he, Asher, have to prove himself somehow before Josiah would be a true friend?

You'd probably run the other way if you knew my doubts about YAH, Asher told himself. *For now, I'll play along. If it doesn't work out between us, no big loss.*

Chapter Nine

The house was quiet. Uncle Ezekiel lay on his bed, Aunt Elisheva at his side. Benaiah stood nearby, looking at nothing.

Ezekiel's eyes were open, one brown, the other—still blue.

"How is he?" Asher asked. He shivered, even though the room was warm.

"The same," his aunt whispered. "I've gotten him to swallow some water."

"Where are Azarel and Tirzah?"

"At the shop," Benaiah said. "There was no reason for them to waste a day here when they could be working. They'll be home soon."

"What should we do?" Asher asked.

"Wait and pray," Elisheva replied. "And take care of him."

"How was your work?" Benaiah asked.

"The same as yesterday."

"I can smell you. Wash up, and then fetch some water."

Tirzah arrived just as Asher was going to the well. She said Azarel would be along later; he was meeting friends for a cup of palm wine.

"That good-for-nothing," his father complained. "No telling when he'll be back, probably drunk."

When Asher returned, the physician was there. He examined Ezekiel again, declared himself satisfied that he would wake up soon, and not to worry.

Elisheva smiled and thanked him. Then she announced she was going to prepare the evening meal; Tirzah went to help her. Before long, the smell of a cookfire and a vegetable stew filled the house.

Asher joined his father, keeping watch near Ezekiel's side. He wanted to share what Josiah claimed: YAH had sent a vision, but he hesitated. There was no telling how Benaiah would react to such a crazy idea. Instead, Asher mentioned how the Lady Iltani had offered him a job. He was quick to point out how his pay would be three times that of a field worker, and how such a position could lead to better things later. The lady had not told him that, but Asher figured it couldn't hurt to make the strongest case.

"What would you do?" Benaiah asked.

"Whatever the lady asks. Serve her meals. Take messages. Talk with her."

"She has slaves for such tasks! You want to be one of them?"

"Shoveling manure around date palms is slave's work," Asher retorted. "The manure is from swine as well as oxen. Do you want me to bring pig shit into our house every evening?"

"Watch your mouth! I don't allow talk like that."

"Sorry. I want to help the family and to make something of myself, too."

"And you can't see how working in the field will help your dreams come true."

"Dreams?"

"Most young men have dreams—of wealth, power, finding a virtuous wife, obedient children . . ."

"What about Azarel?"

"He dreams of the next cup of palm wine!"

"That's not fair. He works hard at the shop."

"I know, but you can tell how much he hates it. The way you did."

"Maybe he'll find something he likes better."

"Maybe. There's nothing wrong with him that going home wouldn't fix."

"One day we will," Asher assured him.

"One day," his father echoed, his voice flat. "I'll bet that most people in our village share that dream, but dreams don't always come true."

"May I work in the lady's house?"

"Do what you like." He went to the bed. "Wake up, brother," he said, touching his forehead. "Please wake up."

Tirzah appeared in the doorway. "The food's ready. Elisheva is bringing broth to see if Uncle will take some."

Benaiah lifted Ezekiel to a sitting position. He didn't resist, but he didn't help, either. Elisheva spooned some broth into his mouth. He accepted it, and then he drank some water. Still no words, just a look of intense concentration.

When he was done, Elisheva told them to eat; she would stay in case he awakened.

The stew and warm bread tasted delicious. Benaiah ate in silence. Tirzah tried to chat about the day, who had come into the shop, what had been sold, how much she liked one certain pot she'd painted.

As they were finishing, someone knocked at the door. Asher was surprised to see Josiah. With him here two men whom he introduced as his father, Eliezer, and his grandfather, Simeon.

"Shalom to this house and all who dwell here," Eliezer said.

"Shalom," Benaiah replied. "We welcome you. Please come in."

The men entered. Elisheva appeared and greeted them, too, and offered them food, which they politely refused.

Asher caught Josiah's eye, wanting to know what was going on. Josiah, for his part, was beaming.

Asher explained that he and Josiah worked together and that he'd told Josiah about Ezekiel.

"We are priests," Eliezer explained. "My father used to listen to his teachings. In Jerusalem, he prayed for many others when they were ill. He was always in the temple, sharing his wisdom and his compassion with those in need. When Josiah told us he'd seen a vision from YAH, we wanted to come pray for him. Would that be all right?"

"A vision?" Benaiah asked. "Who says it was a vision?"

"I did," Josiah replied.

"How do you know that?"

"Asher said his uncle's eye turned blue. That must mean your brother has seen a vision. He's a prophet."

Benaiah let out a deep sigh. "Very well. Please, come. We welcome your prayers."

Everyone crowded into the small room. The older man, Simeon, went to the bedside and touched the sleeping man's hand. "My brother, can you hear me?"

Josiah, who stood next to Asher, began to pray softly.

"He seems not to hear anything," Elisheva explained. "But he drank some broth and some water."

"A good sign," Simeon said. "Ezekiel, wake up. Come back to us. To those who love you."

Eliezer began to pray, too. For a few moments, the murmuring of the priests was the only sound in the room.

"Wake up," Simeon said again. This time it was not a polite request. It was a command.

Ezekiel's body jolted, and he sat up so quickly that everyone startled.

"My darling!" Elisheva cried. "Listen to the priest. It's time to come back."

Ezekiel looked at her, and recognition came into his eyes. He touched her cheek with the back of his hand.

"I knew he'd be all right," Josiah told Asher.

Ezekiel pivoted on the bed, putting his legs over the side. He tried to stand but was too weak. Benaiah and Eliezer were right there to catch him, and they helped him sit. Again, Ezekiel tried to stand, and this time, he was steady enough that he was able to walk with help. He gestured that he wanted to go into the courtyard.

Elisheva brought more water, and this time Ezekiel was able to drink a little on his own. He let her give him more broth but was too weak to help himself.

Simeon took one of Ezekiel's hands. "Can you tell us what you saw?"

Ezekiel looked puzzled.

"In your vision."

"You sure it was a vision?" Benaiah challenged.

"Yes, sir! I knew the moment Asher told me what had happened," Josiah assured him. "Father and Grandfather agree."

"Tell us what you saw," Simeon repeated. "It's all right. You are safe."

Ezekiel took a breath. Closed both eyes, opened them again. Looked at the old priest, held his gaze.

"YAH," he said at last. "I saw YAH."

"I told you!" Josiah crowed. "I was right! Didn't I say so, Asher? Tell them!"

"Josiah, quiet!" his father commanded.

"Sorry. Sorry, everyone. But I did say it."

Ezekiel didn't seem to have heard Josiah's outburst. He sat as before.

Benaiah went to his brother. "Ezekiel," he began. "It' true, you saw a vision of YAH?"

Ezekiel nodded.

"Can you tell us what you saw?"

The man shook his head. In a moment, he made as if to stand, but his legs still would not hold him. He tried again, and they half-carried him back to his bed, where he immediately fell asleep.

Josiah kept whispering to Asher, "I told you!" He looked as if he wanted to dance.

"Is it possible that my brother really did have a vision of YAH?" Benaiah asked the two priests.

Eliezer nodded enthusiastically. "Without a doubt! You say that his eye changed color?"

"Yes," Benaiah told him. "Before, both his eyes were brown. I don't understand it."

"YAH has changed his eye to prove the vision was from him. Who else has the power to do that to a man?"

"No one else," Simeon declared. "Only YAH."

The two men's certainty made Asher uncomfortable. He felt them looking at him.

"Your uncle's eyes are like yours now," Eliezer said, stating the obvious. "Have yours always been this way?"

Here we go again, Asher thought. "Yes, I was born this way."

"That means he's a prophet too," Josiah broke in.

"I'm not!"

"He can't see it yet," Josiah continued, "but I'm sure he will, in time—"

Asher didn't hear any more. Without warning, the truth came rushing at him: the darkness, the dazzling light—the faces—the wheels covered in eyes . . .

It *was* a vision. Certainly not as staggering as what his uncle had seen—but a vision, nonetheless . . .

The other men's faces and bodies blurred. Light dazzling as the sun filled his eyes. The head of an ox rushed at him, then swerved away just before it seemed sure to strike him with full force. A human face with one brown eye and the other radiantly blue took its place. It hovered an arm's distance away, smiled knowingly, then melted at his feet.

"Asher?" he heard someone ask in a faraway voice.

Then came wheels spinning faster than those on a chariot at full speed. Wheels covered with eyes, most of them brown, but some blue.

He saw his uncle's face before him. As he watched, unable to look away, the man's right eye changed from brown to blue, and Uncle Ezekiel began to weep . . .

"Asher, what's wrong?" a distant voice cried.

And then he beheld his own face, as if reflected in a pool of still water. First, he recognized his brown eye, looking just as a normal eye looks, but then his blue eye--much larger, much brighter--grew until it shone like a sun, blinding him but lighting his steps forward . . .

It all went dark, and the last thing he recalled was hitting his head on something hard.

Chapter Ten

Asher woke up lying on his bed. The room was dark, but an oil lamp provided feeble light. His head hurt, and when he touched it, he found a bandage.

"You awake?" someone asked.

"Azarel?"

"Yeah." He came close, lamp in his hand. "How are you?"

"My head is sore."

"No wonder. They say you cracked it good."

"How long have I been out?"

"A pretty long time. It'll be dawn soon. Father asked me to stay up to make sure you're okay."

"I think I am. How's Uncle Ezekiel?"

Azarel shrugged. "He was asleep when I got home, but Father said he'd roused when those priest guys came over. Told everyone he'd had a vision of YAH."

"Yeah. They got all excited."

"They'll be back in the morning to wait for him to wake up again and explain what he saw."

Asher sighed. "I hope that won't take long."

"I know what you mean. We don't need any more excitement around here. But what about you?"

"One second I was okay, and the next, I felt strange, and then everything got dark and I kind of remember falling and hitting my head . . ."

"What about Ezekiel's eye?" Azarel asked. "They told me it's turned blue, like yours."

"I can't explain that."

"I'm trying to understand things. Uncle goes all weird, gets an eye exchange, claims that he's seen YAH . . . And you say you two were caught in a storm and there was darkness and bright lights and wind that knocked you on your backsides . . . but there wasn't any storm, not really, so you imagined it all . . ."

Asher didn't respond.

"What aren't you telling me? If Ezekiel really saw YAH, then he's a prophet, isn't he? And what about you?"

"No way! I don't want to talk about it anymore."

"Okay. Maybe later. You want some water?"

"Please."

Azarel held the lamp to Asher's face. "You've bled through the bandage. Let me change it."

Asher nodded. His brother could be a jerk, but now he was being kind.

"You've got a nasty gash there," Azarel informed him. "Let me put pressure on it."

All at once, Asher began to cry.

"Hey, buddy, what's wrong? No need to blubber. Big brother Azarel is here."

"It's just that . . ."

"Yeah?"

"I remember how Mother used to look after us. That time I slipped and smashed my face into a rock when we were climbing around Reuel's pasture? There was a lot of blood."

"And you were convinced you were dying. I had to carry you all the way back into the city. Good thing you were such a skinny little runt. Still are!" Azarel kept pressure on the cut. "You miss her, don't you?"

"More than anything. You?"

Azarel nodded. "I pray every day that I'll meet up with the soldier who murdered her so I can cut *his* throat. It's why I always carry a knife, but don't tell the old man. He'd try to take it away and give me a big lecture on forgiveness and stuff."

"I promise. Just don't do anything stupid. If you kill a Babylonian, you'll be dead in an hour. Remember what happened to Elkanah."

"How could I forget? They threw him off the wall near the Ishtar Gate. Wouldn't let his family retrieve his body."

"I hate them," Asher declared.

"But Father said you're gonna start as some rich old lady's houseboy. How will you manage that if you hate them?"

"Pretend. Steal as much as I can. I don't know."

"You're the one who'd better watch it. You know what they do to thieves."

"Cut off their hands."

"Don't do anything stupid, either."

"Has the bleeding stopped?"

Azarel held the lamp near the cut. "Yeah. I'll tie on a clean bandage and you'll be as good as new."

"Will there be scar?"

"And mess up your pretty face? I don't think so. But if there is, remember that girls like dangerous-looking men."

"How would you know?"

"That's my secret."

"You're so full of it!"

"What a thing to say, after I've been so nice to you!"

"You have been," Asher admitted. "Thanks."

Azarel finished with the bandage. "Now try and get a little more sleep. I'm gonna do the same."

* * *

In the morning, Ezekiel was awake and able to eat. He recognized everyone but still did not speak. "You're going to be all better soon," Elisheva assured him. YAH is faithful."

When Asher left the house, he found Josiah waiting at the door. His face fell when he noticed Asher wearing his best clothes. "You didn't change your mind. I was hoping you would."

"We need money to pay the physician," Asher explained. "I have to try it. Father said it's all right."

"My grandfather and some of the other priests are coming over today to sit with your uncle. They'll pray and wait for him to reveal his vision."

"Why do they think he'll do that?"

"When YAH calls a prophet, he has to tell what he's seen and heard. You should know that."

"Even if he doesn't want to?"

"He has no choice. Do you think anyone can stand against YAH's will?"

"I guess not," he said.

They came to the plantation. The Lady Iltani was at her place, greeting the parade of workers streaming through the gate. Asher and Josiah approached her. Josiah gave him a searching look. "You're sure?" he asked. "There's still time. You don't have to do this."

"Come to the house this evening," Asher told him. "I know what I'm doing."

"I wonder. May YAH protect you from evil." With that, he went with the crowd, heading for another day of shoveling manure.

"Good morning, My Lady," Asher said.

"So you've decided. Those are your best clothes?"

"Yes."

"We'll find you something decent to wear. I can't have you looking like a street urchin."

He could have walked away then, followed Josiah back to the fields, but he didn't.

"Why is your forehead bandaged? Were you in a fight?"

"I tripped and fell," he lied. "It's nothing. I'm all right. It just aches a little."

"Please be careful. I don't like to see my people looking like thugs."

"The bandage can come off soon."

"That's good. Now: are you ready to begin?"

He nodded.

"Very well. I think it's best if you go to the house and meet my servants." She reached into the beaded pouch at her waist and came up with a clay cylinder etched with markings. "It's my seal. I have others, but if you lose this one, you lose your position, as well."

"What does it do?"

"You roll it over damp clay, which takes the impression. Then you can see the images. It's Our Lady Ishtar standing on a lion, holding her bow to show her power. Two ibexes in combat, to show that life is a daily battle. A date palm to remind us of the gods' blessings."

A compliment seemed in order. "It becomes a great lady such as yourself."

"It does indeed. Keep it safe and use it only if you have to."

"I will protect it."

"See that you do! Can you find your way in the city?"

"Not well. I've been there a few times, but we don't have reason to visit."

"Then you'll need to get directions. Take the Marduk Road and ask the way. I doubt anyone will challenge you once you identify yourself as belonging to my household."

"Yes, My Lady."

"You may call me that now."

"Yes, My Lady."

"When you get there, go to the alley on the right, turn left, and you'll see the back gate. Someone will admit you. I will return later. Do you understand?"

"I do."

"Go, and Marduk protect you."

Asher crossed the bridge over the canal. He was questioned by the city guards, but just as Iltani had promised, one glimpse of her seal won him permission to enter the city and a ready answer to his request for directions.

Inside the city walls, crowds jammed the streets, haggling with vendors in the food markets, buying cloth, pottery, metalwork, jewelry, sandals, tunics, perfumes, and wine in the shops. Asher saw men and women with skin darker than earth and hair black as ebony. Gorgeously dressed young women with painted pale skin and lips as red as plum juice stood in doorways, calling out to men to come inside and enjoy themselves. There were soldiers, priests, brick masons, carpenters, and beggars. Children, many in rags, scrounged the streets and doorways of shops looking for things to scavenge or, perhaps, to steal.

The air was saturated with smells of all kinds: cooking food, smoke, incense, flowers, perfumes, the sweat from thousands of bodies packed together under the hot sun.

The sounds of talking, laughter, quarrels, of harps and tambourines, drunken voices singing lewd songs. Tinkling bells, the chanting of priests marching in procession to one of the temples, the wailing of professional mourners following a recently dead citizen whose corpse was being carried to a cemetery outside the city.

And everywhere, slaves. Asher recognized them easily because they were branded—women, men, and children—on their arms, either on the shoulder or on the forearm, and a few on the face. Unlike free citizens of the city, slaves did not loiter about, chatting with one another or enjoying a cup of palm wine. They worked at every kind of task. Asher saw some making bricks, just as his own ancestors had done for Pharaoh; others plastered walls with wet clay that would harden and then be whitewashed or painted. Slaves were building flat roofs made of palm logs covered with layers of mud and palm branches. They carried pots overflowing with human waste to be dumped into the canal. They did the hardest, dirtiest, and most dangerous work the city needed done, with no time to rest and eat a meal.

At first, Asher was caught up in the bustle and energy of the city. Everywhere he looked, new things caught his eye. He understood now why Tirzah was so fascinated by Babylon, and why their father never tired of warning them against it and predicting their ruin if they would not listen to him. Asher passed another doorway where three seductively dressed women looked him over. One spoke, telling him how handsome he was and how much she would like to give him pleasure. Her price, she said, was cheap. Then another of the girls whispered something to her, pointing at Asher's face.

His eyes again.

The first girl stared, then turned away. She probably did not want to sell her favors to a freak.

Asher looked straight ahead, walking fast. He couldn't help but wonder if his brother visited such places and spent money on women like that.

He got lost a few times. He hesitated to use the Lady Iltani's seal, afraid that someone would snatch it from him. He asked people who seemed to be like himself--not rich or important--if they could help him. Everyone did.

Eventually, he located the estate. A slave boy let him through the back gate, and Asher found himself inside a walled garden. He hadn't thought he'd be working in a household with slaves. The lady had not mentioned it; perhaps it never occurred to her that there was reason. Slavery was simply how things were.

"I am Kuri," the boy told him. "Welcome to the house of our Lady Iltani."

"I'm Asher."

"Yes. We were told so."

"You're not Babylonian," Asher said. "You have a different accent."

"You are not Babylonian, either. I'm not the only one with a different accent."

"Where are you from?"

The boy shrugged. "I don't remember, but they say I am from Akkad, to the north. And you are an Israelite."

"How did you know that?"

"As I said. We were told you might come to work here."

So the lady had been sure of him—sure enough to inform her household of his arrival.

Kuri looked at him hard, and Asher sensed what was on his mind. Might as well get it over with and have some fun at his expense. "My eyes, right? You want to know about them."

"Oh, sorry. It's just that—"

"I'll tell you, if you're sure you want to know."

Kuri nodded.

"In my country, we have bands of roaming prophets, mostly men, but some women, too, called by YAH, our god, to see things others cannot see." Asher looked around, pretending he had to make sure no one could overhear him. "I have to whisper. No one else can know my secrets."

Kuri's eyes were wide. He obeyed when Asher summoned him with a finger.

"Are *you* a prophet?"

"Indeed I am. I have the mark: one brown eye, and one blue. It's how I was born."

"What can you see?"

"Oh, many things. If I choose, I can see what people in other rooms are doing, even when doors are closed. I can tell what other people are thinking. And sometimes, I know what will happen before it does."

Kuri stared at him in awe. "Really? You can tell the future?"

"Sometimes. When YAH desires it."

"Can you tell *my* future?"

"Perhaps. What do you want to know?"

Kuri's brow wrinkled. "Uh—"

"Yes?" Asher urged.

"Will I always be a slave?"

Asher wasn't expecting that. Of course, he didn't know the answer, but he didn't like slavery. "No," he declared. "One day you will be free."

"Your god told you that? What is his name?"

"YAH. Yes, he told me." Asher hated to lie to the boy, but really, what could it hurt? Maybe one day Kuri *could* get free. Asher had heard that the laws of Babylon made it possible for slaves to buy their freedom—if they ever accumulated enough money. Trouble was, earning money wasn't part of the deal for most slaves.

"Oh, just one more thing: like I said, sometimes I can see what people are doing in other rooms, or on the other side of walls. That means I might see if you aren't doing your work, or if you're tempted to take something that's not yours. Better behave yourself, okay?"

Kuri nodded.

I've done him a favor, Asher thought. *He'll never steal or shirk his duties. That way, he'll avoid a beating.*

For once, his freakish eyes might have done some good.

Chapter Eleven

Kuri led Asher to the back door of the house.

A woman met them. "So here he is," she said, looking him over. "A blue-eyed Israelite! I never thought I'd see the day."

"Only one of my eyes is blue," Asher told her. "The other is as brown as yours."

The woman snorted. "Do you think I'm blind? I can see that quite well, thank you."

Then why don't you say that I'm a brown-eyed Israelite?

"This is Rubati, our cook," Kuri put in. "She makes great breads and honey cakes."

"The best in Babylon," Rubati boasted.

"Asher's ready to work," Kuri said.

"And work he will! Find Ahiyababa and then get back to your own tasks, or you'll go hungry today."

"Yes, Rubati. Right away."

Kuri led the way into the house. They came first to another courtyard where the cooking was done. Beyond that, a passage with rooms on either side.

"Wait here," Kuri said. "I'll find Ahiyababa."

Asher looked around. The walls of the passage were smooth and painted in bright colors. Unlike the floor in his own house, which was packed earth, this floor was made of glazed tiles.

In a moment, a big man came toward him, followed by Kuri. "You are my lady's new houseboy," he declared, stating the obvious. He was tall and broad, his hair carefully curled, his beard the same. He wore a plain, short-sleeved tunic of fine linen. A thin band of what looked like gold encircled his right arm, and he wore a ring with a blue stone on his left hand.

"I am Ahiyababa, steward in this house. I am responsible for seeing that everything runs without problems. I have authority over all who work here, free and slave. As long as you are in service to the Lady Iltani, she will direct you, but you answer to me. Do you understand?"

"Yes, sir."

"Do you steal?"

"No, sir." *What a dumb question*, Asher thought. *If I did steal, does the man think I'd admit it?*

"Are you lazy?"

Another stupid question.

"No, sir."

"Dishonest?"

"No."

"Are you a liar?"

Asher knew that he did lie about many things. But he lied that no, he was not.

"If I discover that you steal, or fail to perform your duties, or lie to cover up mistakes you make, you'll find yourself thrown out and back in your miserable village. Do you understand?"

"Yes, sir."

"I don't know why the Lady Iltani has taken a fancy to you; she must see something in you that I don't. Serve her faithfully, and you will be treated fairly. If you fail her, you'll wish you hadn't."

"Yes, sir."

"Very well. Boy, show Asher the servants' quarters and then bring him back to me."

Kuri took Asher to a small, windowless room with a packed earth floor, bare brick walls, two narrow beds, and two low stools. "This is where I sleep," he explained. "Ahiyababa says you can use this room if you have any free time. But don't expect much. They always keep you jumping in this house."

"What do you do?"

"Whatever they tell me. Anything and everything. They say I should feel grateful that Iltani bought me."

"Are you?"

"Sometimes. I get enough to eat and decent clothes and a place to sleep. It's better than what my old master used to give me. He beat me, too. So far, no one here has done that. But I'm still a slave."

"What will *I* do?"

"Whatever the lady wants. Ahiyababa will explain it. Let's get back to him. He doesn't like to be kept waiting."

Ahiyababa dismissed Kuri and showed Asher the rest of the house. It was a sprawling maze of courtyards, passageways, and rooms. Outside stairs led to a second story and on top of that, a terrace.

When they came downstairs again, Ahiyababa took Asher to a door painted with images of fruit trees, flowering vines, and birds. On either side were fired clay statues of dogs, sacred to Gula, as Asher remembered. "My Lady's rooms," Ahiyababa explained. "Here, by this door, you will spend much of your time, waiting to be summoned. When she calls for you, you will enter, stand ready to serve her, and then do what she asks quickly, completely, and no questions. Her wishes are more important than any other task you might be doing, so if you are occupied and learn she that she wants you, go immediately. Is that understood?"

The room on the other side of the painted door was more splendid than any Asher had ever seen. The walls were covered with paintings of serpents, scorpions, dogs, ibexes, lions, horses, oxen, and some other animals unfamiliar to him. Scenes of battle, a flood covering a city and its people, a huge boat on an empty sea, a kingly figure mourning over the body of another man. Statues of the gods stood in shrines along the walls. Asher recognized Marduk and Ishtar, but others he had never seen. Oil lamps burned in front of some of the images, and the air smelled of incense.

Beyond this room was a courtyard, in whose center was a pool with a fountain. There were strange birds in cages, and Asher caught sight of a cat slinking among the flowerpots.

At the far side was another door, this one guarded on either side by images of Ishtar, bow in hand, standing upon a lion, a star behind her head, just like her image on the seal in Asher's tunic pocket.

"Her private quarters," Ahiyababa explained, "where My Lady sleeps and dresses. It is unlikely that you will ever be summoned beyond that door. The last houseboy never was. It has been a long time since I have passed inside. My lady's closest friends sometimes visit her there, but it is forbidden to men."

"Does Lady Iltani live here alone?"

"She does," the steward replied shortly.

"What happened to the rest of the family?"

"Dead from the plague, so Iltani prays every day, presents offerings in the temples, consults seers. Despite what you told her, she is convinced you have second sight, and perhaps healing powers, as well."

This was unwelcome news. He was no seer . . .

Even if he were, how could he stop a plague?

"Do you have questions?" the man asked.

"Do I come to the back gate in the mornings?"

"Yes, and be here early. She likes to arrive at the plantation even before the workers do."

"When does my day end so I can go home?"

"When you are dismissed! You must be prepared to stay here overnight if she has need of you."

"I can't do that, sir. I have my own family, and just now, my uncle is very sick."

The steward raised an eyebrow. "Sick with what?"

"We don't know, but it's not plague or fever. The physician says he will get well, and we must be patient."

"Decide: if you are Iltani's houseboy, your first loyalty is to her."

"I understand."

"Do you want to leave? If so, I will explain your decision."

"Would I still have my work at the plantation?"

"No."

"May I go home this evening?"

"As far as I know."

"I'll stay," Asher told him.

Ahiyababa returned him to the back of the house, where Asher met some of the others. They were all slaves except for the head gardener. They cleaned the latrines, swept floors, patched and repainted walls, cleaned out the cook ovens and discarded the ashes. Slaves brought in dried palm wood and branches for burning in those ovens. Slaves assisted the cook. They washed plates, cups, and pots. Slaves accompanied Rubati to the market each morning and carried back to the house what she chose for the day's meals.

Ahiyababa ordered Asher to help Rubati until Iltani returned from the plantation. He was put to work grinding grain. The work was unfamiliar and he felt clumsy, but the cook seemed satisfied with his efforts.

Mid-morning, Iltani summoned Asher to her courtyard. She asked how he was getting along, and he told her, truthfully enough, that things had gone well. Then she decided that he needed some better clothes. A trip to the tailor was in order.

Accompanied by Kuri, Asher again found himself in the noisy streets. At the shop, he showed the lady's seal and explained what was required. The man inspected him carefully, memorizing his size so that he could sew the required tunics. In the meantime, he gave Asher two new loincloths and a tunic. The tunic was a bit big, but it would do. He also provided a pair of sandals, the best Asher had ever owned. The tailor said to return in two days.

Back at the estate, Asher was informed that he was to have his hair cut and bathe before waiting on his lady. In the servants' courtyard, two slave girls tended to him. Both were young and beautiful, and they smiled and giggled a lot. One cut Asher's hair with a razor; when she was done, the other admired him and told him he looked a proper young Babylonian now. Then the girls led him to a pool. They told him to undress and that they would wash him. Asher objected. He'd never been seen naked by any woman except for his mother, and that was a long time ago, when he was still a child.

The girls insisted. With many smiles and sidelong glances, they got him out of his tunic and then his loincloth. Asher's impulse was to cover himself, but he gave it up and stood before them just as he was. The warm water provided some covering, and it felt wonderful. When was the last time he'd enjoyed a bath? Pools for bathing were reserved for the houses of the rich in Jerusalem, not working people.

The girls used cloths to scrub his skin, and before he knew it, Asher was laughing along with them and even found himself splashing them playfully. For the first time he could remember, he was having fun. But what would his father and uncle say about a son of Israel sporting naked with two slave girls?

Not to mention YAH's opinion . . .

When the bath was done, the girls dried him and rubbed herb-scented oil into his skin. He dressed, and the girl who had cut his hair rubbed a different oil into it and arranged it to her liking. The other tied his new sandals on his feet. Finally, the first girl used a piece of reed dipped in a thick black liquid and drew fine lines on his eyelids and beneath his eyes.

The two inspected him and seemed delighted with their labors. One produced something Asher had heard of but had never seen, let alone used: a mirror. Its handle was shaped like Ishtar in her bold nakedness. The girls offered it, and Asher had the first clear look at himself in all his sixteen years of life.

He didn't know what to make of it. Reflected in the polished metal surface was the face of a handsome young man, hair styled in the Babylonian fashion, clear light brown skin, the beginnings of a beard on his upper lip and chin, one eye sky blue, the other earth brown. Both eyes were accented by the makeup the girls had applied.

He kept gazing at himself and realized he was pleased. No one had every told him he was handsome, but these two desirable girls had flirted with him, touched him, and awakened things in him he could not deny.

The image before him looked for all the world like that of a Babylonian in his young, manly prime.

But he was no Babylonian.

Not yet, anyway.

Chapter Twelve

Iltani called for him to attend her. He found her sitting beside the fountain; a cup and a plate of fruit sat on a table of inlaid wood.

"Let me have a good look at you," she told him. "Come, stand in the light where I can see you."

Asher obeyed.

"Turn around."

He did.

"Face me."

The lady scanned him head to feet, and Asher found himself feeling as he'd felt the other day—like a prized piece of livestock.

She nodded her approval. "Yes, you will do."

"Thank you, My Lady."

"In fact, you are a handsome fellow, better looking than I had hoped you'd be once you'd been properly cleaned up! I don't suppose you were accustomed to being anointed when you were back in Jerusalem?"

"No, but we Israelites know about anointing. Our priests and kings—"

"Are of no interest to me," she broke in. "What of my young maidens?"

"Very beautiful. They were good to me."

"And you visited the tailor?"

"My new clothes will be ready in two days."

"Good. Rubati should have my meal prepared. I'm ready to eat."

Asher brought food, which included pieces of grilled fish and duck, luxuries that never appeared on the table back at home.

The lady told him where to stand. He offered her plates of fruits, vegetables, and rounds of bread. He kept her cup of palm wine filled and held up a clean napkin each time she asked for it. A slave girl appeared and played softly on a hand harp.

Lady Iltani ate sparingly, and her manners were dainty. She dined without hurry and clearly enjoyed her meal. When she was done, Asher presented a basin of scented water and a napkin. Returning the dishes to the kitchen, he noticed a morsel of grilled duck. Why not help himself? Since the day he was forced from Jerusalem, nothing had tasted as delicious as that sliver of meat.

In the afternoon, the lady took her mid-day rest, and Asher was told to report again to the kitchen. But Rubati herself was sleeping, so he had free time. He found his room, lay down on the bed, and slept until Kuri woke him and said he was wanted.

The lady lounged by the fountain. "So how do you like it here?" she asked.

"Fine."

"And my girls, Damkina and Anatu, how do you like them?"

He felt himself blush. The lady smiled knowingly.

"I thought so," she declared. "They find you highly acceptable. Tell me: have you been with a woman yet?"

He blushed again. "No! It's not the custom in my country—"

"To enjoy oneself?"

"To lie with a woman before marriage."

"Ah. Your god must be stern."

"He is."

"You are innocent! If you want Damkina or Anatu, take one. Take them both. They're willing. Enjoy youth and beauty while you can before the evil days come. They *will* come, I promise you that."

"Yes, My Lady."

"You may go."

As he pushed his way through bustling streets, Asher felt himself shaking. He knew he should hurry home, scrub himself, and put on his own clothes. He must never return to the estate, where temptation crouched like a hungry lion.

Where two beautiful young women wanted him.

The idea frightened him--and excited him.

He must never again venture inside the maze where dangers waited everywhere.

He wanted nothing more than to return there and encounter Damkina or Anatu in the darkness.

* * *

Elisheva met him at the door. "Asher, is that you? Or is this a prince of Babylon? Your tunic! New sandals. Your hair. And do I smell perfume?"

"It's me," he admitted, embarrassed, "and you know it."

"What happened to your eyes? That's not kohl!"

Asher grimaced. "It is. The woman I work for wants me to look my best."

Elisheva smiled. "You mean she wants you to look like a male prostitute, the ones our prophets condemn!"

"It's not like that!" he protested. "I didn't know what they were going to do to me."

"I know what you're going to do to *yourself* right now. Get that stuff off your eyes. You'll have enough explaining to do when your father gets a whiff of your perfumed body."

"How is Ezekiel?" Asher asked.

"Better. He can walk, and he will drink water and eat some porridge."

"Has he said anything?"

"Not yet."

"Has the physician been here?"

"Yes. He says we must be patient. Nothing else can be done."

"Why are *they* here?"

"Eliezer and Simeon? They came this morning and said they'll wait for Ezekiel to speak what YAH has shown him. They are no trouble. Go on, now. Everyone will be back from the shop soon enough."

Asher washed himself, and he mussed his hair. He put away his new tunic and put on his own clothes. When his family got home, his father and brother noticed nothing different, but Tirzah's expression proved she was on to him.

The priests took their leave but promised to return in the morning.

The family ate, and Asher was grateful his aunt had done the cooking. It was good but compared to the feast he had served Iltani, this plain stew of grain and vegetables seemed dull. Ezekiel allowed Elisheva to help him eat, then he went to rest.

Benaiah watched him go. "I don't know what to think," he said grimly. "It troubles me."

"Trust YAH," Elisheva urged him. "Your brother *will* return to us."

Benaiah shook his head. "I hope you're right."

Just then, someone knocked, Josiah wanting to know if Asher could join him for a walk.

"I want to see the place where YAH showed himself to your uncle," Josiah explained.

The spot looked just the same. Josiah gazed toward the north, searching the sky. "I'd like to have a vision," he explained. "Then I'd know for sure."

"Know what?"

Josiah hesitated.

"Know what?" Asher repeated.

"Promise you won't say anything to anyone."

"I promise."

"Then I'd know for sure that YAH is real."

Asher was shocked. "You doubt it, too? I thought I was the only one."

"I try so hard to have perfect faith," Josiah admitted, "but when I see what's happening to our people, I wonder."

Asher's irritation with Josiah drained away, replaced by a feeling of closeness. Someone understood! He just never thought it would be Josiah.

The two kept looking north as day gradually faded toward dusk.

Josiah broke the silence. "I keep smelling something good. It's not you, is it?"

"I don't think so."

"It *is* you! What'd they do, douse you in frankincense?"

Asher sighed. "Yeah, they did. I got a bath, too. And a tailor is making me new clothes."

He decided *not* to mention that he'd been bathed by Damkina and Anatu, or that they'd shown him his handsome self in the mirror--or that they were his for the taking.

Josiah smiled. "Your lady would definitely not want *me* around, then. I smell more like dung than fancy perfumes. What else happened?"

Asher described his day, and as he did so, he realized he had little to show for it. He hadn't made anything, the way he did back in the pottery shop, even if his cups and plates were ugly. He hadn't used his muscles to fertilize date palms so that they could provide food for people. No—he'd helped a wealthy old woman spend her time in pleasure.

In return, he'd be paid—and not just in money. Damkina and Anatu. "Take one, take them both," Iltani had offered.

Josiah listened without interrupting. Then, "Are you going back?"

"Yes. Disappointed?"

"Sure, but what can I say? You're stubborn. Just be careful or you'll find yourself worshiping their idols. The old bag *does* have idols in her house, doesn't she? I've heard they all do."

"Some. I can ignore them. They're just statues."

"That's what my father and grandfather say, but YAH still won't tolerate them. I'll pray to him to show you the right way."

"You still believe enough to pray?"

He shrugged. "I sometimes doubt, but yes. Besides, I can't imagine *not* praying. That's scary."

The northern sky revealed no visions of YAH, and the two walked home.

That night, when everyone in the house was asleep, Asher buried the little clay dog, sacred to Gula, beside the door. The earth was packed solid, so it took him what seemed a long time of hard digging to make a hole large enough. The entire time, he expected someone to come along and catch him. He packed down the dirt so no one would notice. Now his house was under the protection not only of YAH, but also of Gula, goddess of healing.

The next four days passed, one much like the other. Ezekiel slept, sat in the courtyard, peered into empty space, and allowed himself to be tended by Eliezer, Simeon, and other priestly brothers who came to stand vigil by him.

Asher got his new tunics. The slave girls gave him fragrant oil and a jar of kohl, so he learned how make himself presentable. His time at Iltani's quickly fell into a routine: he had to appear first thing each morning to escort the lady to the plantation. There, he ran errands such as summoning certain people to come speak to her. If she felt thirsty, he'd bring drink. Hungry, he'd bring her favorite honey cakes with sesame seeds. In the late mornings, Iltani would return home, and there Asher would serve her food and listen to her gossip about people he didn't know. After the mid-day meal, she would nap, so Asher often had some time to himself. He usually slept, too. After her rest, the lady would sit with the plantation accountant or sometimes visit a friend. Once, she went to the market to amuse herself, she said, seeing what was for sale even though she needed nothing. But she bought things anyway, expensive luxuries: cloth, jewelry, a new fragrant oil.

She had her favorite merchants ready to show her their latest wares. That day, Asher carried home an armful of her gifts to herself.

Soon, Iltani seemed to take his presence for granted. He was there when she called for him, silent unless spoken to, seemingly invisible to the other household workers.

Asher felt alone in the bustling household. Had he offended anyone? But then he overheard two of the slave girls talking. They couldn't understand why their lady had hired him. They resented the fact that although his tasks were light, he was well paid. "To hold down the floor," one joked. "And to lie to the old hag about how lovely she is."

"He is handsome, though," the first one said. "I'll have to admit that. Good looking piece of flesh, even if he is one of those stinking Israelites."

So that was it. He wasn't liked—no, worse than that—he was resented and looked down upon because of who—or what—he was.

He didn't care, he told himself. Let those stupid, jealous girls talk. But they were right about one thing: he *was* handsome, and he knew it. Seeing himself in the mirror convinced him of that.

On the fourth day, Iltani informed him he'd have to spend the next night at the estate. She was entertaining some friends—widows her age—and she wanted to show off her strapping young houseboy. Those were her words. Asher felt embarrassed, but more pleased. He told his father where he would be and added that he would be paid extra for the overnight hours. To Asher's surprise, Benaiah agreed without an argument. But he did make Asher promise one thing: he needed to have the weekly Sabbath Day at home. If his mistress wouldn't agree to those terms, then Asher could no longer work for her.

The lady made no objection to his request. "You please me," she told him. "I can't lose you because I'm too stingy to allow you one day each week with your family."

The evening of the party, a dozen Babylonian women, all dripping jewelry and wearing the finest linens and silks, enjoyed the banquet. Asher was kept busy filling their cups and offering them dainties. He overheard some of them whispering about how good looking he was, and how his lady had a fine thing on her hands. His pride swelled; even so, he was somewhat embarrassed when one of the women, an aged thing wearing a fancy wig and too much makeup, pinched his bottom and asked if he wouldn't like to escort her home.

The party lasted until nearly midnight; the ladies all declared themselves stuffed, tipsy, overtired from having stayed up too late, and ready to drop on their feet. Litter bearers were summoned and quickly the house was quiet. Damkina and Anatu appeared to help their lady prepare for bed, and Asher was told he was no longer needed.

He was tired, too. Kuri was not in the room they shared during the day, and Asher wondered where he was sleeping. He undressed and lay down. Before he was fully asleep, Damkina appeared at the door, which she shut behind herself. Then she lay down beside him, and Asher eagerly gave himself up to the pleasures of lying with a woman.

Chapter Thirteen

He woke only when Kuri roused him. It was late, and he hurried to be ready in time. Iltani gossiped about her friends at the party, who had eaten too much, drunk too much, had worn too much makeup. Asher pretended to be interested, but his mind was on the previous night. He thought of Damkina and wanted her again. He asked himself if he felt shame and realized he did not. *At least I don't worship their idols,* Asher assured himself. Then he recalled the clay dog he'd buried at home . . .

Asher was released early that day so he could help prepare for the Sabbath. Before he left, Iltani called for him. Ahiyababa was with her, and at her instruction, he paid Asher his wages. They were more than he had expected.

"For a job well done," Iltani told him.

"Thank you, My Lady."

"""Enjoy your day of rest. Be here on time the day after."

The village streets were bustling with people buying food; tantalizing aromas filled the air. Women were hanging laundry to dry before the sun set and they could do no more work. Children were sweeping the street in front of their houses. Girls stood in line by the fountains to fill water jars. Sounds of laughter and conversation met Asher on every side, and people greeted him with cries of "Shabbat shalom!"

It felt comfortable. It felt right. Here, after all, was where he belonged, not in a Babylonian house. But then he felt his pay in his pocket, and he knew how pleased his father would be to receive such a generous sum.

At home, Asher was surprised to find a small crowd in the courtyard: Ezekiel surrounded by priests. Two scribes sat cross-legged on the ground near him, both with papyrus and their writing boxes of reed pens and ink. Benaiah stood by him, whispering into his ear. Toward the back, Asher spotted Azarel, who looked grumpy. Tirzah moved among the men, offering cups of water. The air was hot, and it smelled of sweat and dust.

Elisheva met him. "Isn't it wonderful, Asher!" she exclaimed, her face glowing. "Ezekiel came to himself early today. He has bathed and changed clothes, and he has called for scribes. Eliezer and Simeon have summed these other priests."

"What's going on?"

"He's going to share what he saw the day you were with him. That's what he's been telling people. Now we are waiting. Would you like to speak with him?"

He was glad that Ezekiel had come to himself, but suddenly he felt shy.

"Come," Elisheva urged.

The crowd opened before them, and Asher found himself face to face with the man he loved so well. "Uncle?" he asked.

Ezekiel looked him up and down, and Asher wished he could change into his own clothes and remove the fragrance of scented oil from his skin. At least he'd remembered to wash the kohl from his eyes.

Ezekiel frowned slightly, then smiled and opened his arms. Asher dropped onto his knees in front of him and allowed his uncle to embrace him. The visiting priests murmured their approval.

"I was so afraid you wouldn't come back," Asher whispered.

"I have a lot to share, and we have things to discuss, just the two of us. After all, you were there, too."

"When?"

"When YAH spoke to me. I saw him, Asher!"

So it was true.

"Later," Uncle Ezekiel promised him.

It was nearly sunset when Ezekiel asked the crowd to get quiet. "Shabbat begins soon," he began, "and you may need to return home. If so, please do."

There was talk among some of the priests.

"I asked that these scribes be given permission to write down what I say, even though YAH's laws forbid work on Shabbat. Do they have your blessing, Simeon?"

The old man conferred with his brother priests. "They do," he replied. "The law makes provision for breaking Shabbat when there is great need, and this is one of those moments."

"Thank you. As I said, anyone who must go, please do so. You'll hear what I have to say soon enough."

At that, three men took their leave, all of them embracing this new prophet. Azarel left, too.

Those who remained found places on the ground, where Tirzah had spread mats. Most of them were priests, but Josiah appeared, bringing with him the faint odor of animal dung. Ezekiel nodded his welcome.

The sun set and the lamps of Shabbat were lighted. The priests chanted their prayers, and the gathering waited in silent expectation.

Then Ezekiel began to speak. His words were soft, so Asher had to strain to hear him. As soon as he began, the two scribes got to work.

"I was by the canal," he began, "with my nephew. Suddenly, the hand of YAH was upon me, and I saw a storm, a cloud, lightning, brightness like the sun, like the coals at the heart of blazing fire."

At the mention of YAH, some of the priests murmured. Asher felt a shiver run down his back. He had seen the same things.

Ezekiel paused, then put his hands over his eyes, as if to shield them from light too bright for them.

No one spoke. No one moved.

"Then—creatures," Ezekiel cried. "Four—one with the face of an eagle. Another of an ox. A lion. A man. And bodies—with wings like those of great birds. The creatures had feet, but not like ours—but hoofs like those of calves. And they all gleamed like devouring fire!"

As he spoke, his voice became louder, the words tumbling out faster and faster.

"Slow down," one of the scribes asked him. "We can't keep up."

Ezekiel did not hear him.

"Beneath their wings—hands, hands like ours. And the wings of each creature touched the wings of another. It seemed that they stood at the four corners of a square. Then they moved. Sometimes forward, sometimes to the side. Like torches. Fiery torches lighting up the sky, brighter than the sun. I can't tell you what it was—how it looked. I have no words!"

Ezekiel sat forward in his chair. He was shaking.

Asher felt the fine hair on his arms standing up straight. The more his uncle said, the more uneasy he became.

Ezekiel sat up again so violently that one of the scribes dropped his pen.

"Wheels!" he exclaimed. "Wheels beneath the creatures, but not touching them. The creatures moved, raced from place to place, and the wheels went with them, but they did not touch the ground. The wheels! They sparkled like chrysolite, and within each wheel was another—a wheel within a wheel. And . . ."

Ezekiel covered his face, as if to block out what he was seeing.

"Eyes. Eyes covering the wheels. Eyes that see—everything."

Asher edged toward the door. The otherworldly faces of animals and of a human being, the fire, the darkness, the eyes--*he had seen those things, too*—not the way his uncle had seen them, fully face to face, but from the side, so to speak, like looking into a room through the narrow space left when a door is opened a crack.

At the door, Asher stopped. A few of the men had turned to see what he was doing, but most kept their faces fixed on his uncle, whose words came pouring out. He repeated things he had already said. He tried to explain what he had witnessed but kept crying out that there were no words. He wept. He fell off his stool and had to be lifted back.

Ezekiel was silent for what seemed a long time, and Asher wondered if he had anything more to tell.

He did.

Once again, his voice was low and soft. "Above the four creatures I saw—a platform. Beneath it the creatures moved, soaring on their wings, covering their nakedness with two and flying with the others. The sound—like the uproar in the middle of a storm. Above the platform, brightness like that of the most precious gems. Sapphires, amber."

He paused. The scribes wrote furiously.

Ezekiel stood up, and for a moment he tottered. Several hands reached out to support him. He fell onto his knees. He raised his face toward the darkened sky, his eyes fixed and staring.

Asher moved another step back. He wanted to be gone from this place, to find safety where the all-seeing eyes could not find him. But he also wanted to hear—he *had* to hear—everything.

"Go on," Benaiah urged. "It's all right, Ezekiel. We're with you. Nothing can hurt you."

Ezekiel sighed. He kept his face turned upward, but his eyes were now closed. "On the platform, a throne. On the throne, one like . . ." Again, he searched for words to express himself. "One like a human. From his waist up he was sheer radiance, like the rainbow after a storm. All around, brightness, glory—the glory of YAH."

The men murmured again. One or two cried out praise to the god of Israel.

Ezekiel began to speak more loudly, more rapidly. The voice coming out of him sounded scarcely human. In it were the sounds of storm winds, and the shouts of armies going into battle, and women crying out in the pains of childbirth, and of Asher's father keening over the body of his slain wife. The sounds of priests chanting in the house of YAH back in Jerusalem. The glad songs of Zion sung to the accompaniment of harps and tambourines. The cries of the wild jackal, the lowing of oxen, the cooing of the turtledove. The voice coming through Asher's uncle was all of these, none of these, and more than these.

Two of the priests got up and brushed past Asher, apparently unable to stand anything more. One old man began to cry. The man next to him offered comfort.

Asher stayed put, unable to budge. He knew somehow that the voice he was hearing was not that of his uncle, or of any human.

"'Man, stand on your feet and I shall speak to you,'" Ezekiel began. He stood. "'I am sending you to a nation of rebels and traitors. They have gone from me just as their fathers and forefathers did. Like a rebellious town, they have fought against me, their king. You will speak to them whether they listen or not, and they will not listen, for they are rebels.'"

One of the priests began to groan. Another scratched some dust from the hardpacked earth and sprinkled it on his head.

"'Do not fear them,'" the voice went on. "'Speak what I tell you, and do not be like them. Open your mouth and eat what I will give you.'"

Ezekiel spoke again in his own voice: "He put a scroll in my mouth and fed it to me. Like a child, I ate. On it were written laments for the dead, dirges, prophecies of destruction! I thought the taste would be bitter, but in my stomach, it tasted sweet as honey."

Then once again, his voice was not his own: "'I am sending you to the exiles, your own people. They are a house of rebellion and will not listen, but I am giving you a brow like a diamond, harder than flint. Do not fear them. When you hear a word of warning from me, speak it to the wicked. If the wicked repent after you have warned them, they will save their own lives, and you will save your own. But if I speak a word of warning to the wicked and you do *not* speak it to them, then the wicked will perish in their sins and I will hold you accountable.'"

Ezekiel collapsed onto his chair. His head dropped onto his chest, and he seemed to have fallen into a faint.

"Brother?" Benaiah touched his shoulder, trying to rouse him.

"That's all?" one of the priests asked. "No words of judgment against our captors, these detestable Babylonian dogs?"

"How are *we* rebels, our faces set against YAH?" added another. "Are we not faithful? Do we not keep all the laws written in the book found in the temple in the days of King Josiah, blessed be his memory?"

The men got to their feet.

"He's mad," another priest declared. Some agreed. "What he saw—animal faces, wheels, eyes—the ravings of a lunatic!"

"Not a vision from YAH," put in another. "A vision of demons, more likely!"

Asher listened as the men's complaints and condemnation of his uncle grew stronger. He wanted to shout that Ezekiel was telling the truth. He knew because he himself had witnessed part of it.

"I keep the laws of YAH!" cried one. "He will never have cause to warn *me* through any so-called prophet. Benaiah, keep watch on your brother. He's dangerous."

The men began to leave.

"Brothers!" shouted Simeon. "Let me speak."

The crowd got quiet. Simeon was the oldest among them, respected by all. "Be careful before you condemn this man. Has there ever been a true prophet who spoke honeyed words and declared that all was well? What about our brother, Jeremiah? The lying prophets surrounding the king kept telling his majesty what he wanted to hear, and they tried to kill the prophet for speaking the true words of YAH."

"Bah!" cried one of the others. "Jeremiah's another madman, counseling us to settle here and make this hole our home for many years. I've heard enough from these so-called prophets who speak only doom. Haven't we repented enough? Don't we strive to love YAH and keep his commandments? Why would he condemn *us*?"

"Hear me!" cried Simeon. But the crowd was done. They pushed their way past Asher, who wanted to shout insults in their faces.

Soon, everyone had left except for Simeon, Eliezer, and Josiah. Ezekiel remained on his chair. He hadn't spoken again or tried to keep the men from leaving.

Elisheva came to the rescue. "Here it is, well past mealtime! Tirzah, help me. We'll have the food ready to serve in just a few moments."

The food, prepared before sunset, was ready. Josiah's family accepted Elisheva's invitation to share the meal, and they enjoyed her delicious cooking as the stars came out.

Ezekiel roused and seemed himself. He ate with appetite, and over the meal, asked about the small things of village life—was anyone sick? Any births? Marriages? How was the garden coming along?—as if he'd been on a long journey and needed to catch up on the local news.

In a way, he *had* been on such a journey.

"Don't despair that they don't believe you," Eliezer told Ezekiel. "It has always been that way with true prophets. Jeremiah spoke the truth about YAH's judgment, and they persecuted him. For all we know, they might have killed him by now."

"What about his letter to us?" Benaiah asked. "He advises that we settle in for a long exile."

"Josiah, you believe YAH is going to free us soon," Asher said. "Isn't that what you told me at the plantation?"

Josiah looked embarrassed. "I did say that."

"And where did you hear such a promise?" his father asked, not unkindly.

"Nowhere. I—just feel it's going to be soon."

"Who can tell?" Simeon said. "Hope isn't wrong. But whether we go home soon or stay here a long time, we must stay true to who we are. We're Israelites, not Babylonians."

"No wonder every prophet tries to escape the call of YAH," Ezekiel said. "'I'm just a boy!' 'I'm only a farmer!' 'I s-st-t-t-t-tutter!'" He laughed, and suddenly everyone relaxed. Even Elisheva smiled.

"YAH himself told you they won't listen," Simeon reminded him. "That should be a comfort to you, Ezekiel."

"No, brother. If anything, it fills me with sadness."

"YAH also told you not to be afraid," Eliezer added. "He has called you, and he will protect you."

Ezekiel glanced at his wife. "Of course he will. I put my trust in him."

"What will you do now?" Eliezer asked him.

Ezekiel shrugged. "I don't know. Wait, I suppose."

"For what?" Asher asked.

Ezekiel gave him another penetrating look. "For YAH to command me what to do next."

The meal done, Josiah and his family left. In the street, Josiah took Asher aside. He looked troubled.

"What's wrong?" Asher asked him.

"Oh, I don't know. Don't get me wrong: it's wonderful that YAH spoke to Ezekiel. It's just that—well—he didn't say what I hoped he would."

"You wanted YAH to announce that we'd be going home to Jerusalem soon. Am I right?"

Josiah nodded. "I haven't given up hope! I'm sure we need to hear what YAH is saying—about repenting and all—and he never said he's *not* going to take us home. Still . . ."

"I'm sorry," Asher said. "You—"

"Come along," Josiah's father called to him. "Help us explain to your mother why we all missed the Shabbat dinner she prepared for us."

"We'll have to eat again," Josiah told Asher, with a smile. "Don't worry about me. I'll see you soon."

Asher watched his friend catch up with his father and grandfather. Then he turned back toward the house and found his uncle waiting for him at the door.

Chapter Fourteen

"We have a lot to talk about," Ezekiel began. "Let's walk."

Asher knew where they were going.

Now that night had fallen, it was quiet along the canal. In silence, they made their way through the Ishtar grove, then on to the flatland beyond it. The stars twinkled in a black sky, and a pair of nighthawks called to one another high above.

At the place, Ezekiel stopped. Gazing straight ahead into the darkness, he asked, "What did you see?"

There was no lying his way out of this one.

"Tell me," Ezekiel said.

"The storm and darkness. Light as bright as the sun. Then--the faces. The eyes . . . But not what you saw—the One on the throne."

"I know."

"How?"

Ezekiel sighed. "He told me."

"I'm scared."

"I understand, Asher. I'm frightened, too, even though YAH has commanded me not to be."

"Was it really YAH, and not a dream we shared? Not a--nightmare?"

"What do you believe?"

That was the question.

"I don't know," he confessed.

"Then you will be in torment until you decide."

"Why?"

Now his uncle looked at him kindly. "Because like me, you *are* a seer, a visionary, a prophet—I don't think it matters what word we use."

"I'm not! I can't explain what happened, but I didn't see anything for myself. It's like I was spying on what *you* were seeing."

"YAH won't show himself to you in all his glory until you're ready to do what he commands."

"Then I don't want it! I'm only a child!"

"Oh, please. That's what Isaiah said when YAH showed himself in the temple. He couldn't get away with that excuse either."

"I'm not a prophet!" Asher repeated, as much to himself as to his uncle.

"You can't escape who you are. If you try, his fire will consume your bones." Ezekiel put an arm around his shoulder. "I don't mean to frighten you, but I have to speak the truth. I will have to speak the truth from now on. Do you understand?"

Asher shook his head. "I don't want any of this. I hate it. I hate everything!"

Ezekiel nodded. "With good reason. Our lives are destroyed, and we have brought all this evil on ourselves."

"No, we haven't! The Babylonians—they did it! They captured Jerusalem. They made us come here. They killed Mother. I hate them!"

"And yet you've taken your place in a Babylonian house."

"How did you know?"

"I've been awake ever since this morning. Do you think your father and aunt haven't told me what you're doing? Even if they hadn't, the way you're dressed and perfumed tells everyone you're not a fieldhand."

"The lady invited me to be her houseboy. She's paying me triple what I'd have earned in the palm groves. I have nice clothes, delicious food. Maybe I'll be like Joseph and become powerful among the Babylonians."

Ezekiel smiled. "I doubt it. You'll become one of *them*, and YAH will not be able to speak through you."

"And then he'll kill me? Is that what you said—something about his fire consuming me?"

"Your body won't die, but your spirit will. And you'll be left with nothing, including your right mind."

"I'll never become one of them!"

"That's easy to say now when you can feel YAH's eyes on you. And you *can* feel them, can't you?"

"No!"

Ezekiel looked at him, waiting.

"I mean, yes." Asher began to shake. "Help me!"

"No one can hide, Asher. How do you think I've spent most of these past few days?"

"Seeing more visions from YAH?"

"No. Trying to escape. Pretending to YAH that I'd seen nothing. Pretending that YAH *is* nothing. That I'm simply a madman, driven crazy by the horrors of our lives. And there are more to come, Asher. Many, many more."

"You said you haven't seen any new visions."

"That's true, but YAH has told me I will see at least one more, and I'm not going to like it. I tried to refuse, but that's useless. Shall I share what I think it is?"

"No! Tell YAH you're done being his prophet. Tell him to find someone else. Please!"

"I've spent hours doing just that. *He* won't take 'no' for an answer."

"Why doesn't he pick on someone else? He's already tortured our family enough."

Ezekiel rubbed his back the way he used to do when Asher was a child and wouldn't go to sleep. "I don't understand him, Asher. I tried to bargain with him, and I told him flat out I wasn't going to do what he wants. Nothing worked, and so here we are."

"*We?*"

"Prophets. We both have the mark and the call."

"Our eyes? Then let's gouge out the blue ones. We can do it for each other, and then we'll be free!"

Even in the darkness, Asher knew that his uncle was smiling at him—a sad smile.

"You know our eyes are the outer mark of what YAH has called us to be on the inside, where no one can see. There's no escape."

Asher collapsed against his uncle and allowed himself a good cry.

"Feel better?" Ezekiel asked him.

"I don't know," he replied miserably. "Maybe a little."

"Ready to go home?"

Asher nodded. He had a question. "What happens now?"

"I must do what YAH tells me to do. That's decided."

"But how can you agree when you don't know what he might ask?"

Ezekiel squeezed his shoulder. "I think it's called trust."

"I don't want it!"

"Of course not. You'd be crazy if you did. I can't say what YAH has in store for you. You two will have to work that out."

"You mean he might do to me what he did to you?"

"Who can say?"

Asher was getting impatient. "Can't you give me a straight answer?"

"If I could, I would."

"This isn't fair."

"I suppose not, but it's what *is*. Now it's up to us to make the best of it—and do what YAH tells us to do."

They started back home. Asher couldn't think of much to say, even though he had many questions.

Ezekiel broke the awkward silence. "What about your job at the Babylonian woman's house?"

"I don't think you're going to allow me to go back. Not the way you hate the Babylonians."

"I don't hate them, Asher. Their foolish idols, yes. I hate the doom that will fall on them the day they are overthrown."

That got Asher's attention. "When? Soon? I want to see that happen."

"I doubt you will."

"Why? Will I be dead?"

"Probably not, but you'll be old. I can't see that far into the future, certainly not with accuracy. No, I think maybe you'll be home in Jerusalem on the day Babylon falls."

"I hope so! I want to be by the city gates when the messenger arrives with the news."

"Perhaps you will be."

"What should I do now, since I can't work for Lady Iltani?"

"Did I ever say you couldn't? I think you should. My call is our fellow Israelites, not the Babylonians. Maybe you have a calling there. It will be easier if you already have a reason to be living among them."

"I don't to live among them! I come home every night—well, almost every night. And how could I have a 'calling' among them? Their gods are powerful! They have no reason to change and worship YAH. Why would they?"

Ezekiel didn't answer right away. Then he said, so quietly that Asher had to strain to hear his words, "Because he is the true god. The only god. All the rest that you see—the idols, the temples, the worship—they're all lies. We Israelites have been given the truth by the one and only god, who created everything and rules this world."

"If he's real, like you say, and rules everything, then why are we here?"

"Because we've been unfaithful. YAH doesn't allow his people to worship any false gods. That's what I have to tell them, and they're not going to like it."

A pang of fear pierced Asher's chest. "Will they kill you?"

"I don't think so. But I don't expect things to be easy from now on."

"I wish we were in Jerusalem!" Asher exclaimed. "Back where we belong."

"That day will come, as I told you. Until then . . ."

At home, they found the evening meal cleared away and the family on the roof, enjoying some breezes.

Azarel had not come back.

Ezekiel found a place next to Elishava. He put his arm around her, and she leaned her head against his shoulder. "I'm glad you're here," she told him.

"We'll take good care of him, won't we?" Benaiah added.

"Thank you for everything you've done," Ezekiel told him. "I knew what was going on, and sometimes I recognized you. I just couldn't speak. Now I feel much better."

"Want to play the Game of Twenty Squares?" Tirzah asked Asher. She'd never invited him to play before. Always he had to beg.

"Sure, but it's too dark."

"That's what lamps are for." Benaiah handed her one.

They played while the others chatted about this and that.

From the start, luck favored Asher. It seemed that every throw of the dice helped him and made things harder for his sister. He also realized he had a new understanding of the game and its strategy that he'd never felt before. The outcome seemed assured from the earliest moves, and Asher won decisively.

Tirzah took it in good humor. "You must be a prophet!" she complained, half-teasingly.

That got everyone's attention.

"Maybe so," Asher agreed. "But that doesn't mean I'm happy about it."

"No more of this tonight," Elisheva told everyone. "We're all much too tired."

“All right,” Tirzah said. She looked directly at Asher. “Just one thing, though. It’s not fair to use your prophetic powers to figure your moves in Twenty Squares. I can beat Azarel, and I can beat you, too, but I’ll never be able to beat YAH!”

That made everyone laugh. They needed it.

Chapter Fifteen

Because of the Sabbath, Asher got to sleep late. While he was eating, his father and uncle came back from morning prayers.

"You can't do that," Benaiah was telling his brother. "Not on the Sabbath."

"I don't know if it's work, exactly," Ezekiel said. "That doesn't matter, though. I have to do what YAH tells me, and I need your help."

"Can't it wait until tomorrow? You don't want to borrow more trouble after getting everyone riled up last night. Your words made them angry enough. What might happen when you start *doing* things?"

"I don't know. But YAH has promised to protect me. He'll protect you, too, if you help me."

"What's going on?" Asher asked.

"Your uncle says YAH gave him a command and he has to obey it today—now."

"Come with us," Ezekiel said. "We're going to the shop first."

Why not? Asher thought. He'd rather witness what his uncle had in mind than hear about it later.

At the shop, Ezekiel took an unfired brick and some iron pens used for scratching designs into pots before they were fired. He instructed Benaiah to get a basket of wet clay. Then he led them to the village square. There was no commerce, it being the Sabbath, but people were strolling, enjoying a day of rest. Some priests were gathered, probably discussing fine points of the law. Children were playing, and some small girls were doing a circle dance.

In the middle of the square, Ezekiel sat down and began scratching an image on the sides of the clay brick. Asher recognized it: Solomon's temple standing above the king's palace and the other buildings of Jerusalem.

Ezekiel worked diligently, paying no mind to anyone. Asher stood nearby, but not too close. He felt uncomfortable being linked to this strange man sitting in the dirt etching pictures of Jerusalem on a brick.

When Ezekiel was satisfied, he scooped up a mound of earth and put the brick on top. Then he took wet clay and began fashioning siege walls, towers, and ladders. These he placed all around the brick. Soon, his purpose was clear: a model of Jerusalem surrounded by an attacking army. It was all too familiar, a reminder of what had happened four years earlier.

A few children gathered to watch. Two boys snitched some clay and ran off before anyone could stop them. Ezekiel didn't even notice. Then adults joined the children. Before long, the prophet was surrounded by curiosity seekers, who whispered among themselves and pointed at his project.

Asher kept his place. His father had stepped closer to his brother and stood tall and straight, as if protecting the worker from any interference. Some priests showed up. Among them, Asher recognized two who had been at his house. One, an old man with a scraggly beard and an eye clouded by sickly white film, inspected the model of the besieged city. "What are you telling us, prophet? That's what you pretend to be, isn't it? We already know Jerusalem was taken by Nebuchadrezzar, and here we are. What of the *future*?"

Ezekiel made no answer but kept working. Soon, he was done. Before him was a miniature model in wet clay. It was crude, but unmistakable to anyone who had known Jerusalem.

"Tell us what it means!" someone in the crowd cried.

Ezekiel got to his feet. He scanned the faces of his fellow villagers but said nothing. Then he nodded to Benaiah, gathered up the clay-stained basket, and made his way out of the market.

People began buzzing. Asher stayed where he was, hoping to catch what they were saying.

"He told the priests last night that he'd seen a vision from YAH," one woman said.

"He's gone mad," asserted another.

"This is nothing new," complained a man holding a baby. "We all lived through what happened in Jerusalem."

Then Asher recognized Simeon. He gazed down at Ezekiel's work, then looked at the people. "Don't you see?" he asked. "Our brother *is* showing us what will happen. Jerusalem surrounded by her enemies again. Jerusalem besieged! Jerusalem . . ."

"What?" cried several people at once. "Tell us!"

Simeon looked sorrowfully at the clay model. "Jerusalem conquered."

The crowd fell silent.

Asher felt his stomach knot. Simeon had to be wrong. His uncle couldn't be prophesying that the Babylonians would return to Jerusalem and destroy it. Not when the exiles would be going home one day soon. His uncle was mistaken. He had to ask him, beg him, to say that was not what he meant.

The half-blind priest advanced toward Simeon. "You have no right to say such things," he began. "Stirring up the people, making them afraid. Many of us have concurred, and we agree that YAH will soon deliver us and allow us to return to Jerusalem. This so-called 'prophet' is nothing but a troublemaker!" With that, he stomped on the model walls and siege engines Ezekiel had constructed. Then he made the mistake of kicking the clay brick and howled at having injured his toes.

Serves you right, thought Asher.

The priest proceeded to flatten the rest of the siege works. He ordered a child to pick up the brick and dump it in the canal. Then he limped away.

The crowd lost interest, and in a moment, only Asher remained, gazing down at the ruin of his uncle's work. He was angry with the priest but more upset by what he suspected Ezekiel had intended. He didn't want to ask, but he had to know.

At home, he learned that his uncle had taken to his bed. Elisheva said he had nearly collapsed when he came through the door and was already deeply asleep.

He found his father in the courtyard. "Did he say anything?" Asher asked.

"Nothing."

"What did he mean—by what he built?"

"You already know."

He wanted to protest, but there was no fight left in him. His uncle was right, and it was useless to pretend differently. But he hated it, hated everything it might mean.

"Jerusalem will be destroyed," Asher muttered. "That's the message. The Babylonians aren't finished. They'll be back."

"So be it." There was no feeling in his father's words—no anger, no despair. Nothing.

"We have to warn the people in Jerusalem!"

"Oh? And how do you plan to do that? They wouldn't listen to Jeremiah. Do you think they'll listen to your uncle? Or to you?"

"They have to! Then maybe YAH . . ."

"YAH will *what*?"

"Change his mind?"

"Is that a question? Tell me, son. Do you even believe in YAH?"

Utter silence fell on them.

"Look at me!" his father commanded. "Do you believe, or not?"

His head throbbed. "I—I don't know."

"How can you not know! You're a prophet. You saw at least part of what your uncle saw, didn't you?"

Asher kept looking at his father. No words came.

"Tell me!" Benaiah roared.

Elisheva appeared at the door. "Why are you shouting?"

"I'm sorry, but this is between us. We'll be finished in a moment."

"I'll go back to Ezekiel," she said. "Shabbat shalom, brother."

Benaiah turned back to Asher. "It's not good enough to claim 'I don't know'! Make up your mind. Do you believe?"

Asher had to look away.

"Then you had better find out. How can a prophet in Israel not believe in YAH?"

"We're not in Israel now," Asher reminded him.

"Don't be disrespectful."

"And I'm not a prophet."

"You didn't deny it last night! You said 'maybe.' But I suppose that's the coward's way out."

His father's ugly words stung, and he wouldn't let them go unanswered, even if it meant punishment. "What about *you,* Father? Do you believe? You never talk about YAH. I hardly ever see you praying or going to sit with the priests in the evenings."

His father's shoulders slumped and he sighed. "No, I can't claim to believe anymore, not since the day the soldiers murdered your mother. She was a faithful daughter of Israel. I know because we grew up together, fell in love, and married. Your mother never once strayed from the laws of YAH. Never once! She always believed with her whole heart, and as a reward, she was slaughtered by our enemies. So do I—*can* I—honestly believe in YAH now? It tortures me. What god allows an innocent woman like your mother to die the way she did?"

"Father—"

"And now my brother and son turn out to be prophets? And my son doesn't know if he even believes? He willingly works in the house of our oppressors? YAH, is this my punishment for hating you? Do you have no pity?"

Asher stood horrified to hear his father rant at the god he wasn't sure he believed in. But Asher felt the same way. One moment he didn't believe, one moment he wasn't sure, another moment he did believe.

And Josiah had confessed to the same confusion. Asher groped for a way make his father feel better. "I'll quit working for her," he promised. "I know it's not right. I don't want to upset you or my uncle."

"I don't care what you do. You're old enough to decide your own way. I'm going to rest. The Sabbath never lasts long enough."

Asher went to his bed, too, relieved to be alone. He closed his eyes, and the wheels and eyes from his vision appeared. To get rid of them, he had to stare, open-eyed, at the ceiling. Then the awful faces hovered above him, seemingly close enough to touch, but when he reached for them, he found only air—thin air.

* * *

Next morning, Asher woke early to find Ezekiel bustling about the courtyard, measuring grains, which he dumped into a kneading bowl. Elisheva sat nearby, looking bemused.

"Come help me," Ezekiel invited Asher.

"What are you doing?"

"YAH has instructed me to cook some bread." He grimaced. "I reminded him I've never baked a thing in my life."

"I told him I'd do it," Elisheva said grimly, "but your uncle is stubborn."

Ezekiel smiled at her. "Your husband is following orders."

"From YAH, according to you. I never knew he shared recipes."

"Why not? He created the world, so I suppose he knows how to bake a tasty loaf."

"What goes into YAH's secret recipe?" Asher asked.

"Wheat, barley, ground dried beans, dry lentils, millet, and emmer."

"Salt?"

"YAH didn't say so."

"Leavening?" Elisheva asked.

"No," Ezekiel replied. "It must rise on its own."

Elisheva rolled her eyes.

"Now for water," Ezekiel said. He began adding it to the grain mixture, which immediately dissolved into a sticky, grayish-brown soup that looked exactly like the village streets after rain. When Ezekiel was satisfied, he set the bowl in the sun and covered it.

Benaiah appeared from his room. "What's going on?" asked, rubbing sleep from his eyes.

"Ask your brother," Elisheva told him.

Ezekiel proudly showed off the gloppy mess. "We're waiting for it to rise," he announced.

"Looks like you'll have a long wait," Benaiah noted.

"Will it be ready to bake today?" Elisheva asked.

"I don't know. I hope so! Some warm bread would taste good, don't you think?"

Elisheva looked skeptical. "If you're done, please clean up after yourself."

"I'm going to the latrine," Benaiah told them. He left the courtyard, shaking his head.

"Is there enough wood for the oven?" Elisheva asked. "I wasn't planning to bake this morning."

"I'll check," Ezekiel said. He looked in the bin. "Not enough. What now?"

"Someone has to go get some," Elisheva replied. "Asher?"

"I can't. I have to go to work."

"Come with me," Ezekiel told him. "Maybe there's time. I'll help."

In the street, they were met by a slave from the Lady Iltani's house, informing Asher that she was ill and did not require his services that day. When the slave had gone his way, Ezekiel looked pleased. "Now you won't be late. YAH must be looking out for you! Anyway, we won't be needing wood. YAH has something else in mind for fuel."

"What?"

"He told me to use--our own excrement."

"What are you talking about? That's crazy! No one'll eat bread baked on human shit."

Ezekiel smiled. "I didn't say 'shit' when I argued with YAH about it. My chosen word was 'turds.'"

Asher had to laugh. His uncle was either playing a joke on him, or he had truly gone mad. He decided to go along. "You argued with YAH?"

Ezekiel nodded.

"How did that go?"

"I told him I've kept kosher all my life and I didn't intend to eat anything baked in uncleanness now."

"And he said—"

"He said I had a point, so he changed his mind."

"YAH changed his mind? He always does things *his* way. When he gives a command, you have to obey."

"That's what I told you, and I had no reason to think anything different. But believe it or not, he did give in. I still have to cook the bread, but he compromised and said I can use dried animal dung. I wasn't going to press my point after that."

"So why did you tell me about having to use our own . . . droppings?"

"I just felt like messing with you!" Ezekiel looked pleased with himself. There was no figuring the man. He might well be crazy, but he could still joke around. Then he looked perplexed. "Where can get some dung? I've been trying to think of something."

"There's plenty at the plantation. Piles of it for fertilizing the trees."

"That's a brilliant idea. We grab a couple of baskets and find what we need there. Will anyone mind?"

"I doubt it, but we'll have to go and see."

That's what they did. At the gate, the slave boy recognized Asher and seemed unconcerned that Ezekiel was with him. The shit shovelers, which was how Asher now referred to them, didn't care what they did, and in a short time, they had filled two bags.

At home, they found that the dough had not risen a bit, but some bubbles had formed on the surface. They gave it another hour, and when it was obvious that it was not going to do anything more, Ezekiel shaped it into balls and stuck them on iron spits. Then he announced they were going back to the market to bake it. That's when Elisheva decided to fetch Benaiah from the shop, where he, Azarel, and Tirzah had gone to start the day's work.

Benaiah came puffing from running the whole way, and he didn't care one bit for his brother's plan. "You're going to do what?" he challenged. "Cook it over an open fire of animal droppings? Please, Ezekiel! Enough is enough!"

"YAH commands," was the reply.

So they trekked back to the market. In the middle of the square, they built their fire. Soon, the rancid aroma of burning dung filled the air. People turned up, eager to see the next antics in Ezekiel's prophetic show.

When the fire was down to coals, Ezekiel held some bread over them and commenced cooking. He had to keep turning the spits to prevent the sticky balls from charring. Asher joined him.

More and more people gathered to gawk, fascinated to see what would happen next.

When Ezekiel determined that the bread was done, he allowed it to cool and then removed one piece.

"The bread of siege!" he proclaimed. "Thus says YAH, the Lord of Heaven's Armies: 'I am about to remove wholesome bread from Jerusalem. They will eat bread weighed out in small portions and with nausea from the pollution of animal dung. Their water shall be portioned, and they will drink and eat in desolation, each man and his brother, each woman and her sister. They shall rot in their guilt.'"

The crowd began to murmur. Angry voices denounced the so-called prophet's words.

Ezekiel paid no mind. Instead, he bit into the baked ball of dough, chewed, and swallowed. He nodded to Asher to follow suit. He did, and he found the so-called bread to be as nasty as he imagined it would be. Dense, flavorless, still wet and gooey at its center, burnt at its edges.

I can't swallow this, he realized. He tried again, though. With an effort, he got a little down, but that was all. When he tried another bite, he gagged. He dropped the rest onto the ground. Elisheva got Asher's attention and gave him a look that seemed to say, "I knew how it would be."

Ezekiel tried a second mouthful, swallowed, and then let all the rest fall into the dirt. He scattered the remaining coals and used a spit to stir them until they were extinguished.

"The bread of siege," he proclaimed again. "Thus says YAH."

Then he gathered up everything else and headed out of the market. The crowd dispersed, but some spectators—the priests—remained, perhaps to confer about how to deal with this new and troublesome prophet.

Asher stayed, too, somehow compelled to stand guard over the blackened ring of earth. He watched as stray dogs made their way into the square, attracted by the smell of cooked food. They found the discarded balls of bread, sniffed at them, then slunk away. Apparently, there were some things that even half-starved dogs refused to touch.

Chapter Sixteen

At home, while Elisheva prepared a meal, Benaiah raised the question that was perhaps on everyone's mind.

"So what next?" he asked Ezekiel. "Another stunt to get attention?"

"Benaiah," Elisheva scolded. "That's unkind."

"It's all right," Ezekiel told her. "YAH does seem to have a flair for the dramatic."

"All your talk about YAH!" Benaiah exclaimed. "Maybe it's all in your head."

Ezekiel shook the head in question. "If you mean I'm making things up, then you credit me with more imagination that I've ever had in my life. And how do you explain what your son saw?"

"Asher?" his father asked. "Is there anything more to tell us? You and your uncle aren't playing some joke on everyone?"

"No, sir. Like I told you—I saw a little bit. If you believe one of us, you have to believe us both."

Benaiah sighed. "I see there's no getting around you two. Wherever all this came from, one thing is sure."

"What's that?" Ezekiel asked.

"You've made some powerful enemies. That's a shame because people used to respect you and listen to your wise words. It's a good thing Simeon vouches for you now. Even our corrupt priests respect his opinion."

"Corrupt priests?" Asher asked. "What do you mean?"

"The ones who care only about themselves. Who want only one thing: that we all get to return home soon so they can take up their lives of wealth and privilege. They stir up hopes of freedom without caring a thing about the people. Even your friend Josiah and his family are tempted to believe them. All this nonsense about the Babylonians freeing us! Tell me: if you were King Nebuchadrezzar and had easily conquered Jerusalem and brought thousands of its best people to serve you here, would you let them go back?"

"I guess not."

"You guess not! Did Pharaoh let our ancestors go just because they were homesick for Canaan?"

"No."

"And neither will the almighty king of Babylon let *us* go. We don't even have a Moses to lead us. All we have are . . ."

"Crazy prophets like me," Ezekiel finished for him.

"I wasn't going to say that."

"But you thought it. It's all right. I don't mind." He took Elisheva's hand. "I'm blessed, no matter what happens."

"And what do you think will happen?"

Ezekiel shook his head. "I don't know."

"And now?" Benaiah asked.

"We wait to see what YAH has in mind."

No one spoke, but Asher noticed that everyone was looking at Ezekiel.

"I'm not going to grow wings!" he exclaimed, the familiar humor in his voice. "But I am going to help my lady clean up our meal. Then let's go to the shop. I have the feeling I'll do better with clay than bread dough today!"

* * *

That night, Asher was awakened when Azarel stumbled into their room, crashed against his bed, and groaned.

"What's wrong?" Asher asked. "You drunk?"

"No. I'm hurt. You have to help me."

Asher went for a lamp. When he came back, he found Azarel had pulled off his tunic, revealing a long slash along the left side of his torso.

"Get some water and rags," Azarel whispered urgently. "And for YAH's sake, don't wake anyone. I don't want to have to explain this yet."

Asher felt his way in the darkness, certain that he was making enough racket to rouse everyone in the house and the neighbors, too. But there was no sound.

Azarel washed the wound. "Hold a cloth on it," he said. "We have to stop it bleeding."

Asher did. The first cloth was quickly red. A second one took longer, but a third stopped the flow.

"It's not deep," Azarel assured him. "I'm not going to die on you, if that's what you're afraid of."

"What happened?"

"I'll tell you in a minute."

"You can't keep this from Father," Asher warned him. "He'll find out. Look at all this blood!"

"I know. But I need time to decide what to say. Get some more clean rags so we can bind the cut. Then I'll put my tunic on and hopefully we can make it 'til morning."

"You're sure you're not bleeding to death?"

"Hey, I'm tough! It hurts like anything, but like I said, it's not deep."

Asher made Azarel lie down while he cleaned up the mess. When he was done, he sat on his bed, watching and waiting to see if the wound would bleed again, in which case he'd already decided that he would wake their father.

"I'll tell you what really happened if you swear to keep your mouth shut. You can't tell our family, nor those people you work for. No one. You swear?"

"Yes. What's going on?"

"Everyone in the family thinks I go out nights to drink and find women. That's what the old man says, right?"

"Yeah."

"Good. I want him to keep believing that. It's safer for all of you."

"How do you mean?"

"When I go out, I don't go drinking and whoring, which is what everyone thinks. I join up with some other guys from our villages. Guys like me, who hate the guts of every Babylonian we see. I swore I'd kill the soldiers who murdered our mother. I don't know if I'll ever come across them, so I make other Babylonians pay for their crimes. It doesn't matter if they're not the ones who actually did it. They're all guilty in my eyes, and they all deserve to die."

"What are you talking about? What do you do?"

"We meet up. I can't tell you where, and it doesn't matter, because it's never the same place twice in a row. We don't have an exact plan, but we're pledged to hurt anyone or anything that we find, especially guys about our own age."

A shiver of horror ran down Asher's backbone. "You—*kill* people?"

"Not people, Asher. Babylonians! There's a difference."

"Who have you killed?"

"Does it matter? It happens mostly in the dark anyway, so I don't usually see any faces. I don't care to see or to know. They're all mongrels anyway."

This can't be true, Asher thought. *It's too horrible to be true.*

"You shocked?" Azarel asked him.

"Yes! And scared. Who else is with you?"

"You wouldn't know them. There is one, though. Someone you *do* know."

"Not—Josiah?"

"The very same. He's one of our best warriors. Without fear. Totally committed to our cause. Good with a knife, too."

"You're lying!"

"I'm not. It's totally true."

"You'll all be caught and executed!"

"Keep your voice down. Maybe we will, but that's no worse than living here, like this."

"It's not so bad here. We're making it."

"Slaves usually find a way to 'make it,' Asher. But that's not living. I have to live free, not like a bird in a cage."

"Why'd you tell me any of this?"

"I needed your help," he said, touching his side. "And I appreciate it."

"You could have lied to me, like you're going to lie to the family. What will you tell them?"

"That I was drinking with friends—"

"In Babylon?"

"Naw. Right here in town. A lot of that goes on, little brother. You just don't know about it because you're such a good boy."

A good boy who slept with a slave girl, Asher said to himself.

"I'll tell them that a guy picked a fight with me and before I knew it, he'd cut me. I'll say a couple of my buddies brought me home and I woke you up because I didn't think it was all that serious and I knew the family had a hard day and I wanted to let everyone sleep."

Asher just looked at him.

"What's the problem?"

"Do you hear how crazy that sounds? They're going to be suspicious. Not only that; Father can check your story. He'll want to know which tavern, and he can go there and—"

"Let him. The guy who owns the place will cover for me. We go there a lot, Asher. We're not out killing Babylonians *every* night." He chuckled.

Those words were more chilling than any others his brother had spoken.

"It's my story and I'll stick to it. Remember, you swore."

"You've got to stop! You'll get caught. I can't believe the night guards haven't arrested you already. When they do, you'll be tortured to death."

"Babylon's a big place, Asher. Lots of dark streets. Lots of places to hide in ambush. Lots of stupid drunk people staggering around in the dead of night when they should be at home in bed."

"Like you! You could have been killed tonight."

"But I wasn't. We can't stop fighting our enemies, ever. Listen to me: our uncle believes YAH is going to keep punishing us and is using the Babylonians to do it. He may be right; I can't say, but some of us are done living like slaves."

"Do you even believe in YAH?" Someone had recently asked him the same hard question.

"I don't know—I guess so. Ezekiel can believe what he wants about YAH; I won't argue with him. What's the point? But I agree with him on the other thing: Babylon is not done with us Israelites. It's just a matter of time before they decide to pay another visit to Jerusalem and finish what they began—unless we stop them first. In the meantime, we've got to avenge ourselves for every drop of our blood they've already shed. For our mother's blood, Asher! Don't you get that? I'll stop when *I* think it's time to stop. Not when some god tells me to."

"I wish you hadn't come home tonight," Asher said. "Why didn't you go to the physician right away? Father will make you go first thing in the morning. And why did you tell me all this? You didn't have to. I'm sorry I swore anything."

"But you'll keep your oath," Azarel assured him. "Like me, you have honor."

"You? Honor? A murderer?"

"A *soldier*, brother. Fighting for my people the best way I know how."

"Then I can't have anything to do with it. I'll back you up like I promised, but I don't want to know anything else, ever. Get me?"

Azarel lay back down. "Yeah, I do. By the gods, I'm hurting. Take my advice: don't ever get yourself sliced up. It's awful."

"Let me look at your bandage."

Some blood had seeped through, but not much.

"You should try and rest," Asher told him. "Morning'll come soon enough."

But his brother was already asleep.

Chapter Seventeen

Azarel lied convincingly about his misadventure—and everyone accepted his story. Benaiah reacted with a mixture of anger and relief: anger that his older son was a drunken lout and relief that he hadn't been stabbed to death in a tavern brawl. He insisted on taking Azarel to the physician even though in the daylight, the wound didn't look all that bad.

As far as Asher could tell, no one suspected the truth of what *he* knew. He earned praise for taking such good care of his brother, but Elisheva scolded him gently for not rousing her. He'd done a decent job, but she asserted that a woman's skillful touch would have been a comfort to the wounded man.

Asher was glad he had to leave for work. He wasn't really surprised when Josiah appeared. "How's Azarel this morning?"

"My father took him to the physician. He's going to be all right. How do you know about it? Your family doesn't let you go to taverns."

"Why are you angry?"

"You weren't out drinking together."

"I was! I sneak out at night. Sometimes I just walk around, and sometimes I get wine at the tavern. The owner knows me, and he looks out for me. Wine helps me sleep."

"Quit lying! Azarel told me everything. You gang up with other guys and kill people in Babylon."

Josiah put up his hands. "Shhh! What are you talking about?"

"Assuming it's true, why would someone like *you* be part of it? You—a murderer? Come on, Josiah. Tell me the truth."

Josiah took in a deep breath. "Keep walking," he advised. "And promise me you'll stay calm."

Asher promised. Then he shared with Josiah what Azarel had told him. "How much of it's true, Josiah? None of it? Some? All of it?"

He didn't answer right away. Then, in a whisper: "All of it."

Asher had to stop. Around them, people made their way through the village streets, hurrying to the day's tasks. But it felt as though he and Josiah were all alone on a distant mountaintop.

"*Why*?"

"We're obeying YAH."

"YAH told you to kill people?"

"Yes. Just the way he told Joshua to slay everyone—men, women, children—when our ancestors conquered Canaan."

"YAH commanded you," Asher repeated, trying to make sense of what he'd heard.

"Yes. And he must be obeyed."

"You told me just a couple days ago that you don't always believe in YAH! Remember?"

Josiah nodded.

"But you kill in his name? You kill anyway?"

"I wonder about Him sometimes, and when I do, He disciplines me. He guides me back to His way of thinking, reminds me that I'm a soldier sworn to obey his superiors."

"Like when you're wiping blood off the knife you just used to murder an innocent man? Azarel told me you're lethal with a sharp blade. He said you're fearless—and merciless."

"He said that?" Josiah puffed out his chest.

"You're proud?"

He looked Asher in the eye. "Yes. And humble that YAH has chosen me to help liberate our people. To help liberate *you*."

"I don't want that kind of liberation!"

"What will you do, then? Wait for YAH to come swooping down from the heavens and carry us on eagles' wings back to Judah? You're going to have a long wait."

"You told me you believe that very thing. That it'll be a happy day. And then you sang pilgrims' songs all afternoon like you're about to go up to Jerusalem for the feasts."

Josiah chuckled—the same way Azarel had just a few hours earlier. "I had you fooled, didn't I? You believed I'm just a harmless boy without the guts to fight back when he's kicked in the face. Those days are over, Asher. We have a plan."

"Who? What plan?"

"I can't tell you—not yet, at least. If I ever do, it'll be after you've proven yourself."

"No, thanks! I'm not proving myself to anyone."

"But you're curious, aren't you?"

"Stop it! Quit messing with me."

"Admit it, Asher. You want to know. Admit you hate your life here. Anyone with eyes can see that."

He couldn't deny it. He'd felt that way a long time, until he snagged the job for Iltani. Then things started looking up. Decent clothes. Excellent food. The luxuries of a fine house, even if it didn't belong to him. A beautiful girl to share his bed . . .

All part of the bargain he'd made--with the people his brother and his friend were sworn to slaughter.

"What are you thinking?" Josiah asked.

"That I wish you'd go away and leave me alone. I've heard enough."

"Poor Asher! Feeling sorry for himself. It's time you grew up, friend."

"Friend? I hardly knew the person you said you were. And now you're someone—something!—completely different. You and I—we've got nothing in common."

"Only that we're Israelites exiled from our homeland, doomed to stay here until we find the guts to fight back and regain our freedom."

"Fight back? Against this?" He opened his arms wide as if to embrace all of Babylon. "You can't do anything, Josiah, except try and shed enough blood to satisfy your hatred."

"Are you done? Do you think I haven't heard all that before? My fellow warriors and I say the same things to each other all the time. We have to speak them out loud. That's the only way we can test the lies you just spouted against the truth of what YAH has ordered us to do. We can't stop any more than your uncle can stop what's happening to him."

"Which is . . .?"

"The voice inside his head: the voice he believes is YAH's. You saw what Ezekiel's already done. That's just the beginning. I'm sure there's more to come."

"And what about me?"

Josiah shrugged. "Only you can answer your question."

"Ezekiel says we Israelites are being punished for our sins against YAH. He believes YAH is going to keep punishing us unless we repent and quit worshiping idols. If he's right, there's nothing you can do to change that, no matter how many Babylonians you slaughter."

"I heard him, too, remember? It's a shame his so-called vision isn't helpful to our cause. He's blaming us for our enslavement when he should be condemning our Babylonian overlords. Most of our priests feel the same way."

"What about your father and grandfather?"

"They defend Ezekiel, but they're wrong."

"And you pretend to agree with them?"

"That's not your worry. Next time I pray, I'll ask that your uncle actually hears from YAH, not his own imagination—that we must have more warriors to fight this war."

"He could never say that!"

"Why not? I thought true prophets are bound to speak whatever YAH tells them, even if it gets them into trouble. You *do* believe your uncle is a true prophet, don't you?"

Asher didn't like being baited, and that's exactly how he felt. But he was having a hard time answering his friend's taunts. "Ezekiel would be arrested for speaking against the Babylonians," he told Josiah. "You might not care about that, since you don't care about anything except murdering people who've done you no wrong. If he prophesies in public that the Babylonians are going to be punished and overthrown, they'll get rid of him, no questions asked. He'll end up in some prison or hanging from a gallows. *My uncle*, whom I happen to love."

"In war, personal feelings don't matter, Asher. The *cause* matters. It's the only thing that does."

They were approaching the road Asher had to take to get to his job. "I've got to go," he told Josiah. "I don't know if I want to talk to you anymore."

Josiah grabbed the sleeve of his fine tunic. "Listen," he told him. "You're an Israelite. Nothing can change that. Why not quit acting sorry for yourself and do something to help us?"

"Like what? Grab a knife and cut people's throats? No, thanks."

"Nothing like that. I thought about you last night. There's a reason you've been hired to work in a house of our enemies. You can be our eyes and ears. That's all you have to do. Pay attention to what goes on there. Listen in on their conversations if you can. Find out what they're saying. Especially if they ever mention how some of their people are being killed. Listen to hear what's happening with King Jeconiah and the royal family. See if Nebuchadrezzar is planning another war against Judah."

"They wouldn't know that! That's a military secret."

"There are no secrets, Asher. Just important information that hasn't been uncovered yet. Listen, watch, and if you can, tell me if there's anything we might need to know."

"In other words, be a spy."

Josiah nodded. "Exactly. Like the others we've planted throughout the city—even in Nebuchadrezzar's palace."

"What do you think you're going to accomplish, with all these so-called spies?"

"I said I can't tell you now. Maybe if I come to believe you can be trusted—"

"One more thing," Asher broke in. "Why did my brother tell me everything? Why have you?"

"To save you, brother."

"From what?"

"From becoming a whore in willing service to our enemies."

"Take that back!"

Josiah just looked at him.

Asher glared at him. "For all you know, I'm going directly to the Babylonians and report you."

"And Azarel, too?"

Asher had no answer.

"We thought carefully about telling you," Josiah said. "Azarel was against it at first. Wanted to protect you and your family. But we convinced him we need all the soldiers we can recruit. I knew it was risky. I don't really know you any better than you know me. You may be a traitor, even though Azarel insists you can be trusted."

For some reason, it pleased him to hear that. "That's what he told you?"

"Maybe he's right; I don't know. If you betray us, it's on your conscience. If being an Israelite means anything, you'll do what I say. But remember: if we learn you've blabbed, we'll consider you our enemy. In war, you take care of your enemy so he can't cause you any more trouble."

"You bastard! You're threatening me?"

Josiah gave him a steady look. "Let's not call it that. Let's just say I'm telling you how things might be."

"I have to go," Asher broke in. "See you around." He hurried away before he smashed his fist in Josiah's smug face.

So much for getting his thoughts together! If only he could escape to somewhere quiet, peaceful—somewhere without any other people. But that was impossible. He arrived at his lady's house just in time to accompany her to the plantation. She took her usual seat, he nearby, waiting for any orders. Before long, Josiah appeared. He gave Asher a steady look before disappearing into the crowd of workers facing another day of drudgery among the date palms.

Lady Iltani spoke to many people. She had words with one of her overseers, scolding him for being too hard on workers he disliked and too soft on those he did. Treat them alike, she warned, if he wanted to keep his job.

When the last stragglers had passed through the gate, the lady went to her litter. "Walk by me," she told Asher. "Tell me the news."

"What would you like to know?"

"How is your uncle? You said he was taken ill."

"Much better. He came to himself, and now he's well."

"Well enough to make a scene in your village, from what I hear."

"I don't know what—"

"Don't play dumb! You know what I mean. What's this about his making some kind of clay model of your city and then putting up a siege around it? A grown man playing in the mud?"

"He's a fine potter."

"That's not important. What did he *mean* by it? And then, cooking lumps of soggy dough over a fire of animal droppings! Has the man lost his mind?"

He was nervous about saying anything. "He's all right. He's doing what our god has ordered him to do."

"Then your god has lost *his* mind!"

"My Lady, please—"

"Put me down," she ordered her bearers. They obeyed without a word, without a glance that revealed they'd heard anything or wondered at their mistress's command.

"My uncle . . ."

"Yes? His name?"

"Ezekiel."

"Ah, yes, Ezekiel! I was right. He told some of your priests that the armies of Babylon will invade your nation again and destroy your cities."

How could she know that? True, Ezekiel had declared that the charred lumps of bread were the food of starvation in a besieged city, but that's all he'd said to the crowd in the market. He'd shared his full vision only with those few men gathered at the house. Someone who'd been in their house and heard his uncle prophesy was . . .

A betrayer.

A spy for the Babylonians.

Just as he himself had only a few minutes earlier been asked to spy for the Israelites against those same Babylonians.

"What's the matter?" Iltani challenged. "Are you surprised I know things about what goes on in your village?"

He could only nod.

"What did your uncle say?"

"Nothing against you!" Asher exclaimed. "Nothing against you or your people. He said that YAH, our god, is punishing *us* for our faithlessness to his covenant."

"What covenant? I don't know your religion."

"That he would be our god and protect us as long as we obey his commandments. Including his command not to worship other gods."

"You mentioned that to me. And I repeat what I told you then: this mighty god of yours isn't worth much."

Now he wished this mocking woman could have seen what his uncle saw in his vision. Then the lady would change her tune.

He had been granted a glimpse of the YAH's glory, and *he* still doubted. Why should a pagan woman believe anything he told her about his god?

"Your uncle—this so-called prophet—doesn't he call for the overthrow of Babylon?"

"No, my lady."

"But he does predict another siege against your city—what do you call it?"

"Jerusalem." A fleeting image of YAH's temple, proudly crowning Mt. Zion and gleaming in the sunshine, flashed in his mind. The enemy had already desecrated it once. What worse disaster lay in the future? He knew the answer—if his uncle were right. But he wouldn't accept it. Another siege—capture—destruction—those could never happen.

"Your own prophets predict its destruction," Iltani told him. Do they have spies inside Nebuchadrezzar's inner circle of advisors and generals?"

At the moment, that seemed possible. Almost anything seemed possible.

"No, My Lady! Your king would sense it and discover such men."

"On that we agree!"

"Yes."

"Home!" she called to the litter bearers. They obeyed.

Asher was dismissed as soon as they arrived at the estate, but Iltani told him to be at her call; she was not yet done speaking with him.

He was summoned to serve her the mid-day meal. When they were alone, she informed him that his presence was required the following evening; she'd be entertaining friends, including two distinguished guests he would want to meet. That's all she would say. Iltani also informed him that the New Year's Festival was coming up in a few days. She would attend, as always, and he would accompany her as her servant.

Asher agreed to everything. He longed for another night with Damkina and could only hope she would appear as she had the last time.

The day dragged. Iltani spent the afternoon with her slave girls, subjecting herself to beauty treatments ahead of hosting her friends the following evening. She had no use for Asher, who was dismissed early.

He wasn't sure what to do, so he simply wandered through the maze of streets. He had a bit of money and spent it on a cup of palm wine, which made him hot and drowsy. Every so often, he checked his pockets to make sure the lady's seal was not lost or stolen. Hungry, he bought bread and some dates, then found a comparatively quiet street where he sat, his back against a mud brick wall, and tried to think.

Many things spun in his mind, but one crowded out all the others: Asher the spy. *Asher the double spy.*

Josiah and his band of cutthroats wanted him to spy on the Babylonians, find out what they were saying and thinking about their Israelite captives.

The Babylonians would want the same. It was only a matter of time before Iltani would ask him to tell more of what he knew about events in his village, especially anything involving his uncle. She had powerful friends. She herself was formidable; he realized that now: mistress of a large, wealthy plantation. Perhaps her "distinguished guests" were women from Nebuchadrezzar's court. You couldn't go much higher than that unless you were discussing the royal family itself. Everyone knew Nebuchadrezzar had many wives and many more children. All would be wealthy, influential. Would some of them be at Iltani's party?

He munched on the tender bread, so different from the muck his uncle had tried to bake. The dates were sweet and chewy. As his belly filled, he felt himself relaxing, ready to doze in the afternoon sunshine. But that was a sure way to get robbed, or at least stepped on.

He roused himself and thought hard about what to do. Did he want to help the Babylonians?

No.

Did he want to help Azarel, Josiah, and their gang?

Again, no.

Did he want to help anyone?

Yes, he decided. His uncle.

Who else?

The answer, when it came, was obvious.

Himself.

Chapter Eighteen

At home, things seemed almost normal. Azarel was on his bed, resting. Benaiah wouldn't allow him at the shop, saying he needed time to heal. They'd gotten into an ugly quarrel, which ended only when Azarel promised never to leave the house again at night.

"A promise I won't keep," he told Asher grimly. "I'll lay low for a few nights, lull the old man into believing I'm reformed, then . . ."

"You'd be a fool to keep on. Josiah talked to me. Those guys are fanatics! They're going to get caught sooner or later and put to death. If anything happened to you, Father would kill himself. Do you want our whole family destroyed?"

"Don't worry. I won't ever be caught. I'm too smart. I know the city, and I've made some useful friends."

"I can't hear anything else."

Azarel ignored that. "Did Josiah ask you to spy for us?"

"How'd you know? He said he thought of it just this morning."

"We discussed it and agreed you might be persuaded if the idea didn't come from me. I told him you never do a thing I ask."

"Thanks a lot."

"What'd you tell him?"

"I said I would. What else could I do?"

"He can be--persuasive. Well, that's good news. We need every bit of help we can get."

Asher was bone tired of the subject. He lay down and threw an arm over his eyes. If only he could blot out the world!

"Take a nap," Azarel suggested. "You'll feel better after you do."

"No, thanks. I'm not sleepy."

"See what I told you! You never do one thing I suggest."

"Maybe that's because your suggestions are so awful."

"Aw, now you've hurt my feelings, little brother."

"Just leave me alone!"

"Okay. But this isn't finished."

Asher hated that Azarel was right, and there was nothing he could do to change it.

* * *

Benaiah, Ezekiel, and Tirzah returned from the shop at the usual time. They'd been mobbed all day, waiting on people claiming they needed a cup or a new bowl for one they'd broken, or a new jar for olive oil.

"They really wanted a look at their crazy neighbor," Ezekiel joked. "The guy who makes mud models and tries to cook lumps of soggy dough on skewers over a turd fire. Never mind if his pottery is second-rate."

"You create beautiful things," Elisheva assured him. "Beautiful things." She put her arms around him.

Asher wasn't sure what to make of his uncle. After the drama of the past days, he seemed so—normal, his old self again.

Asher prayed that night—his first prayer in many nights—asking YAH to please leave his uncle alone. Ezekiel had done what YAH commanded him. What more was required? Now it was up to the people to listen and change their ways.

After the meal, everyone was too tired to sit on the terrace and talk. Azarel admitted that his wound burned and he needed sleep. Soon afterward, they all went to bed.

Asher dreamed. A figure without a face came at him, brandishing a knife of iron. Asher tried to run, but his feet were fixed to the spot. The assassin advanced, raised his blade, and slashed at Asher's throat. "No!" he cried out. "Stop!"

"Hey," Azarel said, shaking his shoulder. "You're having a nightmare."

He sat up, his heart beating furiously. Relief washed over him.

"You all right?"

"Yeah. Just a dream."

"Here," Azarel offered, reaching under his mattress and coming up with a stoppered clay vial. "Have a sip. It'll help you sleep."

Asher asked no questions. The liquid was bitter, but he didn't care.

"Whoa!" Azarel exclaimed. "Just a little. Too much'll knock you on your ass all day tomorrow."

"Thanks."

"Everything's all right. I'll stay awake until you're asleep."

His brother had looked after him, and it was a comfort. Asher lay down and pulled the thin blanket over himself. He didn't need it for warmth, but it provided a kind of defense between him and the world.

"Azarel?"

"Go to sleep."

"I will. But I just proved you wrong."

"About what?"

"You claimed I never do what you ask."

"Yeah, and—"

"Well, I just did. Thanks for the medicine."

"I know best, kid. Keep listening to me, and you won't go wrong."

Asher wondered about that.

* * *

Next morning, Azarel announced he was going to the shop, and Benaiah didn't try and stop him. Ezekiel went, too, just as if nothing unusual had been happening. Asher left the house on time, reminding Elisheva that he'd be gone that night. He expected Josiah to be waiting for him, but he didn't show up.

The Lady Iltani was excited about having guests, and Asher was kept busy all day long. She even told him to get a bath and wash his hair. He was disappointed that Damkina and Anatu did not attend him. Perhaps they had too many other tasks.

Evening came, and so did the lady's guests. Asher remembered some of them, including the one who had pinched his rear end and told him she wished he would come and work for her.

Slaves played music, and Anatu danced. The women laughed, gossiped, ate, and drank. Among them were two Asher didn't recognize. They weren't dressed in the Babylonian style, and their clothes, although fine, were not elaborate. The older one sat and talked with Iltani a good bit, but the younger, who seemed not much older than Asher himself, sat apart, looking uncomfortable.

Asher served food. He refilled cups. Removed platters when the ladies were done with them. Delivered short messages from one woman to another, for the ladies seemed too fatigued to get up and walk across the room themselves.

Then Iltani summoned him with the slightest movement of a finger, something he'd learned to recognize and obey.

He nodded to the strange woman at Iltani's side. She received his gesture of respect without responding. Iltani gave him the appraising look he'd also come to recognize. He hoped he passed inspection, dressed, perfumed, and made up as he was, in the best Babylonian style.

"This is the boy I was telling you about," Iltani said to the other woman. "He looks well, doesn't he?"

Asher didn't like two pair of eyes on him.

Iltani gestured toward him. "I present Asher, one of your own, from Jerusalem, like you."

He still didn't know the other woman's identity. Unsure what to do or say, he just stood, feeling foolish.

Iltani smiled. "I thought you might have recognized her, Asher. Nehushta, mother of your former king, Jehoiachin, whom I believe some of you call Jeconiah."

He didn't need to be told what to do next, but dropped to one knee, bowed his head, and said, "Your Majesty."

The queen mother still did not speak, and he kept his eyes on the polished tiled floor.

"He knows his manners," he heard Iltani say. "I've instructed him, but he has an instinct for doing the gallant thing. That cannot be taught."

"Indeed not," Queen Nehushta agreed. "Get up," she told him.

He stood, his eyes till downcast.

"Look at me," the queen commanded.

He knew what was coming.

"Your eyes. Strange, yet handsome, somehow. They say your uncle bears the same mark."

He wasn't sure if that was a statement or a question. Many of the women had gotten quiet and were looking in his direction. He hoped no one would notice that his legs were trembling.

"Well?" Queen Nehushta asked. "He bears the same mark as you?"

"He does, Your Majesty."

"And that this—*thing* came upon him only recently, whereas you have carried it all your life?"

How did she know all that?

"I was born this way, Your Majesty. I don't know how or why."

"And you're a seer?"

"No, just a freak."

"Oh, come now," Lady Iltani said. "Don't be so dramatic. You've done well for yourself, no matter the colors of your eyes."

"Thank you, My Lady."

"What's your father's name?" the queen asked him.

"Benaiah."

"Tell me, Asher ben-Benaiah, who is the true king of Israel?"

There was no right answer, and he felt trapped. He knew Jehoiachin—Jeconiah, that was—had been deposed by King Nebuchadrezzar and exiled here, just as Asher's family had been. Then Nebuchadrezzar had placed Jeconiah's uncle, Zedekiah, on the throne in Jerusalem. As Ezekiel had once joked, YAH must hold his people in high favor to grant them not one king, but two.

At the moment, there was nothing funny about that. Whichever answer he gave, he would offend one of the two women interrogating him.

"Well?" the queen mother asked again.

Think! he commanded himself.

He felt the room grow completely silent. If only the tiled floor would open and the earth swallow him up! A drop of sweat ran down the bridge of his nose, hung there a moment, then dropped to the floor.

He had to say something.

"It is not for me to determine that," he began, his voice a whisper. "I'm just a boy. I don't know the mind of my god or of King Nebuchadrezzar, but they are both wise and powerful and must have their reasons for what they do. I try to serve them as best I can."

"Go back to your gossiping," Iltani said to her other guests. "Don't let us spoil your pleasure."

They obeyed.

"I told you he's a born diplomat," she said to the Queen Mother.

Nehushta smiled. "That he is," she told her hostess, "even though he has not answered my question. Diplomats seldom give straight answers. They value their own necks too highly."

"If you and I held such posts, I dare say everyone would know our opinions!"

Both women laughed.

"You see that girl on the other side of the room?" the Queen Mother asked Asher. "Have her come here."

He did. The girl got up to follow him, and he realized that she was expecting a child.

Queen Nehushta took the young woman's hand. "This is my daughter-in-law, the Princess Sherah. Before long, she will bear the king a son, and the line of David will continue. One day the child will rule from Jerusalem. YAH will answer our prayers."

"My dear, he must be a clever god if he can do all that," Iltani exclaimed. "Your son lives here as our guest, but his uncle Zedekiah sits on the throne in Jerusalem—for Nebuchadrezzar so wills it. How will your god answer your prayers?"

"I do not know," Nehushta replied, "but I trust him."

"You Israelites! All this talk about your powerful god and your faith in him. Will you open your eyes and see the truth? Perhaps you will never believe in *our* gods—that's your business--but you must believe in what you see all around you! Nebuchadrezzar is king of the world, and he commands its mightiest army. If you doubt, go ask the Pharaoh of Egypt or the rabble who now inhabit the ruins of Nineveh. They will bear witness to the true power that rules the world."

The Queen Mother looked at Sherah, and Asher saw pity in her eyes. "We thank you for your generosity," she told Iltani. "Not all conquerors are as gracious as your king. We are happy to enjoy his favor. Every day, my son tells me so. Nebuchadrezzar could have chosen another way to deal with us and our people."

Iltani patted her hand. "Now, now. We've had this conversation before. Since they've not yet asked us *women* to rule our lands, let's leave the affairs of state to the men and enjoy ourselves this evening. And you, my young lady, how is your child?"

"Well," Sherah said. "Growing, moving. He's thoughtful, though. When I need to rest, he senses it, and then he sleeps. I look forward to holding him in my arms—soon."

All this time, Asher stood squirming. The women seemed to have forgotten his presence. But he'd promised Josiah and his brother to be their spy—find out what the Babylonians were saying. Here was his first chance to prove himself.

He was grateful when there were calls for more wine from a circle of over-dressed and perfumed women on the other side of the room.

The evening lasted a long time, or so it seemed. When the guests left, Asher was stationed in the street, helping Ahiyababa locate the ladies' litters and assist them, tipsy as most of them were, into the correct ones.

Last to come out were the Queen Mother and her daughter-in-law. "Leave us a moment," the queen told Ahiyababa. "Here are our litters; the young man will assist us."

The steward looked none too pleased to be ordered around by someone not his mistress, but he said nothing.

When they were alone, Nehushta summoned Asher to stand close to her. "You handled yourself well this evening," she told him. "Of course, I know your loyalty is to my son as rightful king of Judah, not his uncle Zedekiah, the lackey of this tyrant Nebuchadrezzar."

He hadn't thought about being loyal to either man, but this was not the time to say so.

"Can I trust you?" she went on.

"Yes, Your Majesty." That also seemed the correct thing to say.

"Good. Will you promise me? Remember, you are an Israelite first and always, not a servant in a den of vicious old crones pretending to be young and lovely again."

Asher had to keep from smiling. He'd thought something very similar several times during the evening.

"What can I do?" he asked.

She glanced around. Ahiyababa stood watch by the gate, too far away to hear what she was telling Asher, but perhaps all the more curious for that. "Nothing particular," she said. "Keep your eyes and ears open. If you learn anything having to do with my son or his station here, let me know. Especially if you come to think he's in danger."

"How can I do that?"

"Take this." She produced an amulet on a thin leather cord. "We live inside the palace grounds, along with other conquered kings and their families. At the gate to our compound, you will find a guard sympathetic to our cause."

"What cause, your majesty?"

"The restoration of my son to his throne in Jerusalem."

"How will I know him?"

"Hunzuu is a huge man, a famous warrior, but he lost his right hand in battle. Nebuchadrezzar rewarded his service by making him head guard over us." She placed the amulet into his hand. "Show him this, and he will convey any messages you might have."

"But he's a Babylonian."

She nodded. "Yet he's on our side. I can't explain why just now, but trust me. Hunzuu is a faithful friend. Will you do as I ask?"

"Yes, Your Majesty."

She pressed his hand. "Then you a true son of Israel. Shalom, Asher ben-Benaiah."

Asher helped the queen and her daughter-in-law into their litters and said goodnight. When he got back to the door, Ahiyababa gave him a searching look, but Asher kept going. Inside, a slave informed him that the lady required his presence.

He found her in the party room, fingering the beads of one of her bracelets.

"You called for me?" he began.

"How did you like your queen?"

The question seemed innocent enough, but Asher sensed it was not. "See seems kind," he replied. "But my opinion is not important."

"It is when I ask for it," she retorted. "What did you think?"

He searched for something to say that was both true and not likely to offend.

"Well?"

He looked at the floor. "She is sad, I think. Queen Sherah, as well."

"It doesn't take a seer to know that!" his lady shot back. "What queen would not be sad to lose her station, her city—her country?"

"I don't know."

"Come now, Asher! Imagine it for yourself."

"I can't. I'm neither a woman nor of royal blood. I'm just an ordinary Israelite."

"But you also had to leave your city. You told me that members of your family died on the journey here. Aren't you ever sad?"

He nodded. "Yes," he whispered. "Often." *And full of hatred, too,* he thought.

"Then it's time to get over it," she told him. "How long have you been here?"

"Four years."

"Plenty of time to mourn. Now your life can go on if you have courage. It took me a long time to heal from my losses—when the plague took my husband, one of my brothers, my son, and both my daughters. It was hard, terribly hard, but what was the other choice? Death? Not for me! Not after I survived the sickness myself. I told the gods I wasn't ready to die, and if they tried to take me again, I would fight back. They would receive no more prayers from me, no more offerings! I would be done with them and take my punishment in the afterlife."

She chuckled. "I think I frightened them! At any rate, they let me live, and now you see me—withered, proud, cunning-- but still here and ready to fight."

"My Lady is brave," Asher said. He meant it.

"Life requires it. This so-called queen mother is indeed kind—kinder than I. But she is a fool to dream that her son will ever reclaim his throne, or that she will ever leave this city. Instead, she ought to enjoy her new life. King Nebuchadrezzar treats his captive kings with great generosity. They eat at his table. He pays their expenses. These defeated monarchs are better off now than they ever were. Here, at least, no enemies plot against them, hoping to seize their thrones. Nehushta should be thanking our gods—or hers—for her blessings."

He could think of no answer. In fact, the lady's words made a kind of sense.

"What did she say to you outside?" Iltani asked. "She had to have made some private request. That's why I arranged for her to leave last and have a moment alone with you." She threw him a challenging look. He realized she spoke the truth, and that she was, indeed, cunning.

"Nothing, My Lady," he lied. "She asked nothing. She said she'd heard about my uncle Ezekiel and asked me to give him her greeting of peace. That's all."

His lady raised an eyebrow. "That's all—truly?"

"Yes," he lied.

"Then be sure to do so."

"I will."

"You are dismissed. Be on time to escort me in the morning."

Asher went to his room. The slave boy Kuri was not there, but Damkina was.

Chapter Nineteen

The next evening, Asher came home to chaos. His uncle was frantically stuffing a bag with clothing, a blanket, extra sandals, his plate and cup, a water skin, rounds of bread—everything he could lay his hands on. Elisheva and Tirzah stood by, helpless.

"What's happening now?" he asked. "What's wrong?"

"He won't say!" Elisheva cried. "Ezekiel, please stop and talk to us."

"No time," he gasped. "Where's the pickaxe? Never mind. I'll get it." He disappeared toward the back of the house.

"Asher, follow him," Elisheva pleaded.

He started, but ran into Ezekiel on his way back, pickaxe in hand. "Come on," he urged. "We have to go now." With that, he advanced on the front wall of the house, to the left of the door, and began attacking it. "We must go!" he shouted. "Now!"

Elisheva tried to stop him. "Ezekiel, no! Let's talk about it. Tell us what's going on."

He shook her off. Then he turned and glared at them. "Gather your things," he ordered. "You'll need them."

"Tirzah, run and get your father," Elisheva said. "Hurry."

Ezekiel resumed his assault on the wall. Mud bricks shattered under each blow. Pieces flew. The air filled with dust.

"Uncle," Asher cried. "Stop! You'll bring down the wall."

"No! Break through it. Please, help me."

Asher didn't know what to do. When he looked at his uncle's expression—determined, mouth set, eyes fixed on something he alone seemed able to see—he knew what was happening.

A new set of orders from YAH.

Asher grabbed his uncle's arm. Ezekiel shoved him away. He focused his energy on one spot, each blow cutting more and more deeply into the bricks.

They watched, horrifed, unable to stop him.

At last, Elisheva took Asher's sleeve and pulled him toward to door. "Outside," she said. "Before the wall and roof collapse."

They watched from the other side of the street. Asher winced at the sounds of the blows. They stopped for a moment, then continued, rhythmic, unrelenting.

Benaiah and Azarel appeared. By this time, curious neighbors had gathered, too.

"What is YAH's name is he doing?" Benaiah demanded.

"He won't tell us," Elisheva cried. "Why did he come home early?"

"I don't know. He just said he had something to do. Azarel and I were tending the kiln and couldn't leave, so we didn't follow." He lowered his voice. "I don't believe we could have stopped him. I pray this isn't another—"

The sound of a shattering blow stopped him. The point of the pickaxe appeared through the wall, then disappeared, only to appear again with the next stroke.

Benaiah advanced into the house, Azarel right behind. Asher tried to follow, but Elisheva stopped him.

The noise of a scuffle came from inside, made worse by angry shouting. There was a cry, a crash, and then another blow against the wall; the middle of it gave way in an avalanche of mud bricks and choking dust. The roof, unsupported, began to sag.

Elisheva cried out. Asher broke away and rushed to the door. Inside, he found his father on the floor, Azarel bending over him and begging him to get up.

Ezekiel stood unmoving, axe in hand, panting.

"Help me get him out of here," Azarel ordered Asher, nodding at their father. "Before the whole place comes down."

Asher squeezed his hands in under his father's head and lifted him as well as he could. Azarel pulled his legs, and they managed to get him into the street, where more gawkers had gathered. People gasped when Benaiah appeared, his head bleeding and his nose, too.

Elisheva and Tirzah hurried to tend him, calling for their neighbors to bring water and cloths.

Ezekiel had not appeared.

When he did, he pushed through the opening in the wall, his refugee's bag slung over his shoulder. He stared at the crowd. People got quiet, staring back.

Then he spoke: "As I have done," he began, "so it will be done to them."

He paused, then began again, but now the voice was not his own, rather the voice Asher had heard the evening Ezekiel spoke to the priests gathered at their house: "Thus says the Lord: 'The prince and his followers will break through the wall trying to escape. But I will cast my net over him, and he shall be caught like a bird in a snare. I will bring him here, to Babylon, but he shall not see it, and here he shall die. And I will scatter his people and his army to the winds, and they shall die by the sword. Only a few shall remain to tell of their crimes among the nations to which I have exiled them.'"

Ezekiel sighed, picked up his sack, and made his way through the crowd.

Then everyone began to talk at once:

"He's mad."

"What did he mean?"

"He speaks only doom. Who can stand it?"

"Someone should shut him up for good!"

"Why don't his people keep him inside?"

"Take him to the priests and let them cast demons out of him."

"What's he going to do next?"

Asher heard it all, and it sickened him.

"Go after him," Elisheva pleaded with Azarel. "Asher, you, too."

"Let's try the market first," Asher suggested, but Ezekiel wasn't there. They looked up and down the side streets, asking people if they'd seen him. No one had.

"I think I know where's gone," Asher said. "By the canal. Where he saw the first thing."

They set off at a trot. They hurried through the grove of Ishtar and came out at the far side. Sure enough, Ezekiel was there, standing like a statue facing north, his bag of belongings in the dust at his feet.

"Let me," Azarel told Asher. "Stay here." He approached Ezekiel from the side. "Uncle?" he asked. "It's Azarel. Do you know me?"

Ezekiel nodded.

"Are you all right?"

He looked around, as if uncertain where he was or how he'd gotten there.

"Come home with us," Azarel told him. His tone was gentle. "Let us help you."

Ezekiel nodded again. Asher took up the journey bag, surprised at its weight. Just as Asher had helped guide his uncle home the last time, now Azarel did the same.

As they entered the village, people gathered around them, nosy as always. By the time they came to their own street, a motley band of fellow citizens, including many children, trailed behind them. Asher heard one mother warn her son not to get too close to "that crazy man."

They found their family in the street. Neighbors were already bringing posts to brace the tumbled wall and other, longer ones to shore up the roof. Elisheva threw her arms around her husband and drew him inside the house, away from the ruin he had created.

Benaiah was sitting in the street, holding a wet rag over his nose. Someone had tended to the hurt place on his forehead. "Is he all right?" Benaiah asked. "Where was he?"

They explained.

"Go and help our friends," he told them. "We can't spend the night in the street."

It was long after dark when the repairs were completed well enough and there was no danger of anything collapsing. Neighbors went to their own homes, some whispering, others shaking their heads. Inside, Ezekiel had long since fallen asleep, Elisheva at his side.

The rest of the family gathered in the court, unwilling to try their luck on the roof terrace.

"I'm frantic about him," Benaiah began. "He attacked *me*, his own brother! Punched me square in the nose. Who knows what he'll do next? I overheard someone suggest that we keep him in chains."

"Never!" Azarel exclaimed. "He's not insane."

"Then what is he?"

"A prophet?" Asher muttered.

Benaiah shook his head. "What other explanation can there be? I just didn't want to accept it. But what if he gets into serious trouble? What if he'd broken through someone else's wall? It's bad enough that he's offended the priests and frightened mothers who think he's going to eat their children."

"We'll take care of him," Azarel declared. "I promise."

* * *

Azarel didn't go out that night; instead, he went to bed when Asher did, then in whispers interrogated him about his conversation with Josiah and what he'd learned at Lady Iltani's feast.

After answering numerous questions, Asher managed to ask one of his own: "Who's our real king?"

"Whoa! Where'd that come from—and what do *you* care?"

"The Queen Mother asked me—right in front of Lady Iltani. I didn't know how to answer."

"So what'd you say?"

"Managed something about being only a boy whose opinion would be worthless."

"Let me guess: you used your most humble voice and kept your eyes on the floor."

"Exactly! How'd you know?"

"I know *you*, little brother. You're good at playing the 'I'm just a kid' part."

"Whatever it takes, *big* brother. You haven't answered my question about who's king."

"It all depends on who you ask. The Queen Mother naturally believes it's Jeconiah. He *is* her son."

"Yeah, and she assumed I agree with her."

"Do you?"

"I dunno."

"Then you *were* telling the truth when you played dumb."

"I'm not dumb."

"Didn't say you were. Matter of fact, I think you're a smart guy. It doesn't matter to me what you told her, but it's time you make up your mind for yourself."

"How so?"

"Look, Asher. Things are heating up. If they go the way we hope, there could be a revolt, right here in Babylon. I'll tell you about it if you swear you won't tell anyone."

Asher swore his best oath. "Revolt?" he asked. "Who? Revolt against Nebuchadrezzar? That's impossible!"

"Is it? Pharaoh thought he'd keep our people slaves forever, but look what YAH did to Egypt to help that poor fool see things a different way."

"I get your point. But I still don't see how it matters who the true king is."

"Then let me explain, my slow-witted one."

"Hey, take that back!"

"Just joking. YAH knows we could use something to laugh about."

Asher had to agree. "All right. So please enlighten me, O wise brother!"

"Okay, listen and learn. Who's our true king? Take your pick. These filthy Babylonians believe that son of a whore, Nebuchadrezzar, is king of Israel. After all, he did conquer it. Let them go on thinking he's king if it makes them feel good. They'll change their minds when we cut their throats."

"Do you have to talk that way?"

"Sorry. I forgot how tenderhearted you are."

"Thanks. *You* don't think Nebuchadrezzar is our rightful king."

"Do I look like a Babylonian?"

Asher nodded. "Fair enough. Go on."

"Some would say Zedekiah is king because he sits on David's throne in Jerusalem-- because Nebuchadrezzar *allows* him to sit there, as long as he licks his rear end. Zedekiah's gonna find out sooner or later that Nebuchadrezzar cares more for his pet dogs than he does for any so-called Israelite king in Jerusalem."

Azarel pushed himself up and sat on the side of his bed.

"Be careful!" Asher whispered. "Remember your wound."

"I'm all right. Sit up."

Asher obeyed.

"Bring the lamp and give it to me."

Asher obeyed.

Azarel held the lamp between them. They were so close that their knees touched. "Look at me," he told Asher.

Again, Asher obeyed. "What's going on?"

"I need to see your face for the rest of this. When you answer my questions, I have to know if you're telling me the truth."

He met his brother's gaze.

"All right," Azarel told him. "I'll answer the Queen Mother's question about the true king of Israel. Like I said, she believes it's her son. I agree with her—up to a point."

"What do you mean?"

"Jeconiah is King Josiah's son, and since his older brother is dead, the throne is rightfully his."

"Then the true king of Israel is Jeconiah. His mother is right."

"No, Asher. The true King of Israel is YAH. Do you hear me? *He's* our king, and he has the power to make big things happen."

"You sound like a priest," Asher said. "They say that kind of stuff."

"One day, brother, when we're back home where we belong, I'm going to study and become a priest."

"You? A lot of the time, you act you don't even believe in YAH."

"I was bluffing, just like I pretend to be a drunk who's wasting his life pursuing whores. All that was to keep everyone, including you, from knowing the real me."

As Asher looked into his brother's eyes, he could tell that Azarel spoke the truth. "What happens now?" he asked.

"YAH is the eternal king of Israel, but he lives in the heavens, so he depends on us to carry out his will. He's revealed that he's about to overthrow Nebuchadrezzar. Many of his own soldiers, including some of his generals, are tired of his constant campaigns and wars. Men are dying by the thousands to feed the king's lust for power. They're going to revolt and put one of his generals on the throne instead. They've promised peace after that."

"What has that got to do with us?"

"We've been in touch with the generals who are going to lead the revolt. They'll need all the men they can get, so they welcome us to fight beside them. When they win, they've pledged to free us and to put Jeconiah on the throne in Jerusalem. YAH has promised ff we fight, we'll win. And when we win, we can go home!"

Asher let it sink it.

It was a crazy dream. No power could overthrow Nebuchadrezzar. Many would die, including Israelites who fought with Babylonians against him.

"You're not saying anything," Azarel said.

"I don't know where to begin."

"Take your time. We're not going into battle tonight."

"When?"

"Soon."

"You said you had some things to ask me. What are they?" Asher asked.

"You sure you want to hear them now, after all I've told you?"

"I think so," he said. *But I'm terrified*, is what he didn't say. "Ask me."

"Who is the true King of Israel?"

A lot depended on his answer. There was no doubt what it had to be: "YAH."

"That's right."

"Are we done?"

"Not yet. I've got two more questions. They're harder than the first."

Asher had come this far, and there was no turning back. "Go on," he told his brother. "I'm as ready as I'm ever going to be."

"Is YAH *your* king?"

Asher wanted to look away, but he couldn't. It seemed as if the eyes in his vision, not his brother's, were probing his mind, seeking an answer.

"Is he *your* king?" Azarel repeated.

"Yes," Asher whispered. He wanted to weep.

Azarel squeezed his shoulder. "Good man! Now for the final question: when it comes time to fight, will you obey *your* king, even if it means killing our sworn enemies?"

Chapter Twenty

"I don't know," Asher muttered. He felt like a child—small and lost in the dark.

"Fair enough," Azarel said. "It's a big question. No one knows for sure what he'll do on the battlefield."

"I'm sorry," Asher said.

"Don't be. You have a lot to think about. Maybe I said too much."

"No, you didn't. You treated me like—"

"A brother?"

"Yeah."

Asher was suddenly exhausted. "I have to sleep. You should, too."

The dim flame of the oil lamp flickered as a faint breeze moved through the room.

"It's going to storm," Azarel said.

"How do you know?"

He shrugged. "Just do. I've always been able to predict the weather."

The back of Asher's neck prickled. "You never told me that. Are you a prophet, too?"

"Never thought about it. You know how old people go on about their joints aching before it rains? I'm not the only one who can predict the weather. It's no big deal."

Azarel blew out the lamp and lay down. Almost right away, he was breathing deeply and slowly. How could he fall asleep so easily, after everything he'd shared? Topple Nebuchadrezzar from the throne of Babylon? To accomplish that, they'd have to defeat his soldiers, capture him, and then . . .

Put him to death, along with all the men in his family.

That's how YAH intended to answer his people's prayers and let them return home? Through a sea not of water, but of blood?

How many Egyptians had once died so that YAH could bring about the freedom of his people?

Asher preferred not to think about that.

He knew that if the time came, his brother would be among those fighting for freedom. Josiah would be right there, too, wielding a sword. He was ruthless with such a weapon, according to Azarel.

Asher preferred not to think about that, either.

What about himself? What would he do?

He spent a long time in the blackness of the room searching for an answer. Meanwhile, the wind picked up, the air grew chilly, and then came the first rumblings of thunder. Soon, lightning cracked and the sound of pouring rain penetrated the shattered brick wall where Ezekiel had played the part of a refugee desperate to escape an invading army.

Asher did sleep, though—after the storm had moved on toward the south.

In the morning, raised voices awakened him. Azarel remained lost to the world as only he could. Asher went into the courtyard, where he found his uncle stropping a barber's razor. Elisheva was pleading with him to stop what he was doing, for he'd already shaved off his beard and all the thick, curly shoulder-length hair from one side of his head. Benaiah stood by, apparently unwilling to interfere. One look at his swollen nose and bruised face suggested why. Tirzah, a water jug in hand, seemed uncertain what to do.

"Asher, try and talk some sense into him," Elisheva begged. "None of us is getting anywhere. Ezekiel, you have no reason to shave your face and your hair. We're not in mourning."

He put his arm down and allowed the sharpened blade to hang at his side. "*I* am," he told her.

"For whom?"

"For us. For our people. Our land. Our cities. For the rulers, our priests, old men and women, young men and maidens, our children."

"Why?"

"For what will happen."

"What?"

"Jerusalem," he said.

"That again!" his brother cried. "Always harping on Jerusalem. Listen to me," Benaiah ordered, keeping his distance from the razor. "Nothing is going to happen there! Nebuchadrezzar has already won. He's put Zedekiah on the throne, whether we like it or not. Zedekiah's not stupid. He'll do what he's told and the Babylonians will leave Jerusalem alone."

Ezekiel glared at him. "Until they return to finish raiding the temple, stripping anything of value that remains and bringing it here to build another shrine to their Lord Marduk."

"I don't like it any more than you do," Benaiah shot back, "but isn't that better than killing more of us?"

"You tell me," Ezekiel said. "It's your wife they murdered."

Benaiah lunged at him. Ezekiel's arm went up, the razor challenging him to come closer.

"Stop it, both of you!" Elisheva shouted. "I can't take any more."

Asher grabbed his father and pushed him back. Just then, Azarel appeared. He seemed to understand what was happening, and in a second, he was pushing Ezekiel back, razor or no razor.

The brothers eyed one another warily.

"I'm going to the shop," Benaiah said wearily.

"Your meal?" Elisheva asked.

"I'll buy something at the market."

"I'll get water," Tirzah said.

She went to the front door. No one else moved.

"Your head looks ridiculous half-shaved," Elisheva told her husband. "Please finish what you've started, and then I'll sweep up."

"Don't do anything with my hair," Ezekiel told her.

"Why not? It's going to get everywhere and make a mess."

"YAH tells me to keep it."

"Very well. I'll get the fire going."

Just then, Tirzah came back into the courtyard. "The storm made a mess in the front room," she told them. "Rain must have blown through the gaps in the wall. The floor's soaked. And look what I found just beside the door." She held up Gula's little dog, whose duty was to keep evil away from the house. "The rain must have uncovered it, but it looks like it was buried by the doorpost on purpose."

Ezekiel seized the delicate figurine, dropped it on the hard-packed earthen floor, and stomped it to pieces. "YAH, forgive us," he pleaded. "In this house, we worship no idols." He scraped up the shards with his hands and dropped them into the cook fire.

"Whoever lived here before we did must have buried it by the door," Benaiah replied. "These Babylonians practice such superstitions."

"Very likely," Ezekiel muttered. "But let's not forget that this very moment, women of Israel mourn for the god Tammuz and men bow to the rising sun—in the temple of YAH! And you dare suggest, brother, that all will be well with our land and our people, when our own priests and rulers practice unspeakable abominations in the house where our King dwells?"

Asher could only hope no one noticed him trembling. If he had confessed to planting Gula's dog by the doorpost, his uncle might have attacked *him*, just the way he'd smashed his brother in the face.

He is dangerous, Asher admitted.

When it was time to leave for his work, he found Josiah waiting a few paces down the street.

"You all right?" Josiah asked. "You look terrible."

"You would, too, if someone tried to tear down your house last night and then you couldn't sleep because of all the crazy stuff running around in your head."

"I heard about your uncle's latest antics. Everybody's talking about them. We didn't find out for a long time, and then my father said it was too late to come see you. He and Grandfather will visit your uncle today and talk to him."

"Good luck to them if they try and change his mind about anything. He won't listen. Ask my father."

"Ezekiel punched him in the nose, didn't he?"

"Does everything get spread all over the village?"

Josiah smiled. "Just the scandals. You know there aren't any secrets."

Asher thought of the ceramic dog. *There's at least one,* he hoped.

It didn't take Josiah long to share what was on his mind. "Did Azarel talk to you last night?"

"About what?"

"About our plans."

"What plans?" he asked innocently.

"To go fishing this evening," Josiah said. "What do you think?"

Asher could see a faint smile on his friend's face. "Oh, sure. In the river right after work."

"If you want to. But that's not what I mean."

"I know."

"What *do* I mean?" Josiah asked.

Asher glanced around. The street was teeming with people on their way to their jobs, but no one was paying them any mind. "You mean the plan to revolt against the king, and that some of our people are going to join them?"

Josiah just looked at him. Then, "What are you talking about?"

"Don't mess with me," Asher said. "That's exactly what you mean."

"If you ever tell anyone, I'll deny it. I'll say you're just as crazy as that uncle of yours."

"I was just thinking the same thing about you. We're agreed, then: neither of us knows what the other means."

Josiah nodded. "Good. I thought I could trust you but had to make sure."

"One thing, though," Asher said. "I pray that it never comes to my being questioned."

"You'd be stupid if you *didn't* pray that. They say Nebuchadrezzar's torturers can break any man—sooner or later."

"Thanks a lot! *Not* what I wanted to hear."

"I know. But you have to consider it. We're not kids playing soldier. This is serious, Asher."

"Like I don't know that? But don't worry. I won't say anything."

"Good. Did he—ask you anything?"

Asher nodded. "If I would stand with you when the time came."

"And what'd you tell him?"

"The same thing I'm going to tell you now: I don't know."

"Yes, you do, even if you can't say it in words. When the time comes, you'll fight."

"How can you be so sure?"

"Because you're a prophet, like it or not. You're a son of Israel underneath your soft tunic and scented oils. Because—"

"What? Tell me."

"You're a man now."

* * *

They went their own ways, and Asher arrived just in time to escort Iltani to the plantation. She was in a happy mood because the great New

Year's Festival was coming up in a few days, and that, she reminded Asher, meant days and evenings of feasting, gifts of free food to the poor, and the grand processional of the gods along the Sacred Way, through the Ishtar Gate, and then to the temples. The king and the royal family would watch from the city walls, and so would all Nebuchadrezzar's defeated enemies and their wives.

"Your deposed king—"

"Jeconiah, My Lady."

"Yes, Jeconiah. And the new king, the one installed by Nebuchadrezzar?"

"Zedekiah."

"Ah, yes. I don't suppose I will ever lay eyes on him. Imagine me, making the journey to your country. What's there to see or do there, anyway? I must admit, I don't understand why the Queen Mother Nehushta goes on and on about the 'beautiful city of Jerusalem.' Our generals who've been there report that it's all right, for a provincial town. They allow that the temple to your god is handsome in its own modest way, and it did yield a sizeable amount of gold."

The woman was annoying him. Her memory for Israelite names seemed to have deserted her, or maybe it wasn't worth her time to bother to learn them.

"Do you know why Nebuchadrezzar invites all the conquered kings to watch the grand parade from the walls of Babylon?"

"I really can't say." He had an idea, but he didn't feel like discussing things. Why wouldn't she leave him alone?

"To demonstrate his power—Babylon's power—*our* power, of course! Only kings wise and powerful enough can afford to show their conquered enemies mercy and favor instead of slaughtering them as they deserve. This so-called king of yours—wait, don't remind me—this Jeconiah, although no longer a true king--will enjoy a seat of honor at the grand procession, along with the deposed kings of Syria, Phoenicia, Akkadia, and Assyria. After the procession is over, they will dine at the king's table, and their wives will have their seats among the women in the banqueting hall. Nebuchadrezzar has no wish to humiliate or anger them. Why should he, now that he has conquered their lands?"

Asher wished they could make faster progress toward the plantation, but the streets were jammed this morning. At last they arrived, and Iltani took her place beside the gates. Asher stood behind his mistress, at attention, silent, observing everything going on in the plaza.

He was first to notice, then, the man making his way toward Lady Iltani, moving calmly and deliberately. The fellow looked like all the other workers, the same shabby tunic, worn-out sandals, head covering made of woven palm leaves. As he approached, he moved faster, and in an instant, he was racing toward the woman.

That's when Asher saw he was brandishing a long knife, the kind the workers used to cut dead palm fronds from the treetops. He was running now, the knife raised—

There came out of him a terrible noise—a scream, a cry of rage--

Asher jumped forward and threw himself between the attacker and his intended victim. He tackled the man and knocked him backwards onto the ground. Iltani screamed, and from every side people rushed forward to shield her.

Asher had the man flat on his back, trying to pin his arms, but he was too late to keep the assassin from slashing at his arm. The blade bit into his flesh and opened a wound that burned and poured hot blood.

Asher let go and tried to get away before the man could cut him again. Instantly others piled on the assailant. Asher rolled onto his back, his right hand pressing against his left upper arm, trying to stanch the blood.

All around him, people were shouting, crying out, urging the men who had taken Asher's place to kill the man who had attacked their lady. And that's exactly what they did. Asher was told later that one of the men, a guard, had wrestled the knife out of the attacker's hands and driven it into his heart while other men pinned his arms to the ground.

Then Asher blacked out, certain that he was bleeding to death.

* * *

He found himself lying on a soft bed in a fine room he didn't recognize. The air smelled of sweet incense.

His left shoulder throbbed. He touched it and was surprised to find, instead of his own skin, a thick bandage.

Then he remembered it all: standing in his place, noticing the assassin emerge from the crowd—the glint of the knife blade, the man's shriek—his own lunge forward, without a second's chance to decide what to do or how to do it—just the sure knowledge that it was *his* job—and no one else's—to defend his mistress with everything he had, including his life.

He didn't move, but tears came to his eyes, welled over, and ran down each side of his face.

"You're awake," said a nearby voice. A man appeared above him, a young man with a closely-trimmed black beard and curly dark hair. "How do you feel? Terrible, I'm guessing."

"Who are you, and where am I?"

"I'm Isiratuu, physician to the Lady Iltani. You are in her house, in a room usually reserved for guests." The man offered him a friendly smile and laid a hand on his forehead. "No fever, thanks be to Gula. That means your wound is probably not infected, and you will get well."

"My wound?" Asher touched the heavy bandage again.

"Your arm. The assassin cut you badly. I had to sew the wound shut, after I washed it and applied healing balm. If it does not become infected, you'll recover, but you'll always have a scar to remind you of what you did."

"What day is it? Have I been asleep a long time?"

"It's afternoon of the same day. When they got you here, I gave you something to deaden your pain and help you sleep while I stitched up your wound. Skin doesn't like to be pierced with a bone needle, even when the needle is being used for good."

Asher looked into Isiratuu's kind face. The physician laid his hand on his forehead again, then patted his head the way a man comforts a sick child. The gentleness brought more tears to Asher's eyes, and he realized all at once how close he had come to losing his life.

"It's all right," Isiratuu told him. "No shame in tears. You've had a bad day, but you saved a life, and Lady Iltani will not soon forget your courage."

"Was I brave?"

"Everyone says so."

"It all happened so fast! I didn't stop to think about anything. I just did it."

"That showed your character. Another man might have done nothing—out of fear or confusion. Let me give you some advice: when people fuss over you, tell you how brave you were, thank them. Don't be too humble. You've earned respect. That's something you can't buy with money."

"Thank you."

Isiratuu smiled. "I'll charge Iltani, but my advice to you—that's free."

Just then, the lady herself appeared. She looked old and exhausted, but she glowed when she saw that Asher was awake. "My young hero has returned!" she exclaimed to Isiratuu. "Are you all right, Asher?" She came to the bed and touched his uninjured shoulder.

"Yes, My Lady. The physician is taking good care of me."

"He is the greatest in all Babylon," she boasted. "He tends the king himself! When I sent word to Nebuchadrezzar, he dispatched Isiratuu immediately. His Majesty declared that no expense, no physician's skill, be withheld from the man who saved my life."

Asher felt tears coming again, but he blinked them back.

"I sent for your family. They're waiting in the next room, eager to see you, but I told them I had to thank you first for giving an old woman a little more time to live. I praise Lord Marduk that you didn't die defending me. That injustice would have been more than I could stand."

She put her hand over Asher's. "I won't forget that I'm in your debt."

Iltani left the room, and Asher's family appeared. Elisheva wept over him, and Tirzah told him how brave he was and how proud she was to be his sister.

Benaiah asked the physician many questions about how Asher was being treated, and he was grateful for Isiratuu's skillful care. Azarel complimented his brother for not getting killed and said he always knew he was a clever fellow. Ezekiel, his head and beard shaven, said little but paced back and forth, as if the room were too small to contain him.

They insisted on hearing the whole story, and they expressed their pride and admiration at all the right places. Asher surprised himself by realizing how much he was enjoying relating the tale of his adventure—one he realized he would be retelling for some days to come.

The moment Asher finished his story, Ezekiel thanked Isiratuu for his services and announced that they would be taking Asher home.

"I advise against that," the physician told him. "He shouldn't be moved."

"Why not?" Ezekiel shot back. "We can take care of him in our own place, where he belongs."

"I'm certain you can, but I'm instructed by Lady Iltani to stay with the young man tonight, to be sure the wound stays closed and that he doesn't lose more blood. Also, I have medicines to give him should a fever develop."

"He's not a Babylonian," Ezekiel said forcefully. "He's an *Israelite*, and he belongs in an Israelite house, where his own family can care for him."

"He belongs where he can receive the best care possible," Isiratuu replied. "And that's here. You want him to get well, don't you?"

"Of course we do! But we want him home, with us."

"The boy stays here," Benaiah broke in. "The physician is right. Asher will get better care here than we can give him in the village."

"Stop and think!" Ezekiel exclaimed. "Remember where we are. Remember *who* we are! What would YAH want us to do?"

"I don't know, and I don't care," Benaiah retorted. "What I do know is that Asher is my child, and I'm bound to do whatever is best for him. And the best is that he stays here until the physician recommends that he can come home."

"You're making a bad mistake," Ezekiel told him. "This is temptation, brother! Temptation to turn to them—" he pointed an accusing finger at Isiratuu—"when we should be turning to YAH for everything."

"Maybe YAH has answered our prayers for Asher's recovery by sending this man to take care of him. But let's hear what Asher wants."

He felt everyone's eyes on him. "I want to stay here."

"It won't be long," Isiratuu assured them all. "Another day or two, if everything goes well. Lady Iltani says he can remain as long I think it wise."

"Then he stays," Benaiah told Ezekiel. "We respect your opinion, brother, but Asher is *my* son, and I have to do what I think best for him. One day, if you have children of your own, you'll understand."

Ezekiel bowed his head in submission. "It's your decision." He touched Asher's shoulder. "YAH protect and heal you." Then he left the room.

"I'll go with him," Elisheva said.

"My brother doesn't mean to be rude," Benaiah told the physician. "He has strong opinions, that's all."

"I'm not offended," Isiratuu assured him. "If Asher were my son, I'd want him home as soon as possible. I promise you he'll receive the best care in Babylon."

Asher complained of being tired, even though he felt okay, all things considered. But he was ready to have his family gone. They said their goodbyes and promised to check on him the next day.

When they had left, Isiratuu gave him another draught to lessen the pain and help him rest. He slept until evening, when a sumptuous meal was brought to him, along with Damkina, who insisted on feeding him. Isiratuu took his leave, promising to return later and declaring that he obviously wasn't needed at the moment.

The meal made him sleepy, and Asher was dozing when Lady Iltani returned. Satisfied he was doing well, she told him that Damkina would stay with him through the night and waken the physician should there be need.

So Asher slept, not alone, exactly, for the girl arranged pillows on the floor next to his bed. But she did not join him there.

Chapter Twenty-One

In the morning, Isiratuu removed the bandage and examined the wound. Asher felt quivery when he saw the jagged slash. The skin was puckered where the physician's needle had drawn it together. His entire upper arm looked swollen, and now that the injury was exposed, it ached. He felt frightened, more than he had the day before.

"It's bad, isn't it?" Asher asked Isiratuu. "I'm going to die."

"No, you're not! You're doing well. You wouldn't want to see some of the injuries I've had to deal with. Sometimes the king's officers—even his highest commanders—receive terrible wounds. I'm amazed that they're still alive when they get to me. Their wounds are infected and draining ghastly green bile. They teem with maggots. Sometimes bone is sticking through skin and has to be pushed back into place. Shoulders get dislocated, fingers and toes chopped off, heads dented in by maces. One fellow I will always remember: his head was smashed open and I could see his brain! I patched him up as best I could, and do you know that the man recovered? He returned to the army and got killed the next campaign season by a spear through the heart. Believe me, Asher, you've been hurt, but your wound is not nearly as bad as many I've seen."

If Isiratuu's speech was intended to shame him, it worked. Asher realized how fortunate he'd been. The knife intended for Lady Iltani could have gone through *his* heart instead of his arm.

"I'm going to wash the wound, then apply ointment and put on a clean bandage. After that, you can eat and rest. If you're all right tomorrow morning, you can go home. Your family will be happy."

"I know. My uncle doesn't like me working here at all."

"The fellow with the shaved head and beard?"

"Uh huh."

"What's with him? He didn't look pleased to be here, not even to see you."

Asher wasn't sure how much to tell Isiratuu, but the man had won his trust. "He's a prophet."

"Is that like a priest?"

"Not exactly, but a priest can be a prophet, too. Prophets see things that our god shows them, and then they share what they've seen."

"And what has your god shown your uncle?"

"That he's displeased with our people for worshipping the gods of other nations, so he allowed your people to invade our country and bring many of us here to serve your king."

Isiratuu looked puzzled. "Your god doesn't allow you to worship other gods? Everyone does that! Here is Babylon, we worship Marduk and Gula and Ishtar, of course, but some of us also worship the gods of Egypt. I myself am devoted to Sekhmet, the goddess of healing."

"And Gula doesn't mind?"

Isiratuu chuckled. "If the Lady Gula is jealous, she hasn't said so. I prefer to think that she and Sekhmet are friends. So many people in every country are ill; perhaps the goddesses are glad to share the task of healing them."

Isiratuu's argument sounded reasonable, but Asher knew what his uncle would say: simply another temptation to idolatry.

"*Your* god is the jealous one, not Gula or Sekhmet," Isiratuu went on. "Why doesn't he understand that every nation has its own divinities? There's no harm in worshipping other gods as long as your own receive their due."

"I don't understand it all," Asher told him. "My uncle could explain better."

"Why did he shave himself? Did your god tell him to do that?"

"Yes. Uncle Ezekiel says he's in mourning for our nation and our people."

"That seems reasonable. Your nation is conquered. If another empire were to conquer Babylon, I would grieve."

"My uncle says that Babylon isn't finished with Israel. He thinks Jerusalem will be destroyed one day."

"Then I feel sorry for him, to have such gloomy ideas. Maybe he could ask your god to free him from being a prophet."

"I don't think it works that way."

Isiratuu shrugged. "Probably not. The gods do what they please, even when we do all we can to influence them. For now, at least, the Lord Marduk and his court are blessing Babylon, so I imagine we are in their good graces. Should that ever change, we'll know it."

Everything the man said made a kind of sense. Isiratuu had thought about the same things he, Asher, had, and he'd come up with a way of thinking that seemed reasonable.

And yet . . .

* * *

The day passed pleasantly. Food and drink were brought to him. Damkina tended him as if he were a prince. Iltani looked in on him and asked him ten times if he was all right and if he needed anything. In the afternoon, Elisheva and Tirzah paid a visit, too. Asher caught Elisheva looking at the slave girl with suspicion, and he wondered how much she guessed. He could also see how impressed Tirzah was by the splendor of Iltani's estate.

Isiratuu checked on him and changed his dressing in the afternoon and again in the evening. The wound, while still red and tender, already looked better, and there was no sign of infection.

"You can go home tomorrow," the physician told him, "but I've suggested to your lady that you have a few more days of rest. She's eager to have you back, I don't mind telling you. She wants to show you off to all her friends!"

Asher felt himself blushing.

"I also advise that you allow the girl to tend you tonight, if you know what I mean," Isiratuu went on. "Love is a powerful healer. Just be careful with that arm. Nothing too—strenuous!"

Asher blushed more.

But he took the physician's advice.

* * *

Asher enjoyed a fine welcome when he returned to the house, whose front wall had been restored as if Ezekiel had not tried his best to tear it down. When the evening meal was done, Ezekiel sent Asher to Josiah's house and told him to return with his father and grandfather.

The short walk made him tired, but he was glad to see Josiah.

At home, Ezekiel had built a fire in the courtyard. He welcomed Eliezer and Simeon and invited them to share some wine. When everyone was settled, Ezekiel fetched a mud brick and something wrapped in cheap cloth. He placed the brick in the center of their small circle, next to the fire. He had etched images of Jerusalem on it sides, just as he had done with the first one a few days earlier.

"Jerusalem," murmured Simeon. "Shalom be upon her."

"I wish it were so," Ezekiel said. "But that's impossible. For thus says YAH, the Lord." He unwrapped the bundle, which contained a measuring scale and all the hair he had shaved from his head and face.

"What now?" Benaiah muttered.

Ezekiel proceeded to weigh out his hair, dividing it into three parts. He placed one part all around the brick, then set it afire. "So shall the city burn when the days of siege are done," he told them.

Next, he scattered the second portion of hair on top of the charred remnants of the first, again encircling the brick. From the bundle he produced a hand axe and proceeded to chop the hair into bits.

Asher scanned the faces of his family and friends. His father looked angry. Azarel looked fiercely serious—and disapproving. The old man Simeon had covered his head and was praying in a whisper. Tirzah couldn't take her eyes away from what her uncle was doing. Elisheva covered her mouth with one hand, while the other kept gripping her skirt. Her beautiful face was filled with grief.

When Ezekiel had finished chopping the hair into pieces, he took the third portion and tossed it into the air. An updraft caught several strands and launched them into the sky, where a breeze carried them away. Most of the rest fell back to earth, landing everywhere in the courtyard. Several pieces fell on Asher, and he brushed them off as if they were something unclean. He didn't want any of his uncle's hair on him. That was too close.

Ezekiel then gathered up some of the hair from the ground and wrapped it in the skirt of the long robe he had put on over his tunic.

Then he spoke, not with his own voice, but with what Asher recognized as the voice of YAH speaking through him: "'This is Jerusalem, which I set in the midst of the nations. She rebelled against me and was more wicked than any other nation, rejecting my laws and statutes. Therefore, I am now against her, and I will carry out judgments against her in the sight of all the nations. Therefore, in Jerusalem, fathers shall eat their sons and sons shall eat their fathers, and I will judge the people and scatter them among the nations.'"

Benaiah jumped up. "That's enough!" he cried. "I won't stand for your sickening talk in my house. You speak of abominations and horrors in the temple of YAH, but *you're* the one speaking horrors—fathers and sons eating each other's flesh! If you insist on talking that way—of acting this mad way—you'll have to find somewhere else to live. My children and I can't bear any more!"

Ezekiel took it without a word. Elisheva left the courtyard, pulling Tirzah with her.

"Well?" Benaiah demanded. "You've sickened your wife and your niece. Are you satisfied?"

Ezekiel set his face against his brother. His blue eye seemed to glow. "When the siege comes and Jerusalem runs out of food, a hungry man will eat . . ."

"That nasty muck you made and cooked on a fire animal shit?" Benaiah demanded.

"Not only that, brother. A starving man will eat anything he can lay hands on, even his own child. A starving woman who gives birth will devour the afterbirth in secret so that she does not have to share a morsel with her husband or other children."

"Stop!" Eliezer cried.

"You see?" Benaiah told Ezekiel. "Your words are the true abomination."

"They are not *my* words. Thus says the Master, YAH, the Lord our God."

"We're leaving," Eliezer told them. "Come, father. You don't need to hear more of this."

The old man got to his feet, tottered, and then collapsed.

"See what you've done?" Eliezer demanded of Ezekiel. "If he dies of shock, I will hold you responsible."

Asher brought water and they revived Simeon. With help, he got to his feet, and his son hustled him away. Josiah went with them. As he left, he promised Asher that they would talk soon. Something of importance, he said.

That left only the men of the family.

"Are you satisfied now?" Benaiah began, addressing himself to his brother. "Eliezer and Simeon supported you when all the other priests were again you. Now you've alienated them, too. You have no friends left, Ezekiel. It's you against—everyone."

"I take no satisfaction in that," Ezekiel assured him. "But I must obey YAH when he speaks to me."

"That's *your* problem. I meant what I said: if you persist talking like this, you'll have to find another place to live."

"I hear you. I'll do my best to comply with your wishes, but my master is YAH, not you or any man."

"So you keep telling us. Just remember, as you obey this master of yours: it may cost you a lot."

"Even my family," Ezekiel admitted. "I understand."

"Asher and I are going for a walk," Azarel said.

That was news to Asher, but he was glad for a chance to get away.

"I don't blame you," their father said. "Don't stay out too long. You need rest to help your wound heal."

The brothers made their way to the canal and headed north.

"How's the wound?" Azarel asked.

"It throbs. What about your belly?"

"Much better. Just a scratch compared to what you got. That's a nasty cut."

"I think I would have died if Isiratuu hadn't known how repair it."

"Huh! I admit these Babylonians are clever—more than we Israelites are. Imagine if he could be physician in our village instead of that idiot who pretends to know what he's doing. It feels weird saying this, but I'm glad a Babylonian was able to fix you up."

"He was kind. I like him."

"Funny, isn't it?" Azarel asked, more to himself than to Asher.

"What's funny?"

"That there *are* good people among our enemies. I almost feel sorry that many of them will have to die when their king is overthrown. Men like your physician—fathers—mothers—children . . ."

"Are you still planning the revolt?"

"It's already begun. What we've been doing when I'm out at night—picking off the strays one by one before we attack the whole flock all at once . . . Make them all feel unsafe, like they don't know where or when the next attack will come. Suspicion, fear—those are weapons, too."

"Uncle Ezekiel believes nothing will stop Nebuchadrezzar from going back to Jerusalem and destroying it."

"He can take his visions with him to Sheol, for all I care!"

"Azarel! That's awful."

"And what *he* said isn't awful—parents eating their children? Children returning the favor?"

"It's sick, I know."

"And it won't help us!" Azarel exclaimed. "We don't need people like him telling us that we're doomed to destruction and there's nothing we can do about it. There *is* something! If we don't want these damned Babylonians to march on Jerusalem again, we have to make sure they don't. I want them all dead!"

"You're as bad as Ezekiel is. Some people would say *you're* the crazy one in the family, not him."

"What about you, little brother? Who do *you* think is the crazy one? Him? Me? What about yourself? There are plenty of people right here in our village that would say you're insane for risking your life for that bitch you work for. I've learned some things about her. She makes a fortune selling her precious dates to the army so the soldiers can have food on their campaigns. An army has to eat, right? Dates don't spoil. Maybe some of the soldiers who invaded Jerusalem were eating dates grown on the plantation of your Lady Iltani. Or have you heard how she ordered one of her slaves to be beaten so badly that the boy died? She accused him of stealing one of her idols. He denied it, but they found it hidden in the slave quarters. She ordered him whipped until he confessed, but he wouldn't. He died under the lash."

"She's not like that!"

"Isn't she? Do you know what happened to the houseboy you replaced?"

"He joined the army. She said he wanted to fight for Babylon."

"He raped one of her Egyptian slave girls. He was caught in the act, then castrated by your lady's personal physician—"

"Not Isiratuu!"

"No?"

"He wouldn't do that!"

"He did, though."

"You're lying! You're just making all this up to get me to be part of your stupid plot. I won't do it! You're the one who can go to Sheol!"

Azarel grabbed him by the arm—his wounded arm.

"Let go! You're hurting me!"

"That's exactly my intention, you little jackass! Look at this!" He pulled up his tunic. "Have a good look. I got hurt doing my part to destroy our enemies. To get back at the people who drove our grandparents to their death. Who raped and killed our mother! Now let's look at your injury." He yanked Asher's tunic off his shoulder. "You got hurt protecting one of our mortal enemies, a hag who profits from Babylon's wars against its neighbors. Who watched her slave boy beaten to death. Who had a man's testicles cut off for daring to violate one of her possessions. That's who you saved, so now you're Asher the hero! Asher the brave! Asher the defender of a helpless old woman!"

"Shut up! I've heard enough."

Azarel let him go, then glared at him in disgust. "You're giving it to that Egyptian girl, aren't you?"

"Who told you that?"

"No one had to tell me. Elisheva sensed it the moment she saw how the girl looks at you. You must think you're a pretty big man to have a slave in your bed. Does the Lady Iltani know?"

Asher hung his head. "Yes," he whispered. "It was her idea."

"Then pray she doesn't change her mind about your little dalliance, or you might lose your balls, too."

That's when Asher took a swing at his brother. Azarel wasn't expecting it, and Asher's fist caught him on the jaw. He staggered backwards, pulled himself together, and started for Asher. Then he stopped and stood staring, rubbing his chin and breathing heavily.

"The men of our house had better watch out or we're all going to kill each other," he chuckled. "Our uncle goes after our father and smashes his nose—you attack me for no good reason—"

"For no reason? After what you just said?"

"The truth hurts, doesn't it?"

"I'm going home."

"Not yet, you're not."

"You're going to stop me?"

Azarel grabbed him again. "Get one thing through your stupid head, okay? Don't think just because we're brothers I won't take you apart if you really get on my bad side."

"Am I supposed to be scared?"

"You should be."

"Let me alone."

"Okay, but there's one more thing."

"And what's that?"

"Choose, brother. Who are you going to serve? Your own people, or our oppressors? They may dress you up in their fine clothes and paint your eyes and drench you in fancy perfume and let you be their little performing monkey. Hell, they might even let you screw their slave girls. But they are your *enemies!* If it comes to it, your fine lady will throw you away like a piece of garbage. She just might keep your testicles for a souvenir."

"You're worse than Ezekiel," Asher told him. "From now on, leave me alone."

"I won't until you decide which side you're on. Our uncle can keep his little visions and his sick thoughts, but they're not going to help us get Jerusalem free again, with all of us back home where we belong. But maybe you'd prefer staying here so you can be your fine lady's houseboy. Who knows? You might follow in the footsteps of our ancestor Abraham."

"What do you mean?"

"He slept with an Egyptian slave girl, too. Got her pregnant, just as he and his wife had planned. And you know how all that turned out."

Asher wasn't sure what his brother meant about Father Abraham and a slave girl; maybe he should have listened more carefully when the men told tales of the old days.

In silence, the brothers returned home. Azarel stayed up to talk with Tirzah in the courtyard, so Asher went to an empty room. Compared to where he'd slept the two nights before, his bed felt hard, the straw mattress prickly. Instead of the scent of spices, this room reeked of dust and smoke. Compared to the night before, with a beautiful young girl beside him, this darkness felt empty—and lonely.

"Damkina," he whispered. Her image floated before his eyes. Her dark, lustrous hair, her brown eyes flecked with gold, rimmed with the thinnest line of kohl to make them appear even larger than they were. Her lips, red like a poppy. Her slim body . . .

He wanted her.

Chapter Twenty-Two

The next morning, Asher wondered what he would do with himself all day; his injured arm ached and he felt exhausted despite a dreamless night's sleep. Later, he would go and let Isiratuu examine his wound. He was glad when Josiah appeared and invited him to go fishing.

"You should be at work," Asher told him. "It's not Shabbat."

"I quit," Josiah said. "I can't throw away one more day of my life slaving for my enemies when I don't have to."

"What will you do instead? Your family needs the money."

"YAH will provide for us," Josiah assured him. "Just as he provides for all who put their trust in him."

Please not another sermon, Asher thought. *Every time I turn around, somebody is preaching at me.*

They took fishing gear, water, and some food. At the river, with lines in the water, they waited for the fish to cooperate.

"What happened after we left last night?" Josiah asked.

"You mean after Ezekiel made your grandfather sick to his stomach with his prophecies of cannibalism?"

Josiah nodded. "That's strong stuff. Father says prophets like to exaggerate to get people's attention, but not even Jeremiah talks the way your uncle does."

"He can't help himself."

"He'd better start. There's more you don't know about."

"What?"

"Ezekiel came to our house the other evening, after work, and he brought a scribe with him. He told Father to gather some of the other priests because he had something he needed to share. We got a few together, and your uncle said some really indecent things."

"Worse than fathers eating their own children?"

"In a way, yes. He started raving about how our people are like whores. He claims we go after idols and alliances with pagan nations the way prostitutes go after customers. He said our people run after foreigners with male organs as big as horses' and donkeys' so we can satisfy our lusts. When he started talking that way, Father sent me out of the room, but I sneaked back to the door and listened anyway. What your uncle said was filthy! The priests were sickened, but Ezekiel ordered them to keep listening until YAH was finished. All the time, the scribe was scribbling down everything he said, trying to keep up. I didn't like to hear it, but I made myself stay."

"I don't believe you," Asher protested, but he did believe. His uncle was capable of anything.

"It's true, and you know it," Josiah.

There was no point arguing. "What do the priests think?"

"After Ezekiel left, I listened in on their conversation. They hate what he's saying, but they don't know what to do about him. One priest suggested that he should be silenced in any way necessary—"

"You mean that he should be killed?"

"No, not in so many words. But the others confronted him, reminded him that maybe YAH *is* speaking through him."

"You don't believe that yourself."

Josiah sighed. "I guess not, but I wish I could! The way your uncle is carrying on doesn't help our cause. How do you get men to fight if they're convinced everything's their own fault? If that's true, then we should stop and wait for the next disaster—our city burned. More of our people brought here as exiles. More of our people slaughtered!"

"My uncle doesn't say we should do nothing. He's telling us to repent. He's pleading with us to change our ways, renounce idols!"

Josiah gave him a stern look. "Is that what *you've* been doing—changing your ways, renouncing idols, or honoring them in the house of your Babylonian mistress?"

"I'm not—"

"Yes, you are. But it's not too late. I quit; so can you. Our time is coming soon, and we'll need you."

"I'll think about it."

"What's there to think about? What you're doing is flat wrong, and you know it. You're just as guilty as your uncle says our nation is. Going after idols the way a hot woman goes after a fellow with a huge—"

"Shut up, will you!"

"You're in a rotten mood this morning."

"My brother got on my case last night, and now you! I told him to leave me alone. He told you to lecture me, right?"

"No, but we agree, and we're going to keep after you until you come to your senses and do what you know is right."

Asher dropped his line and stood up. "You can bring the fishing stuff. We're not going to catch anything, and my arm hurts. I'm going home."

"Suit yourself. But do us all a favor."

"What's that?"

"Talk to your uncle. Get him on our side. Get him to see that YAH wants us to be free, just the way he wanted our people free from Pharaoh."

"And who's our Moses? You?"

With that, he walked away. Josiah didn't follow.

* * *

Back at home, Asher found Ezekiel waiting for him. "I need you to come with me," was the first thing he said.

"Another vision?"

Ezekiel nodded.

"I don't want to."

"Please, Asher! I need you to be with me."

"I'm too tired. My arm hurts."

"You can rest later. We have to go—*now*!" Ezekiel looked at him with such imploring eyes—the one clear blue, like his own—that Asher couldn't say no.

"All right," he said, "but I'm scared."

Ezekiel touched his shoulder. "So am I. That's why I need you. You give me courage."

Asher couldn't figure how that was possible.

They took the familiar path along the canal to open land. Ezekiel indicated they should leave the path and find a place to sit, near a field of ripening grain.

Then they waited.

Asher saw it first. This time full-on, not like peering through the crack in a partly opened door. The very same thing he had only glimpsed before, that his uncle had described in detail: the throne of YAH, radiant atop the cherubim pillars, the cherubim with four faces, the ox, the lion, the eagle, the man. The wheels. The eyes.

The eyes. Many glowing brown. Some as blue as sapphires.

"What do you see?" Ezekiel whispered.

Asher began to describe his vision.

"I see the same," Ezekiel cried. "The glory of YAH! His throne in heaven!"

Asher was shaking. He grabbed his uncle's hand and found it as cold as a winter rain and trembling as if it were freezing.

"Courage!" Ezekiel told him.

"Uncle, please—"

"Be brave. YAH won't harm his faithful servants."

Asher wondered if that included himself. Then he could not think of himself, for the vision grew until it filled his sight, filled his mind, filled his *nephesh*—all his inmost being.

The throne of light and fire, the sound of rushing wind, of wings, the radiance so bright that it hid the One on the throne—it hovered above the temple on Mt. Zion, above YAH's chosen dwelling place. Then a cloud brighter than the face of the sun at noonday broke from the threshold of the temple, rose up and up and hovered above the four-faced cherubim. Then they went forth, moving away, away from YAH's house, the place where he had promised to dwell forever.

Asher saw it all. His uncle must be seeing it too, judging from the way he was gripping his hand and from the sobs that rose in his throat. Then Ezekiel began to moan, a cry of desolation even worse than his father's screams of agony when he discovered his wife's violated body.

The sound of the rushing winds engulfed him, and Asher dropped face down on the ground. The tumult continued; this must be how it was inside a whirlwind.

Then it all ceased. Asher lifted his head, scanned the area, and was not surprised to see nothing disturbed, just as nothing had been touched during his first vision.

"Uncle?" he asked. Beside him, Ezekiel sat like a stone.

"Can you hear me?" Asher said.

"It's over," Ezekiel answered. "It's too late."

"What's over?"

"Hope."

"I don't understand."

"Tell me what you saw."

"The same as you."

"Then tell me what it means."

Asher considered the vision, how the moveable throne of YAH had hovered over the temple, as if waiting for the glory of YAH to join it. It did, and after that, the throne moved away. Then he understood, but he did not want to speak the truth.

"Tell me!" Ezekiel repeated. "I know that you know."

"I don't want to."

"You *have* to. I need you to, and then I'll be completely certain it's true."

"YAH has abandoned his temple. He's not going to dwell there anymore."

Ezekiel answered with a sob. "He's gone. And with him—blessing and protection."

"Then *they* can go back and destroy it." He didn't have to say who *they* were.

Ezekiel nodded. Desolation filled his eyes.

"When?" Asher cried.

"I don't know. But it will happen. Unless . . ."

Unless we join with the Babylonian rebels and overthrow the king, Asher wanted to shout, but what was the point?

Trudging home was misery. Ezekiel would not speak or wipe away tears. People looked at them oddly, some with suspicion. Some recognized him, and Asher heard one person declare, "It's only that crazy fellow again. Wonder what's bothering him this time?"

Asher was beyond feeling embarrassed to be seen in his uncle's company, for he felt more wretched than he had in his life, except, perhaps, the moment his father told him that his mother had been murdered. He looked back toward the site of his vision—for it *was* his now, not just Ezekiel's. A memory invaded his mind, as clear as the path before him: the first day of his family's forced march from Jerusalem. That day, he'd kept looking back at the city. Each time, it looked smaller. Finally, no matter how hard he strained his eyes, it was gone.

Asher had wondered then if he would ever see his true home again. He wondered the same thing now. Azarel and Josiah were preparing to fight and die to make a return possible. But with YAH departed from his city, would there be anything left even if the exiles did manage to find their way back?

Chapter Twenty-Three

By the time they got to their own street, Ezekiel was staggering. At home, he collapsed into Elisheva's arms. They managed to get him onto his bed, where he suffered a fit. He thrashed, ground his teeth, and then fell utterly still, seemingly paralyzed, drooling from the corner of his mouth. He roused after a while, gave way to tears, and cried himself to sleep.

Asher explained what had happened, but no words could express what he'd seen. Now, *now* he understood, a little at least, the prophet's burden, for he felt it himself.

Elisheva listened while he tried to describe the glory of YAH's throne, its power to rise into the air, to move around. To receive the Spirit rising from the temple and joining it, then to depart. As he told that part, *he* fell to crying, and he allowed his aunt to lead him to his own bed, where he pulled his blanket over his face, turned on his side, and curled up like a baby in its mother's womb, praying for this terrible dream to go away.

It didn't.

He lay there all day, refusing water or food, his wound aching, his mind trying to erase the memory of what he'd seen.

No good.

Not until evening, when his father and brother returned from the pottery shop, was Asher even able to sit up and talk without breaking down again. They reminded him he was supposed to have gone to Lady Iltani's to see the physician. He was glad he'd forgotten. How could he have explained why he was in such terrible shape, not from the wound, but from something Isiratuu could not have understood?

The members of his family were kind to Asher that evening—except for Azarel. He kept his distance and listened in silence when Asher described what had happened. When the family had gone to bed, Asher could hear Azarel turning restlessly.

"You awake?" Azarel asked at last.

"Yeah. I wish I weren't."

"I've got to go out," Azarel told him. "Swear you won't mention anything to Ezekiel or anyone else."

Asher swore.

"See you later," Azarel whispered. Then he was gone into the night.

* * *

Next morning, Azarel was on his bed, profoundly asleep. Asher wondered, but didn't want to know, where he'd been or who his companions had been. Or what they were planning.

When he sat up, Asher felt his head throb, the way it had the one time in his life he'd drunk too much palm wine. His wound felt all right, and there was no sign of it draining through the bandages. At first, he legs felt wobbly, but he got his balance and was able to walk. No one else was awake, which was strange, because it was not all that early. He could hear his father snoring. In the courtyard, no one had started a fire.

The sound of someone tapping on the front door surprised him. It was a man he didn't recognize.

"What do you want?" Asher asked. "Who are you?"

"Never mind that. Are you Asher?"

"Yes."

You must come with me."

"I don't know you!"

"There's no time to argue. Come now if you want your family to stay safe."

The man didn't wait for an answer.

They walked to the far north side of the village. In a narrow alley, they came to a low door. The man knocked, whispered something to someone on its other side, and went in, gesturing for Asher to follow. He found himself in a dim, cramped room, perhaps used for storage, for there were jars along its wall and sacks of grain hanging from the ceiling to keep rats from getting to them.

Three men sat cross-legged on the floor. All had scarves drawn across the lower halves of their faces. All regarded him with cool interest.

"So you are Asher," one said. "We have heard about you."

"What do you want?"

"In time, my friend."

"I'm not your friend. Who are you?" Asher asked.

"Sit down. We'll ask the questions, not you."

Asher sat.

"I am Joshua," the man said. "It's not my true name. It's my warrior name. This is Gideon," he gestured to the man on his right. "And Caleb," nodding to his left. "Not their given names, either. We are sworn to fight for YAH."

"What do you want with me?"

"First, swear you will never tell anyone that you've been here, that you've ever met any of us."

"I swear." *Again,* he thought.

"Swear that you will never reveal to anyone anything your brother has told you."

"I swear." *And again.*

"Swear you will never mention to anyone anything your friend Josiah has told you."

"I swear." *All I ever do is swear,* he said to himself, somehow amused despite the situation.

No one spoke for a moment. Then someone entered the room from a low door at the back of the room. He, too, had his face covered, but Asher knew quite well who it was.

"He has sworn," the man called Joshua told Josiah.

"I heard. Good."

"What's going on?" Asher asked sharply. "What do you want?"

Josiah would not sit. "Everything, brother. Even your life."

"No."

The man who called himself Gideon jabbed him in the side. "You don't speak to Samson that way."

"Samson?"

Josiah chuckled. "It's a bit of a stretch," he admitted. "That fellow was a fool, but at the end, he killed many Philistines."

"And died doing it," Asher recalled.

"A worthy sacrifice, wouldn't you say?"

"I don't know. You still haven't told me what you want."

"Can't you guess?"

"To kill Babylonians?"

The man called Joshua let out a deep breath.

"If it comes to that, yes."

"I won't do that."

"And why not?"

"They're people just like us."

"There you're wrong," Josiah corrected him. "They are our enemies. In wars, you kill your enemies. You don't stop to think of them as—*people*."

"One of them just saved my life," Asher reminded him. "Our so-called physician in the village would have let me die. He doesn't know enough to help anyone."

Joshua shrugged. "Don't get us wrong, Asher. We're grateful that YAH has saved you. If he can give words to a donkey, he can cause an idolator to serve one of his chosen people. Don't worry. One day, we will possess all the wisdom of these Babylonian dogs, and much more."

"I won't kill anyone," Asher insisted.

"Don't be too quick to announce what you will or won't do," Josiah advised him. "When the time comes, you'll find out what you're capable of doing."

Asher made as if to stand up. Gideon pushed him back to his place.

"We've all been where you are," Josiah-Samson went on. "We've been uncertain. Frightened. I lived three years terrified, until my dream."

"What dream was that?" Asher scoffed. "Something about shoveling shit?"

"You can't offend me, brother. I thank YAH every day for honoring me with the task of 'shoveling shit,' as you put it, because it gave me time—minutes, hours, days—to listen for his voice. To realize what he wants from us. To gain the courage to swear to obey him when he speaks. Do you know, Asher, that YAH allowed me to have a taste of what slavery is? Now I know because I've lived it. So have you, even though you haven't realized it yet. There's so much you haven't realized. You've spent your life feeling sorry for yourself because of that one blue eye, and now that you have the chance to accept your true identity, you fight it."

"And what's my true identity?"

"Prophet. That's why we've given you a new name: Hosea."

"Asher is my name. That's good enough for me."

"Think it over. You'll come to see we're right."

"What do you want? I keep asking, and you won't tell me."

Josiah came across the room and squatted in front him. Then he pulled down his face covering. Their faces were close, so close that Asher could feel the other man's warm breath against his skin. "You've sworn," Josiah reminded him. "If you betray us, you will die."

"So you say."

Josiah took Asher's face between his two hands and kissed him on the right cheek. "Welcome to the war, brother," he said. A single tear fell from his eye.

Asher felt Gideon squeeze his good shoulder.

Josiah moved back across the room and sat on a cushion. "Here's what we want from you. In war, nothing is certain, and things happen quickly. When the day of our attack begins, I can't predict where you will be or what you will have to do. We need for you to be ready to act when the command comes. Do you understand?"

"No."

Josiah smiled. "An honest answer, and the one I expected."

"I'm not a warrior—like you," Asher told him.

"No, but you have two weapons no one else possesses."

"What are those?"

"The amulet Queen Mother Nehushta gave you, for one."

Asher had forgotten he even had it.

"What's important about that?"

"She told you, didn't she, that if you show the amulet to the guard named Hunzuu, he will let you inside the royal palace. At least into the quarters of King Jeconiah."

"All right. So what?"

"You may be carrying information our king needs. The Queen Mother will recognize you, of course, but she might not be there. We have to be ready for anything. King Jeconiah must have accurate information delivered by someone he can trust. That will be you."

Asher felt his heart thumping. "What's the other thing?"

"Something even more valuable. You have the seal of that crone Iltani."

Instinctively, Asher felt in his tunic pocket. It was empty. Had he lost it? He couldn't even recall the last time he'd thought of it. That was a mistake, a terrible one.

"Let me see it," Josiah ordered him.

Asher felt for it again. Nothing.

"I don't have it," he admitted.

"How could you?" Josiah said, producing the seal from his own tunic pocket.

"Where did you get it?" Asher demanded.

"Your brother stole it from you and entrusted it to me. You're careless, Hosea."

"Asher!"

"Asher. In time, you'll accept your new name. You'll treasure it."

"I doubt that. Give them back! You had no right to take my things."

"Sorry, brother, but you don't know how valuable they might be for the war."

"I don't care about that. Give them back!"

"Come get them."

Asher wanted to accept Josiah's challenge; he desperately wanted to, but he knew he was beaten. Josiah had three henchmen; they would kill him without a second thought if they had to protect their leader.

"I can't," he admitted.

"No shame in that. A warrior knows when he's outnumbered. So here." He offered the amulet and seal, and Asher grabbed them. But once they were in his hands, he didn't know what to do with them. In fact, he didn't want them now.

"Put them away," Josiah told him. "You understand the power of that seal, don't you?"

Asher nodded. "Lady Iltani told me it will get me into places I couldn't go without it."

"She's right. It also identifies you as someone she trusts. When the war begins, her estate will be put under guard. We couldn't hope to get by those guarding her—" Josiah paused and gave Asher a penetrating look—"but you can."

"And then what?"

"You'll know what to do. And if you don't, pray to YAH. He will guide you."

"I could never hurt her," Asher told them. "I saved her life the other day."

"We know. Why'd you interfere?"

"What do you mean?"

"Do you know who it was that tried to assassinate her?"

Asher shook his head. "Some madman, we were told."

"One of *our* warriors," Josiah corrected him. "'David,' he called himself. He pledged to give up his life for the honor of enacting YAH's vengeance on that old whore. But you stepped in where you weren't wanted and took away his chance of fulfilling his oath. Now his corpse is being torn apart by the vultures and wild dogs while your fine lady indulgences herself with dainties and sends one of her slaves to your bed as a reward for saving her evil life."

"I won't ever kill her. Do your warriors target women for slaughter?"

"When YAH commands it, yes. Learn your history, Asher! Holy War makes for hard decisions."

"I can't do this," Asher told them. "I have to go."

At the door, he stopped. These fanatics had frightened him, but now he was simply angry. Perhaps he had a way of getting them back. "I still don't accept the idea about my being a prophet," he told them, "but I can tell you what my uncle and I saw yesterday."

Josiah looked interested. "And what was that?"

"A vision of YAH's glory leaving the temple. He's abandoned us, Josiah, or Samson, or whatever you call yourself. Even if you join Nebuchadrezzar's enemies and overthrow him, someone else will finish the job against Jerusalem. You might get to go home one day, but it will be to the burned ruins of our city."

No one spoke or stopped him from leaving.

Outside, early morning sunshine dazzled his eyes. He got confused in the maze of crooked streets in this part of the village. When Asher finally got home, Ezekiel was sitting in the courtyard, an untouched meal of porridge beside him. He looked at Asher and extended a hand. Asher went to him and took it. Ezekiel grasped his hand hard and touched his forehead near his blue eye, not far from where Josiah had kissed him.

Now he had to come up with a lie about where he'd been. No one questioned him when he said he'd waked up at dawn with his arm hurting him, so he'd gone for a walk.

The smell of cooked grain made him feel queasy, and he had no appetite anyway. Everything in him clamored for more sleep, so he threw himself on his bed, telling Elisheva and Tirzah to please let him be.

* * *

That afternoon, Asher made his way to the Lady Iltani's estate. He learned that Isiratuu was not there, but at his own home, where he met with patients. At Isiratuu's dwelling, Asher waited with other people, a small crowd of well-dressed Babylonians, some of whom looked at him oddly. The physician inspected his wound, pronounced him well on the way to recovery, and showed him how to bandage the place for himself.

"You have good reason to be thankful," Isiratuu told him. "Had the assassin's knife cut just a little deeper, no one could have helped you. But praise be to Gula and Sekhmet! They spared you. I suggest you make them an offering to show your appreciation."

"How do I do that?"

"Around the corner I have built them a shrine. You can't miss it. Think of something to give them—some token of appreciation. Then they will remember you next time—should there ever be one, which I pray there will not be."

"Thank you, sir. You saved my life."

"With the skill taught me by my father and his before him—and with the blessing of the gods. Now be on your way, son of Israel! May the gods prosper you."

Asher found the shrine with no trouble. Images of the goddesses standing on pedestals faced the street. At their feet, the faithful had left flowers, fruit, or ceramic pots filled with grain and oil. He saw beaded necklaces, pieces of finely woven cloth, and even a tiny dead bird. And there were many figurines of dogs, Gula's favorites.

Idols. If his uncle were with him, he would spit in the faces of the carved stone goddesses or relieve himself over the offerings of the sick and recovering. Asher felt in his pocket. He had the amulet and the lady's seal, but they were too precious to leave on the ground. There was nothing else he could give—and to make any offering was a sin of idolatry. He was Asher, an Israelite whose god was YAH. His uncle insisted he was a prophet, and he halfway believed it.

What prophet practiced idolatry?

Not one that he knew of.

Leave, he told himself.

That's what he did. Sekmhet and Gula got no offering from Asher ben-Benaiah that day.

From his head, Asher plucked a single hair. He held it up, and when a gust of wind came along, he let it go. The wind carried it up and up, his offering to YAH.

* * *

When Asher returned from Isiratuu's house, he was relieved to find Ezekiel seemingly himself, but gaunt and unkempt. The hair on his head and face was growing back, and the dark stubble made him look grimy, in need of a bath. Asher wanted to discuss their vision, but his uncle flatly refused. "It still hurts too much," is all the explanation he gave. Asher had no choice but to wait until he was ready to talk.

He remained at home, telling himself that he could return to Iltani's the next day. She would certainly fuss over him again, thank him again for saving her life. Yes, he was her savior—savior of an idol worshiper who made a fortune selling food to Babylon's army of conquest, destruction, and death. Savior of a woman who had watched, perhaps enjoyed, seeing one of her slaves whipped to death. Savior of a woman who had ordered the gelding of a houseboy for doing something not too far different from what he himself was doing with Damkina.

That evening, Benaiah came back from the pottery shop full of terrible news. Rumors were running through the village of terroristic attacks on ordinary citizens of Babylon going about their business, not breaking any laws or bothering anyone. Three men had been knifed to death, two women—prostitutes, perhaps—were strangled, and even two boys returning home from fishing had been stabbed through their hearts.

Benaiah had worse to report. Two village men had been murdered during the last night, their bodies discovered concealed under cloth sacks used for moving grain. Both had their throats cut.

"Yes, we knew of that," Elisheva told him. "Word of it has run through the village all day long. Tirzah heard it at the well, and Miriam from across the street shared it with me this afternoon."

"Who were they?" Asher asked, glancing at Azarel, whose face betrayed not a speck of interest in the conversation.

"I heard their names, but I can't remember them now," Elisheva said. "No one we knew."

"Why were they killed?" Asher asked, with another glance toward his brother.

"No one knows," Tirzah said.

"I'm so glad you have a safe job," Elisheva told him. "All this talk of people being murdered. I find myself afraid to go even to the well."

Just what they want you to feel, Asher remembered. *Fear and suspicion. Weapons of war.*

"You've got more than a safe place to work," Tirzah assured him. "Now that you've saved the old lady's life, she's bound to make it pretty cushy for you. Just don't forget your humble little family back here when you're some high and mighty official."

"That's not going to happen," he told her. Tirzah was joking, but he didn't find it funny. And as for working in a safe place . . . When it came—the revolt—who would be safe?

A voice inside him pronounced an answer: *No one.*

Chapter Twenty-Four

The next morning, Asher enjoyed a resplendent welcome at the Lady Iltani's. She had a new tunic and sandals waiting for him, and her girls quickly arranged his hair, darkened his eyes, and anointed him. Feeling like a rare bird in a rich woman's golden cage, he escorted her through the streets and all the way to her "throne" at the plantation, where many people paid their respects to the lady and thanked the young hero for saving her from the assassin's blade.

When they returned to Iltani's estate, she began telling him about Babylon's upcoming New Year's Festival and how Asher would have a wonderful view of the great procession. "Not only that," she enthused. "I have a surprise for you, or should I say a fitting honor for you. I wanted to keep it a secret until the day arrives, but I can't! You're to meet your king, Jeconiah!"

The news stunned him. "How?"

"I ran into his mother at a party, and she wanted to know what happened. She was pleased that one of her own people had protected me, so I suggested her son might like to meet you. She sent me word this morning that Jeconiah has agreed. There's more: he intends to inform King Nebuchadrezzar about what you did, to make the point that Israelites are loyal subjects."

Asher had to keep from laughing in her face. How blind she was! How would she like knowing that some of Nebuchadrezzar's so-called loyal subjects were even now plotting his overthrow?

But he said, "Being presented to Israel's king is an honor beyond my imagining."

Iltani gave him a sly look. "One would think you'd been raised in the courts of the mighty. That's just how they talk to one another. Just tell me 'Thank you,' and we can let it go at that."

He had to smile at how well she understood him.

The day passed pleasantly. Asher stayed near his mistress, ready to do her bidding. Damkina was nearby, too, occupied with a bit of inconsequential sewing or arranging the lady's garments. Asher remembered how Iltani had once told him she enjoyed having beautiful young people near her; it flattered him to think that included him.

In the evening, he was sent home. Ezekiel was still not truly himself. After his first vision, one could see he was fighting to recover. Since then, however, every encounter with YAH left him weaker than before. A terrible thought came to Asher: one of these times, YAH would finish the job and kill him. Asher couldn't stand that, nor could he accept the possibility that the same disaster might engulf him if he ever admitted he, too, was a prophet.

After the meal, he told his family he was going out to walk along the canal. He went the usual way toward the "field of sight." When he arrived at the place, Asher gazed toward the north. Was YAH there now? His glory had abandoned the temple, so where had he gone?

Asher could not remember the last time he'd really prayed. Had he ever prayed since coming to their village outside the walls of proud Babylon?

Not that he could recall.

He had prayed when the Babylonians first revealed their plan: the best families of Jerusalem were going into exile. *Not my family,* he had begged YAH. *We're nothing special. Grandfather is a priest, but not an important one. There are many priests who do not have families. Take them, not us.* But the Babylonian generals pronounced their verdict: Asher's family was chosen. Either YAH had not heard his prayer, or worse, he had heard it and refused his petition.

Had he stopped praying then? No—Asher had prayed that everyone would make it safely to Babylon. If they could survive the journey, they might have the chance for a new life. Not a better life, but life. Then his grandparents died. Not of sickness that anyone could describe, not of an injury. They simply gave up. Died within two days of each other.

Still, he had prayed that their graves, shallow pits dug in desert sand, would not be desecrated. He remembered how bitterly his father had wept when they were forced back onto the road. No turning back, no time to grieve.

Then it came to him: he'd never truly prayed since the day his mother was murdered. Neither had his father, he realized. Asher confessed himself a faithless son of Abraham. Yet YAH claimed him—*him*—as a prophet, just as he had claimed his uncle.

What was YAH thinking? That's what he wanted to find out. That's why he was going to pray.

Trouble was, he'd forgotten how.

Asher walked off the path and found the spot he and Ezekiel had received the last vision. Golden heads of grain were pressed down to the ground where they had seen the glory of YAH.

"Speak to me," he prayed. *But don't show yourself,* he thought. *No visions, please. I can't stand any more.*

Asher waited. YAH did not seem inclined to answer.

"I'm in a bad way," he continued. "I'm scared. Look—I'm in a mess and I don't know what to do. You're killing my uncle. My brother is an assassin, and he wants me to be one, too! My father gave up a long time ago. He doesn't live! He just exists. My friend Josiah also wants me to be a killer, to fight in this revolt they're planning. Do something! Save me and my family, please! I'm begging you."

All around him was quiet as the sun sank toward the horizon.

"I'm not giving up until you answer me," Asher declared. "I'm sorry for doubting you. I'm sorry for thinking there are other gods stronger than you. I'm sorry for thinking there are—*any* gods but you."

He waited. Then he found himself muttering familiar words: "Hear, O Israel, YAH is our God; YAH is one." He prayed again: "Hear, O Israel." For himself. For the first time in his life, just for himself. "YAH is my God. YAH is one."

The *only one.* Not Marduk. Not Ishtar, or Shamash. Or Baal, or Asherah. Or Gula, or Sekhmet. Only YAH.

"I do believe in you," Asher confessed. "Please, help me. I don't know what to do. I'm scared!"

Silence. Then, with a raucous cry, a long-legged marsh bird flew up from the reeds that choked the banks of the canal, flapped its wings, caught an evening breeze, and soared toward the north. Asher watched it disappear into the growing gloom.

He sat waiting a while longer. YAH had heard him—that he wanted to believe—but had chosen not to speak. Perhaps that was for the best. Besides, it was high time to go home. A cloud of ravenous mosquitoes had discovered him.

The next day, preparations for the festival kept Iltani's household busy. On the third day, she informed Asher he would need to stay the night, for she planned a small banquet of her "most intimate friends" and needed him to serve. He didn't object, for he wanted Damkina.

Evening came, and so did the lady's guests. They were eager to praise his bravery in protecting their friend, and he was made to recount his gallant deed so all could hear.

When he was done, the ladies' questions and exclamations flattered him, amused him, and irritated him:

"Such courage in one so young! Just like having our own Gilgamesh, right here in Babylon!" (He didn't know who Gilgamesh was, but he didn't let on.)

"Weren't you frightened?" (He said no, which was true. It had all happened too fast.)

"How did it feel to wrestle the knife from the assassin's hands?" (He hadn't done that but saw no reason to correct the lady's misinformation.)

"Aren't we all glad that the assassin was killed?" said a lady to her companions. "It's getting so that I don't feel safe anywhere, not even near my bodyguards. The rabble need to know that we'll tolerate no more violence against us law-abiding citizens."

"My thoughts exactly," said another. "After all you've done for the poor in this city, Iltani, that anyone would even think of harming you! It's just too much!"

"Quiet, everyone," said a third lady. "My husband told me that the attacker was not one of our own kind. He was—an Israelite!"

The room erupted in general cries of dismay and disbelief. Asher felt sure that all eyes would quickly turn to him and that an entirely different kind of question would be put to him.

"How did they find out about him?" a lady asked.

"He was circumcised," said the first, in a hushed tone.

More indignant chatter followed.

"That doesn't necessarily mean he was an Israelite," Lady Iltani declared. "We have people here from many lands," she went on. "They have their own customs, just as we have ours."

"What does *he* have to say?" a woman dressed all in blue asked. She nodded at Asher, and now his fear had come true: everyone was staring at him.

"It's true that my people practice the custom you've mentioned, but I can't believe that My Lady's attacker was an Israelite. We try to be faithful citizens of Babylon."

"But you people aren't citizens," one woman reminded him.

"We admit it," he said. "We have our own nation, so we yearn to return home. But maybe that day will never arrive. In the meantime, we live as best we can. What good would it do us to repay your generosity with violence?"

Some women nodded their heads in agreement.

"Even if my attacker were an Israelite," Iltani broke in, "so was my savior. We dare not judge an entire people by the act of one madman."

"Why do you call him that?" someone asked.

"The man had no chance of escape! He knew he would die for trying to kill me. Only a madman throws away his own life like that."

More general agreement.

Asher had to keep himself from screaming at these foolish, over-dressed cows. How they would stampede if they suspected that even now, some Israelites were plotting to help overthrow their king! He was grateful when Iltani declared they'd all had enough gloomy conversation. This was a party, not a philosophical discussion.

"I will always be grateful to you, son of Israel," the lady told him. "I drink your health."

She raised her cup of palm wine, and all her guests joined her. "Asher! Asher!" they exclaimed.

He hated every one of them.

* * *

It was late when the party ended and Asher excused. He found Damkina waiting in his room. Urgently, without a word, he went to her. She returned his passion.

The next morning, Asher found Iltani elaborately dressed, her eyes lined with kohl, her cheeks and lips reddened, her hair perfectly arranged. Today she'd chosen a scarlet tunic and necklaces of silver and polished black stones.

"How did you sleep?" she greeted him cheerfully. "Or did you sleep at all?"

Asher felt himself blush.

"I slept well. Thank you for asking."

She raised an eyebrow and smiled. "I have great news," she told him. "Your king will receive you in his rooms this morning. I will accompany you, of course. Go and get yourself ready."

Before long, they were approaching Nebuchadrezzar's palace. At the entrance to the defeated kings' quarters, a gigantic soldier, the biggest man Asher had ever seen, guarded the gate. Asher knew who he was: Hunzuu, the one-handed warrior secretly loyal to the Israelites. Asher felt for the amulet Queen Nehushta had given him, remembering that if he ever wanted to get inside with a message, he should show it.

Hunzuu noticed Asher glance at him, and a flicker of recognition crossed his scarred face. Asher couldn't be sure, but it seemed as though the warrior gave him a slight nod.

Once through the gates, they were escorted to Jeconiah's chambers.

Iltani did not seem inclined to chat, and that gave Asher a chance to inspect the room. The walls were plastered and painted in pale tones of brown and green. The floor was made of fired tiles. Unlike Iltani's elaborately decorated chambers, this room was plain, uninviting. No place to sit and enjoy a cup of wine or a good conversation. It was a room for business. At least there were no idolatrous shrines.

They did not have to wait long. Paneled doors at the far end of the hall opened and a servant announced his master: "His Majesty Jehoiachin ben-Josiah, king of Judah."

A man strode through the doors. Asher fell to one knee and bowed his head. Iltani nodded respectfully.

"Rise," the king told Asher.

Asher was surprised at how young the man was—only a few years older than Azarel. He was dressed simply—a long linen tunic with a short-sleeved robe over it, a single chain of gold around his neck. Unlike fashionably turned-out noblemen of Babylon, the king wore his hair simply, not curled or oiled. His beard was short and uncurled, and he sported no earrings.

"Welcome to the Lady Iltani," he said. "It is always my pleasure to see you."

"Thank you, My Lord," she replied. "King Jeconiah is looking well."

"Only my herald and my wife still call me Jehoiachin these days," he said, smiling. "It can be confusing to have two names. Just between us, I prefer Jeconiah."

"It does have a pleasing sound," Iltani told him.

"Thank you. But to your question: I am well. You are kind to ask."

"And how are your lady and the child?"

"Both eager for him to be born," Jeconiah exclaimed, smiling. "He does not move much now, and my lady teases that's because he's run out of room. Very soon, he will make his appearance."

Asher wondered how the king could be so sure the child would be a boy.

"I wish to present Asher ben-Benaiah to Your Majesty," Iltani told him. "He saved me from the assassin's knife."

"Ah, yes! A valiant son of Israel jumps in to protect the righteous from the hand of the wicked!" The king advanced toward Asher, who bowed his head again. "You have my thanks, Asher ben-Benaiah. Not only have you proven your courage, but you have shown a noble heart devoted to fighting for a righteous cause. I am certain that YAH is pleased with you."

"Thank you, Your Majesty. I did what any Israelite would do."

"I believe you. Let no one say that we children of Israel, although strangers in a strange land, do not desire anything besides its peace and safety. As Babylon prospers, so shall we."

"We people of Babylon welcome your words," Iltani assured him. "They will find their way to Nebuchadrezzar's ear."

"I thank you. Be assured he has heard the same gratitude from me and from all my court. We are grateful for his hospitality and kind treatment of our people. You feel the same way, don't you, Asher?"

"Yes, Your Majesty," he lied. "Our lives here are good. We try to be loyal citizens of Babylon."

"Which is why you acted to defend your mistress," Jeconiah added.

One of the king's attendants stepped forward and whispered something to him.

"I'm sorry, but I need to go," Jeconiah told them. "It was good to see you again, My Lady, and to meet you, Asher. Once again, my thanks to you both."

He nodded at them, turned, and left the room. Servants escorted them to the plaza, and at the gate, Hunzuu saluted them.

Iltani was pleased with the interview, but the more Asher considered what had just happened, the more irritated he felt. Jeconiah cared nothing for the Lady Iltani; he said what was expected and no more. She played up to him as if he were someone with real power, when in truth he was a sad figure: a king with no kingdom, allowed to be a hanger-on in a real king's palace—as long as he behaved like a grateful "guest."

And what had it cost Jeconiah to welcome a nobody like Asher into his quarters?

Nothing.

The entire interview had lasted only a few moments, and then the "king" claimed to have other matters to attend. Perhaps he arranged with his courtiers in advance just how much time he was willing to waste on unimportant people like Asher. The whole thing was a lie. Jeconiah probably hated Nebuchadrezzar, hated Babylon, hated people like Iltani. Perhaps he hated his life just as much as Asher had hated his.

By the time they got back to her estate, Asher almost regretted having saved Iltani. She was a wicked old woman, yet he had saved her life, risking his own to do so.

Chapter Twenty-Five

The night before the New Year's festival, Asher again stayed at Iltani's. He expected Damkina to join him in bed, but she did not appear. At dawn, he bathed, dressed, and was ready to walk behind Iltani's litter as she was carried to Procession Street, the broad avenue leading through the Ishtar Gate.

When they arrived, they were directed inside one of the buildings facing the avenue, where they climbed the stairs. It was slow going because Iltani had little strength. On top of the broad, flat wall, chairs were set out. Iltani took a place of honor.

Asher was directed to stand behind his mistress. Slaves appeared, offering food and drink. One held a parasol over the lady, so Asher was able to catch a bit of shade. More and more Babylonians appeared, until all the seats were taken.

Across the Processional Way, Asher beheld a grand sight: deposed kings, along with their retinues, invited to be awed by the spectacle of Babylon, their conqueror. There was Jeconiah, and beside him, Queen Mother Nehushta. The Israelite king had dressed for the occasion; gone were the modest tunic and robe, the plainly arranged hair and beard. Jeconiah was brilliantly clothed in gold. His jewel-encrusted crown glistened in the morning light, and his hair was curled in the current style. Around him sat other kings, all in the gorgeous costumes of their native countries, all attended by wives, children, and slaves.

Down below, soldiers herded crowds of ordinary people back against the walls. The entire plaza was thronged with revelers from the royal family to the nobility, the priests, rich citizens like Iltani, all the way down to the rabble.

Excited chatter filled the air. Citizens greeted one another with joy, clasped hands, embraced, drank toasts to the gods of Babylon and its king.

Asher had never witnessed Babylon in all its glory. He couldn't stop gazing at the great Ishtar Gate, an enormous archway flanked by taller towers topped with stair-stepped battlements. The walls of the whole complex were covered with bricks glazed in lapis lazuli and images of bulls and dragons in low relief.

The temple in Jerusalem was impressive, but it could not compare to the size and magnificence of the Ishtar Gate.

And this was what Azarel, Josiah, and their comrades hoped to overthrow.

Horns heralded the start of the parade. Then came the deep throbbing of drums, the high squalling of reed pipes. The crowd grew quieter. Now the sounds of approaching musicians were joined by the pounding of marching feet. From a long distance down the Processional Way, Asher could see the approaching parade. Here it came: soldiers in battle regalia, swords and shields at the ready. Robed priests, chanting hymns to the gods.

And then appeared the supreme god Marduk himself, or at least his statue, drawn in a carriage boat, a wheeled vehicle fashioned to look like a river vessel. The boat was covered in sheet gold and adorned with lapis and carnelians. The image of Marduk portrayed him as a man of gigantic size and power. The god was dressed for battle, helmeted, weapons in hand, encased in a golden breastplate and long skirt. His arms were bare, mightily muscled, as was his broad chest.

The people shouted, cheered, and sang as their god passed. The masses of the poor threw themselves to the pavement, heads down, worshiping. The mixed clamor of shouting, marching feet, chanting, and drums created a din so loud Asher could not have heard his mistress speak.

Iltani herself impassively watched the spectacle unfold. She'd acted so excited for this day to come. Was she bored by it all now?

A roar from the crowds meant that something yet more impressive was approaching. Here came not another carriage boat, but a sturdy chariot drawn by three horses. A charioteer held the reins. A slave held aloft a parasol. In the middle--

Nebuchadrezzar in the flesh.

He was arrayed like a general or, rather, like Marduk. Golden breastplate, fringed skirt, sword belt, daggers, a spear with pointed tridents at both ends, just like the statue of Marduk in the palm grove at Iltani's plantation. Asher had been surprised by the youthfulness of King Jeconiah, but Nebuchadrezzar was no young man. His body had the solid, rock-like look of a warrior in middle age.

Now Lady Iltani cried out, along with everyone else. "Hail, Nebuchadrezzar!" she shouted. "Long live the lord and ruler of Babylon! Long live the king!"

The lady's voice was one among thousands, but suddenly, the king signaled a stop. The crowd got quiet. Then Nebuchadrezzar looked up toward where Iltani was sitting. He scanned the faces of his special guests, recognized the lady, and saluted her. Then, for a second, he looked directly at Asher before commanding his driver to go on.

Asher felt lightheaded. Perhaps it was the heat, for on the wall, despite the parasols, it was swelteringly hot. Maybe it was the crowd or the noise. Perhaps he hadn't eaten enough that morning.

Whatever it was, he begged his lady's pardon, took a step back, and sat down hard on the pavement. If Iltani noticed, she gave no sign, but a slave tended him, calling for water and urging him to breathe deeply until the spell passed.

In a few minutes, Asher felt better. He stood, accepted a seed cake, and drank more water. Meanwhile, the procession had continued. More carriage boats, more images of the city's numerous deities, more music, marching, and shouts from the crowd.

"Are you all right?" Iltani asked him, without turning in his direction.

He hadn't thought she'd noticed. "Yes, My Lady."

"Come close."

He stood and took his place at her side.

"The king salutes me every year," she explained quietly. "I always enjoy this seat, and he always seeks me out in the crowd. Can you guess why?"

"No."

"I helped to raise him from his infancy," she replied. "I watched over him in his nursery after his mother died. He never tires of honoring me."

"He must love you very much," Asher said.

"He hates me!" she hissed. "Just as he hates everyone."

"My Lady?"

She brushed aside his question. "Save your astonishment. You wouldn't understand. I've told you too much already. Too much palm wine. Never share what I've just told you with anyone. Do you understand?"

Would people ever stop telling him their secrets and swearing him to say nothing? "I do," he told her. "I will speak to no one."

"Be sure that you don't. Now, tell me. How do you like our little festival?"

He was preparing a lie, but renewed shouts interrupted him. These voices had a different tone: not acclaim, but jeers. The reason soon became apparent; the procession was now of captives, men chained together at their wrists.

"Who are they?" Asher asked, forgetting that he was not to start any conversation with his mistress.

"Elamites," Iltani explained. "Our king's most recent conquest. Here are their best soldiers, having their first glimpse of the power they dared challenge."

Asher fixed his eyes on the soldiers. Then he noticed women and children among them. They weren't chained, but there was no need. These captives had nowhere to run, and they looked so utterly defeated that no one could imagine them trying to escape. The crowd began taunting them. Someone threw a piece of rotten fruit. Others did the same.

The guards keeping the fine citizens of Babylon in their places quickly restored order.

"There's no need for such mockery," Iltani remarked. "It sickens me. Losing a war is humiliating enough, then being forced to leave your homeland, and finding yourselves in a foreign land. And then Babylon welcomes you with this cruel display of power. You understand all that, don't you?"

"Yes, My Lady." He fought to keep his voice calm, for the spectacle on the Processional Way was enough to madden anyone who knew the meaning of pity.

"I will speak to the king," she went on. "Plead with him to stop this embarrassment. Today is supposed to be a day of rejoicing, thankfulness to the gods—not rubbing conquered people's faces in the dust beneath our feet."

Asher glanced at the woman in astonishment. Did she really believe what she was telling him, or was she playing the game of always saying the right thing, just as she had with King Jeconiah?

The Elamites disappeared through the arched gateway. More and more carriage boats appeared, all elaborately decorated, all holding images of the gods and goddesses of the city.

Asher lost interest. He longed to escape this place, but the procession was far from over, and Iltani was invited to Nebuchadrezzar's feast afterwards.

The afternoon was long, hot, and boring. Asher and Iltani's bearers were crowded along with hundreds of other servants into a vast courtyard without shade. It didn't take long for people to claim places on the pavement. Those with parasols used them. Lines soon formed for the latrines. Some people sang. Here and there, quarrels broke out.

At least the lords of Babylon provided some food and drink, but the lines of hungry and thirsty people were longer than those seeking relief for their bowels.

Asher stayed close to Iltani's slaves, who downed cup after cup of cheap palm wine. He pretended to doze and so got to eavesdrop as they complained about what a mean old bitch their mistress was, and how lazy and dishonest their fellow servants were. They both hated their jobs, hated their lives, and hated Babylon, but they had no other choices.

Was there not even one happy person in the world?

Nebuchadrezzar must have spread a magnificent feast for his guests, and they clearly enjoyed themselves that day, for when they sent for their attendants, they were drowsy, bloated with food, and drunk. Iltani was sober, however, and quiet, compared to most of her friends.

It took forever to get her home, for the streets were packed. When they did get back, the lady dismissed Asher for the evening, telling him to go home and not return until the second day. She said she was quite thoroughly exhausted —and she looked it.

Over supper, Asher amused his family with descriptions of drunken Babylonians and their ridiculous idols. He made no mention, though, of the Elamite captives. Many Israelites from Jerusalem had been paraded into the city in much the same way a few years earlier.

Azarel spoke little that evening. He went to bed with the rest of them, but in the morning, he was gone.

Asher was shaken awake by his father. "Get up and get dressed. Something's going on in the city."

Asher didn't have to ask what it was.

"People are running around claiming there's an uprising against the king."

At that moment, someone began pounding on their door. Benaiah hurried to answer it. Asher followed. So did the rest of the family.

Josiah's father, Eliezer, stood there, panting. "It's a revolt!" he cried. "They're saying many of the king's troops are fighting their way toward the palace to take him prisoner and place one of their generals on the throne."

"Death to them all," Benaiah muttered. "Let them kill each other and then we can leave this filthy place forever."

"That won't happen, and you know it." Ezekiel's voice was low, sad.

"How do you know?" Benaiah challenged. "Playing prophet again?"

"There's no time to argue," Ezekiel told him.

"Right now I don't care what they do to each other," Eliezer broke in. "Josiah is missing! He's gone, and we don't know where. I was hoping he was here."

"He's not," Benaiah said. "Neither is Azarel, but that's not anything new. He's probably somewhere sleeping off a drunk."

"Josiah never leaves the house without telling me where he's going," Eliezer continued. "Something's happened to him; I'm sure of it. Something terrible. Asher, he's your friend. Do you know anything?"

For a moment, no one spoke. Asher felt all eyes on him. *Think!* he ordered himself. *You have to say something!*

But what?

He'd become skilled at lying, but no lie would come to his lips. Here, at last, it was time to tell the truth.

"Well?" his father asked. "You know something. Tell us."

"Soldiers who hate Nebuchadrezzar and his endless wars want to get rid of him and raise up a different king. They've been planning a revolt for a long time. It must have started last night."

"That's the rumor I heard in town already," Eliezer said. "What else?"

There was no turning back. *Say it and get it over with. You're in bad trouble, and there's no way out.*

He took a breath. "Some Israelites are in cahoots with the soldiers who hate the king. They're joining them in the revolt. When Nebuchadrezzar is gone, they intend for us to return home and put Jeconiah back on the throne in Jerusalem."

"Is that all?" Benaiah demanded.

"Josiah and Azarel are with them. Josiah is one of the leaders. They've been planning the revolt for a long time. They say they're willing to fight and die for our freedom."

Stunned silence.

"What are you saying?" Benaiah shouted. "You *knew* all this and said nothing?"

"Yes—"

Before he had time to say another word, his father struck him, smashing him to the floor.

"Stop!" Ezekiel cried. "Benaiah, don't!"

But Benaiah did not stop. He dropped to his knees beside his son and began pummeling him in the face. Eliezer and Ezekiel had to pull him off. Benaiah was sobbing, and so was Asher. He looked into his father's eyes, and then, ashamed, turned away.

"If your brother is injured or killed, I will hold you responsible! Do you hear me?"

"Benaiah, please," Eliezer said. "No one could have stopped our sons from doing what they believe they had to do."

Benaiah turned on him. "I would have *tried*! I would have tied him to his bed every night."

"And the next morning he would have disappeared into the city and you'd never have seen him again," Ezekiel said, his voice a whisper.

"What's wrong with all of you?" Benaiah demanded. "Haven't we lost enough already without our sons sacrificing their lives for a hopeless cause? That's what *you* think, isn't it, Ezekiel? That YAH has turned against us, so there's no point in trying to help ourselves? We're simply supposed to wait here and take whatever shit the world throws at us? That's what you believe, isn't it?"

Ezekiel did not answer the question. Instead, he said, "We must try and find them."

"I'll go," Asher volunteered.

"You will not!" his father commanded. "Ezekiel, bring rope!"

Did they really believe they could tie him down? Asher made a break for the door, but Eliezer caught him. He was much stronger than he looked, and he had no trouble wrestling Asher back to the ground. His arm throbbed, and he felt a warm, damp place where it was bandaged.

Ezekiel brought rope.

"Don't resist," Benaiah warned his son. "There are three of us and one of you. If I have to, I'll knock you unconscious before I'll let you out into the streets."

Asher nodded his obedience. The men bound his hands behind his back, then tied him to a seat in the courtyard.

"We're going to find Josiah and Azarel," Benaiah promised Tirzah and Elisheva. "Do not untie him, no matter what he says. He must stay here."

"We will be back with both boys," Eliezer promised. "I don't know when, but we will. Ezekiel, are you coming with us?"

"Yes," he told them. "YAH will help us find them."

Elisheva went with them into the street. When she returned, she had more news. "Miriam told me that there's heavy fighting in the barracks, those loyal to Nebuchadrezzar defending the palace against the rebels. Word is that the rebels are many, and the king is in danger."

"Untie me!" Asher demanded. "I have to go!"

"No!" Elisheva exclaimed angrily. "What you did—knowing about the plot and saying nothing! That was—" she searched for words—"stupid—thoughtless—unforgivable! I can't imagine what you were thinking!"

Elisheva's words stung. Never before had she spoken to him in anger. This was worse than having his father punch his face. "Let me go!" he shouted. "I can help. I can't do anything here!"

But Elisheva would not. Instead, she ran for the physician, who came right away and tended to Asher's injuries. His father's blow had split his upper lip, but there was nothing to be done about that. Without untying him, the physician undid the bandage on Asher's arm; as he had suspected it had reopened a little. He tended it and exclaimed about the excellent job his Babylonian comrade had done, as if he knew anything about Isiratuu's skills.

When he was gone, Asher kept begging Elisheva to free him. She ignored him.

Outside, in the street, they could hear people hurrying by. There were shouts. Some screams. Some villagers came along, singing a song of Zion with all their might.

Asher became frantic. He had to escape. Had to see about his brother and his friend.

The women would not stay near him as he shouted to be untied. He thought he was making progress with them, but then their resolve was no longer required. Someone knocked and without waiting, came through the door. It was Azarel, masked to the eyes.

"What's all this?" he demanded.

"They tied him and ordered us not to let him go," Elisheva explained. "They said they'd be back later."

"Who?"

"Your father. Ezekiel. Eliezer."

"Did they say where they were going?"

"To the city, I suppose. I don't think they knew exactly."

"I'm going to untie you," Azarel told Asher.

"Don't! I promised *I* wouldn't," Elisheva exclaimed. She seemed near to panic.

"Then you've kept your promise," Azarel assured her. "You can say you tried to stop me, but I was too strong for you." In a moment, Asher was free. Elisheva turned away.

"Find a cloth and tie it around your face," Azarel advised him. "And the amulet the queen gave you. Do you have it?" Asher found it in another tunic, along with the seal of Lady Iltani. He pocketed them both.

"Now come with me." It wasn't a polite request.

Once in the street, Asher asked what was happening.

"Our fighters are doing well," Azarel assured him. "We planned the revolt for last night because we knew many of the king's guards would be sleeping off their palm wine. We caught them completely unprepared. We've killed many of Nebuchadrezzar's loyal soldiers, and some have come over to our side. I tell you, brother, we're going to win!" He was shaking with excitement and joy. "You'll see it! The streets by the barracks are red with blood! So's the plaza by Jeconiah's quarters. Our day of liberation is here!"

"Where are we going?" Asher asked. "I need to see if Damkina is safe." He hadn't known he was going to say that.

"Who's that?"

He'd never even mentioned the girl's name to anyone in his family.

"One of Lady Iltani's slave girls."

"Why should you care about her?"

"I love her."

"Don't be stupid! You're sleeping with her. That's not the same thing."

"We can't talk about it now," Asher said. It was true. The village streets were thronged with people. Some were in a party mood. Others, panicked, were simply running around, unsure of where to go or what to do. They came close to the bridge across the canal. It was barricaded by guards apparently loyal to Nebuchadrezzar.

"Just as I figured," Azarel muttered. He pulled Asher onto a side street. "Listen. We need to get a message to King Jeconiah."

"How? No one can get inside the city."

"Yes, they can, and you're gonna do it. Come on."

"Me? I'm not in this! Do it yourself."

"I can't risk being captured or killed. Our cause depends on me."

"You're important but I'm not?"

"Don't get all offended. You're smart enough to understand."

Asher did, but it still hurt.

"Now listen," Azarel said. "You're going to cross the canal and get into the city. Go to the palace where Hunzuu stands guard at King Jeconiah's apartments."

"How do you know about Hunzuu?"

"Never mind now."

"I can't swim."

"Yes, you can."

"No, I can't!"

"It's not far, and it's not deep. You can dog paddle. Trust me, you'll make it."

"I can't!"

Azarel shook him. "You have to! We have a chance to get rid of Nebuchadrezzar and win our freedom. Don't tell me you're not willing to help. If you won't, believe me, you'll regret it as long as you live."

Asher pressed his back against a mudbrick wall. "You're crazy, or you just want me killed. Even if I could do what you say, the guards on the bridge will see me. I'll be target practice for their archers."

"No, you won't! We're going to sneak away from the bridge. That's the best place because there's a drainpipe from the city into the canal that the guards won't suspect. Just be careful, and everything will be fine."

Asher felt himself trembling. This was how his life would end. Either he would drown or he would be discovered and killed. "I can't do it," he whimpered. "Please don't try and make me."

Azarel pulled him right up to his face. "They killed your mother! They've made you their slave. And you won't do just this one little thing? I'm not asking you to grab a sword. Just paddle a few feet, climb into a big pipe, and find your way to Jeconiah's quarters. It's not much."

"It's madness!"

"Maybe so. Maybe it's all madness, but at least I'm trying to do something to end it. Now it's your turn to decide who you are. Please, Asher! I'm begging you."

The brothers stood face to face, gazing into each other's eyes.

"All right," Asher sighed. "Everyone dies sooner or later."

"This isn't your day," Azarel told him.

"How to you know?"

"I'm a prophet, in my own way. Trust me. I know for sure."

"You're not just making that up to get what you want?"

"We can discuss the fine points later, when there's time."

"All right. Let me do it before I change my mind."

They came back to the street that paralleled the canal and headed away from the bridge. There were people around, but no one paid them any mind. Soon, they came to the place. Reeds grew along the canal's edge and on the other side. The water was dark, and the canal seemed to be a hundred cubits wide. Asher's heart sank. There was no way he could succeed.

"It's nothing," Azarel assured him. "Slide down into the reeds, paddle across, and hide in the thickest reeds on the other side. That's where the drainpipe is. Crawl into it until you come to another pipe on the left side. It's big, so it's easy to find. Go that way. In a short distance, there's an overhead pipe. Climb up. It opens into a garden. There shouldn't be anyone there. Go on toward the center of the city and ask directions if you need to. When you get to the quarters of the conquered kings, show Hunzuu the Queen Mother's amulet. He'll make sure you message is delivered."

"That's all? You don't want me to climb to the top of the ziggurat and take Marduk's throne?"

"Not today," Azarel joked.

"This isn't funny."

"One day, when we're old, we'll remember all this over a cup of palm wine. Heck, over several cups! When we're back home again."

"One day," Asher agreed, not believing his own words.

"Ready?"

"Yes, but aren't we forgetting one thing?"

"What's that?"

"The message, you idiot!"

Asher laughed. "Look at us, joking while the world is crashing down around us. Okay, listen carefully: the king and his family are to be ready to escape the moment we can guarantee them safe passage. When our fighters have the upper hand, we'll send an armed escort to lead them out the Shamash gate. That's not too much to remember. Do you have it?"

Asher repeated the words, all the while doubting he'd ever have the chance to deliver them.

Then it was time for him to go.

Azarel kissed his cheek, just as Josiah had. "I love you, brother. YAH protect you. I'll see you later."

"Where?"

"I'll come home to check on things if I can. Otherwise, you'll just have to wait. Take care of the family, all right? I know they're afraid."

"And what about me, after I deliver this message?"

Azarel grimaced. "Good point! I'd hadn't thought about it. But since you mention it . . ."

"Yeah?"

"Come back here the same way you went. You'll be home before you know it."

"Oh, sure. What could be easier?"

Asher smiled regretfully. "You'll figure something out, smart man that you are."

Then there was nothing more to say. Asher slid down the slick bank toward the canal, stepped in, took another step, and couldn't find the bottom. He went under, came up spitting, and started to paddle. For a second, panic threatened, and he felt himself sinking.

"Kick and paddle!" Azarel encouraged. "You can do it."

Two men happened along, scurrying toward the village.

"He tripped and fell in," Azarel explained. "He's all right. He can swim."

The men weren't inclined to stop.

"Keep going," Azarel called. Asher dog paddled desperately, and the next time he looked around, his brother had disappeared.

It's up to you now, he told himself. He made it to the other side, shaking and panting. Asher rooted among the thick reeds, scratching himself on their sharp leaves. The drainpipe was easy to find; getting the courage to climb into it was another matter. Pitch darkness lay ahead, and the daylight behind him faded quickly. Asher felt his way, keeping a hand on the slimy left side, searching for where the other pipe emptied into this one. It wasn't far, but it seemed a long way. Once inside the second pipe, which was smaller than the first, Asher had to fight off panic. What if he got stuck?

Then he would die here unless Azarel rescued him. *Keep going,* he commanded himself. At last, dim light appeared overhead. There was the pipe leading to the surface! He eased his way up into it, stood, and grabbed the top. One big jump, one strong pull with his uninjured arm, and he was back on dry ground. As Azarel had promised, the garden was deserted. He sat, breathing hard, scarcely believing he'd made it. *Thank you, YAH,* were the only words he could form, and he whispered them over and over. If only he could remain here, among flowers and fruit trees, far away from battles and death, away from his problems--but he had a message to deliver.

Asher stood, smoothed out his clothes, ran his fingers through his hair, and wiped off as much muck as he could. The garden was gated, but the gate stood slightly open. He went through and found himself on an unfamiliar street. It was eerily empty, but then he met some people scurrying along and looking terrified. Asher dared not ask anyone for directions, lest he attract attention. But he encountered a boy, alone and bewildered.

Asher stopped him. "How do I get to the king's palace?" he asked.

The child gaped at him.

"I'm not going to hurt you. I'm lost. Tell me the way, please."

The boy looked all around, perhaps seeking for someone to rescue him from this frightening stranger with wet clothes and mud smeared all over his feet, legs, and arms.

"Please!" Asher begged. "It's important. I have a message for the king." He didn't bother to explain *which* king.

The child relented and told him, then ran away. His directions were accurate, and Asher soon came to the walls of the palace. He recognized where he was, but when he came into the plaza before the conquered kings' apartments, he stopped, stunned by what he saw. There had been heavy fighting there not long before, and the pavement was littered with abandoned armor, shields, and swords. Pools of blood turned the brown earth deep maroon.

Dead and dying men lay everywhere. Groaning. Screaming in agony. Crying. Praying to their gods. Begging for mercy.

Asher fell back, fighting the urge to vomit.

He forced himself to look again, and now he realized something that made him want to howl at the sky. Among the Babylonian dead, easily recognizable by their fine armor and weapons, lay other fighters, dressed in ordinary clothes. Asher knew who they were.

Israelites, like himself.

He wanted to run, but there was something he had to know. That's why he wandered among the fallen. Other people, mostly women, were doing the same. Men called out to him, pleading for help. He ignored them. He continued searching. Once or twice, he was forced to turn a man over so that he could be sure.

Then he discovered what he'd feared.

Josiah lay face up, his open eyes gazing into the brilliant blue sky. His own blood soaked his tunic, which had been pulled up to his waist, revealing the gaping wound where his genitals had been hacked from his body.

He was smiling.

Asher prayed that he'd died before his body was so foully desecrated.

That's when Asher screamed.

He attracted the attention of two women tending to the wounded. They approached, but he could not speak with them. He scanned the plaza for the gate to the conquered kings' quarters and ran there as fast as he could, stepping over bodies. Once he tripped on the bloody corpse of a Babylonian soldier. Once he slipped in blood.

At the gate Hunzuu towered over his fellow guards. His expression was blank, and he did not seem surprised when Asher approached and handed him Queen Nehushta's amulet. "A message for King Jeconiah," he panted. "He and his family are to be ready to leave their quarters the moment the rebel soldiers make their way back here. They will provide an escort to the Shamash gate and see to it that the king escapes the city safely."

"Who sent you?"

"My brother, Azarel."

"I know him."

"Tell me: who's winning?"

"Our fighters prevailed here," the giant told him, "and they've moved on closer to Nebuchadrezzar's palace. I had to send my own guards to fight them! Many of them were my friends, who trusted me, and even as I commanded them, I prayed to YAH that they would be defeated! Everything in me wanted to declare myself on your side, to strike a blow for freedom, but I can't—not yet-- not while Jeconiah and his family require protection until they escape the city." He held up his maimed arm. "I thought Babylon's wars had already asked for my greatest sacrifice, but nothing compares to what this new war demands."

"New war?"

"The War between the Sons of Light and the Sons of Darkness! May the light of YAH prevail! Let him arise and scatter his enemies."

"Please, can you help me? My friend Josiah is over there. He's dead. They . . ." He couldn't finish.

Hunzuu's face showed his sorrow. "What do you want?"

"That someone can get him back to our village so we can bury him."

The warrior shook his head. "I can't help you, for that would betray me. Your own people must do it."

"But how can they get here?"

"How did *you* get here?"

"Through some drainage pipes my brother showed me. It's impossible to take a body that way."

"I'm sorry. We must see how the war turns out. If we win—"

"*If*?"

Hunzuu shook his head. "If we win, then we can gather up our dead and bury them properly. If not, Nebuchadrezzar's slaves will cart them away, food for vultures and jackals."

"No!"

"It has always been that way."

"Someone must help me!"

"There's no one. Now go back to your village before you find yourself in trouble. All Israelites will be under suspicion, and if you're caught by the wrong people, you might be harmed."

"But—"

"Go now! And may YAH protect you."

Asher made his way back to Josiah's body and pulled down his tunic, hiding the hideous, shameful wound. He felt in the dead man's blood-drenched pockets and came up with nothing. But next to the body, he found a knife, its keenly sharpened blade sticky with blood. Asher seized it, hoping that it had taken many enemy lives before its owner, in turn, was cut down.

He yearned to lament his dead brother, but he couldn't linger.

Gazing down on his friend's body, he had one question: "Why?"

Chapter Twenty-Six

Asher made his way back to the canal. Behind him rang the faint sounds of battle. Around him, a few people sought shelter. No one spoke. No one challenged him. He managed the drainage pipes without trouble, grateful that they weren't used for human waste. At the canal, he was glad to slip into the water and wash away as much slime as he could. Once he was on the other side, he hurried toward his own street, dreading how his father would punish him for escaping the house, dreading even more the news he had to share.

At first Benaiah berated Asher for disobeying, then held him close and wept that he had him back safe and sound. Asher explained how Azarel had appeared and released him, and he told about his mission to King Jeconiah's quarters.

Then *he* wept, recounting how he'd found Josiah's body.

"What about Azarel?" his father demanded. "He's dead, too, isn't he? You just don't have the courage to tell us."

"No, he's not. He couldn't have gotten to the plaza before I did, so I know he's not there. He must be somewhere else in the city, fighting."

"Someone has to inform Eliezer and Simeon," Benaiah said wearily, "so they have a hope of recovering Josiah's body."

"Let me," Ezekiel said. "You stay here, brother, in case Azarel comes home."

"I'll go with you," Elisheva offered. "Josiah's mother and grandmother will be destroyed."

"I want to help," Tirzah announced.

Elisheva smiled at her sadly. "I'm glad. I'll need you with me."

When they were gone, Benaiah fetched a basin and pitcher. He told Asher to undress, and then he washed his son from head to foot, removing the filth of Babylon. Benaiah did not speak with words, but his gentle touch told Asher more than words could express.

Through it all, Asher mourned quietly. Then he dressed and let his father guide him to his bed, where merciful sleep found him at once.

Evening was approaching when he woke. The house was empty except for his uncle, sitting in the courtyard and gazing at something with unblinking eyes.

"Where is everyone?" Asher asked.

"Your father's gone with some other men from the village to try and recover the bodies of our dead—if such a thing is possible. Elisheva and Tirzah are still at Josiah's, comforting the family."

"Azarel?"

Ezekiel shook his head. "No word."

"Have you—*seen* anything?"

"Visions? No. YAH has cloaked himself in cloud and darkness. What about you?"

"No, and I hope YAH never shows me anything again."

Ezekiel shrugged. "I've prayed the same thing many times, and YAH still does what he will. I try to obey. It hurts, but what else can we do?"

"I don't want to talk about it anymore."

Ezekiel patted his knee. "Of course not. It's not a pleasant topic."

"We have to find Azarel."

Ezekiel sighed. "Another unpleasant topic. But how do you propose to do that?"

"I don't know."

"He'll get in touch with us when it's safe."

They were interrupted by screams of grief not far away. Asher went to the door, expecting to find men carrying his brother's body toward the house, but that wasn't it. Down the street, people were gathered by the house of Joseph, the woodcutter who had helped him that day Ezekiel had his first vision.

Asher hurried to where the sounds of mourning poured through the open door.

"What's wrong?" he asked a woman.

"It's Joseph!" she cried. "He's been killed in the fighting."

"How do you know?"

"His head has been impaled on a stake by the main gate of the city! Two people from the village have seen it! Many heads are there!" The woman was overcome. She dropped to the ground and tore at her clothing.

Joseph? The kind, shy, helpful man who lived alone because his wife had died giving birth to his son? Who always had a treat for the children he met in the streets, who was faithful at prayers?

Joseph, a secret fighter?

Asher's thoughts raced. How many other men from their village were part of the revolt? He'd never have suspected Josiah, and now Joseph?

Shocked, he trudged home to share the news.

Later, Elisheva and Tirzah returned from Josiah's. His mother and grandmother had first given way to hysterical weeping, praying, crying that it wasn't true: Josiah couldn't be a revolutionary! He wouldn't fight or kill. He was a loving, respectful, quiet son who hoped to become a priest. Not a killer. Not Josiah!

If only you knew, Asher thought.

It was late when Benaiah returned. His shoulder slumped, and his eyes were red. "We never made it into the city. Eliezer tried bribing the guards at the gate, but they must be under strict orders. We waited by the bridge, along with many others. When the gates did open, slaves pulled out carts loaded with the bodies of our dead. They told us of orders to dump them in a field near the village. We followed and searched through the corpses as well as we could, but we didn't find Josiah. Where can he be? Some of our neighbors did find the bodies of men they loved. Some had been beheaded, their bodies identifiable only by their clothing or scars. I'll never forget the screams of their families . . ."

A fit of sobbing overcame him. Ezekiel held him until he became calmer. Elisheva brought water, which he accepted, along with a cloth to wipe his face. "Do you want something to eat?" she asked.

Benaiah gently freed himself from his brother's arms. "How can I eat, not knowing where my son is? If he's alive? Wounded? Lying somewhere dying—or under a pile of bodies in that field of death?" He glared at Asher. "You could have prevented this!" he cried. "I will never understand why you didn't say something."

"It's not Asher's fault," Ezekiel said quietly. "We've told you Azarel could not be stopped. If you had known about it and confronted him, he would have found somewhere else to live."

"Always defending him!" Benaiah shot back. "No one in this family ever thinks the boy is wrong—about anything!"

"He's not a boy," Asher said.

"We've had enough of this quarreling," Elisheva told them. "Tirzah, help me with the meal." They prepared it, but no one had an appetite. Soon afterwards, exhausted, they went to bed.

Asher knew there was no point in his trying to sleep. *Please, YAH*, he prayed. *Don't let us find Azarel's head on a stake. Or Josiah's, either.*

When everyone else was quiet, he climbed to the roof and sat all night, looking at the stars, keeping vigil. He suspected his father was awake too, but he doubted he would welcome his company.

In the morning, a bloody and bedraggled Israelite fighter brought the news that Azarel had been captured and was awaiting execution along with other leaders of the revolt, which was being crushed. All at once, Asher realized their only hope of saving Azarel lay with Lady Iltani, if she could be persuaded to help them. He explained his plan to his father and uncle; neither liked it, but reluctantly agreed on the condition that they go with him to her estate.

In a few minutes, they were running through the village, where the streets were deserted and even the houses of mourning silent. As they went, Asher showed them Iltani's seal and explained how he hoped it would get them into the city. As they expected, the bridge over the canal and the gate into the city were still heavily guarded.

"No one can leave the Israelite villages," a guard informed them. "Go home! All you rebels must stay put unless you want to end up in prison."

"Excuse me, sir," Asher panted. "What's happening with the fighting?"

"The king's loyal troops are winning, and then we'll see all the rebels put to death, just as they deserve."

The news felt like a punch to his belly. Behind him, his father cursed.

"I must enter the city," Asher told him. "I have business."

"You? You're just a kid! And why don't these men do your talking?"

"He speaks for us," Benaiah told the guard.

"And you're here because—"

"As I said, I have urgent business in the city," Asher said.

"An Israelite with business in Babylon when they're fighting in the streets? You want to join the rebels, don't you?"

"No, sir! I'm trying to save a life."

"Whose?"

"My brother's."

"Israelite scum!"

"Please, just let me through."

"And disobey a direct order? Not likely. You run along home, little puppy, and take your keepers with you. Or do all three of you want a taste of a Babylonian sword? My men have lost some friends, and they're itching for revenge."

Some of the other guards growled their agreement.

"I *must* be allowed to enter," Asher persisted. "Look!" He held Iltani's seal under the guard's nose. "My lady will be frantic until she knows I'm safe. When she gave me her seal, she promised it would open doors when nothing else could."

"Even the city gates?" asked the guard, amused. "She must be very important, indeed!"

"She is! The Lady Iltani, nurse to King Nebuchadrezzar when he was a child without a mother of his own."

The guard seemed impressed. He inspected it and then summoned another guard to examine it, too. They put their heads together and spoke in a whisper.

"M comrade knows of the Lady Iltani," the first guard explained. "He agrees that the seal is genuine."

"I *must* see her," Asher repeated. "Babylonian lives are at stake, not just my brother's."

The guard paused, then nodded. "Come on, then."

Benaiah took a step forward.

"Not you!" the guard ordered. "Only this fellow."

"Go," Asher told his father. "I'll be safe."

"I don't want to lose you, too," Benaiah cried.

"You won't. Please, Father! Trust me."

"He's right," Ezekiel said. "Let's go home. They'll need us in the village to help bury our dead. Asher is under the protection of YAH."

Asher watched them walk away. He wondered if he would see them again, and if he did, what news he would have to share.

"Come on, you," the guard barked, pulling him toward the gate. "You may not like what you find inside."

So Asher re-entered Babylon, a city at war.

Chapter Twenty-Seven

Chaos ruled inside the walls. Terrified people thronged the streets, some carrying burdens, some asking everyone they met where the battles were, who was winning, and where the dead were being laid out.

He did not come upon any fighting and used side streets to approach Iltani's estate. Peering around a corner, he saw that the front gate was guarded. This time, he would enter that way, not through the back like a slave.

Head held high, he presented himself at the entrance.

"What do you want?" a soldier challenged.

"I belong to the lady's household. Look!" He held out the seal. After a brief discussion on the guards' part, he was allowed to enter. Inside, the servants and slaves wandered about aimlessly. There was nothing they could do except wait: either the rebels would win and they would be lost, or Nebuchadrezzar's loyal troops would prevail and life would go on as before.

He hurried to the servants' quarters and found Damkina helping with the laundry. "You're safe!" she exclaimed. "I'm glad."

"What's happening?"

"I don't know. We're not allowed to leave here."

"I must see your mistress. It's urgent."

But at the door to Iltani's rooms stood Ahiyababa, a sword strapped to his side. "What brings *you* here?" he challenged. "Shouldn't you be with the rebels?"

"I'm not one of them!"

"You're a liar. You're a spy, sent to discover state secrets. The lady—" he gestured toward her door—"is free with her words when she's enjoyed too much wine. Only the gods know how much she's revealed that she shouldn't."

"It's not like that. I'm not a traitor!" Asher started shouting: "My Lady, it's me! I have a message for you. It's life or death! Please, please let me in."

Ahiyababa pulled him away and tried to push him down the corridor. Asher fought back. He kept calling the lady's name, crying that he had to see her.

The door opened, and Iltani, all in black, appeared. "Let him come in," she told Ahiyababa.

"But he's a traitor. A spy! Don't trust him."

"Leave us," she ordered. The steward tried to protest, but she waved him away. "I will call for you when you're needed."

The man slunk away, but Asher suspected he would not go far. He glanced around the room. It looked as it always did; orderly, handsomely decorated, images of gods lining the walls. No civil war had penetrated here yet.

Iltani took her usual seat. "Tell me what you know."

"There is still fighting in the streets. Many men are dead near the quarters of the conquered kings. A guard at the gate said Nebuchadrezzar's soldiers are winning."

"I'm informed that Israelites are among the rebels. Is that true?"

"Yes, My Lady."

"Anyone you know?"

"My friend, Josiah. He's dead. My—brother."

She stood up suddenly and advanced on him. "And what about you, Asher ben-Benaiah? Aren't *you* one of them, too? A would-be revolutionary groomed and sent here to win my trust, learn our secrets, discover our weaknesses?"

She spoke sharply, accusing him.

"No! I'm not one of them. I'm—loyal to Babylon, and to you."

"Liar!" she hissed. "There are no Israelites 'loyal to Babylon'! Not your so-called king, that ridiculous child! Not any of your kind who have wrangled positions at court, who have set up businesses to extort money from honest citizens. Not 'prophets' like that insane uncle of yours!"

Asher was silent.

"This is all such a shame," the lady continued. "I've enjoyed our little flirtation. I will miss you!"

"What are you going to do?"

"Hand you over to the court. We're not barbarians. Those who have taken up arms against Nebuchadrezzar will answer for their crimes after they've been judged according to our laws."

"Do your laws call for castration and impaling heads on pikes?"

She shrugged. "It's regrettable, but sometimes passions overtake even hardened soldiers."

"Josiah wasn't a professional soldier. He was an Israelite my age who wanted to be free. And that's why he was stabbed to death and his genitals torn off."

"You people practice circumcision. That's not barbaric? Perhaps those who killed your friend wanted to finish the work your priests began." She fixed her eyes on his. "You're a handsome fellow, Asher. Those eyes of yours—they still fascinate me. Had I been younger, I'd have taken you to my own bed instead of letting you indulge yourself with a mere slave. I'm certain you're sorry *that* dalliance is over."

"You are a monster," he said.

She smiled. "No—I'm a goddess! Beware of angering me." She turned away and went toward her chair. "I'm thirsty. Bring me wine."

In a second, he drew Josiah's knife, lunged toward the woman, grabbed her from behind, and held the blade to her throat. "I could kill you right now," he threatened. "I want to, and you deserve it."

"And I could scream for help," she reminded him.

"If you do, you'll be dying by the time anyone gets here."

"And then *you* will die. Ahiyababa would take pleasure in choking the life out of you."

Asher kept the pressure against her throat. "I don't want to kill you, but there's a price for your life."

"Of course there is," she replied. "There's always a price. What's yours?"

He was impressed by her cool confidence. If she were afraid of him, she gave no hint.

He let the knife down. She was right: he could kill her, but then he would die, too.

Iltani straightened her robes, smoothed her hair, and returned to her seat. "Let's bargain," she said. "I asked you to bring me wine."

This time, he did.

She sipped it daintily, fingered the beads of her necklaces, and gave him an appraising look, as though he were someone she was about to bid against in the slave market. "Out with it! I haven't all day."

"I saved your life once," he began.

"I have often wondered why," she returned.

"You were generous to me, acted as though you cared. Not long ago, you imagined I might do well in the service of the king. I was grateful."

"I could have accomplished so much for you," she mused. "With your good looks, your intelligence, your smooth way with women—your *deceitfulness*, you could have risen high in the court. A counselor—an ambassador—"

"A slave," Asher retorted.

"Such an unkind word! Where else in the world do so-called slaves enjoy the life you've had here, with me?"

"I don't know or care. Let's finish what we've started, and I'll leave. I admit that you saved my life, too, by having Isiratuu sew up my wound and keep it from infection. We're even."

"So what have you got to bargain with now?"

"Your life again. I mean it when I say I'll kill you unless you agree to my terms. I don't care if I die, but you want to live. You're not ready to give up your riches, your power over other people's lives—your love of pleasures."

The lady smirked. "One must have something to keep herself amused."

"I saved your life once, and I will spare it again, now, but you must send word to the prison where my brother is being held and see that he is released."

She laughed. "I *would* be a goddess if I possessed that much power!"

"You do, and you know it, so don't lie to me." He stepped toward her, the knife pointed at her heart.

"That's much to ask," she said. "I assume there's more."

"After my brother is released, you will guarantee him safe passage away from Babylon—forever."

"And where will he go?"

"Caravans leave the city every day. He can join one of those."

"You've planned it well," she admitted. "I'm impressed, but from the first day I saw you, I suspected you are much cleverer—and more ruthless—than you let on."

"Thank you," he told her. "You've taught me well."

"Men will fear you one day--if I allow you to leave my house alive."

He ignored that. "There's one more thing."

She smirked. "Always one more thing! You drive a hard bargain, Asher-ben-Benaiah."

"I want you to free Damkina and let her go with my brother when he leaves the city. He'll look after her."

"I'm certain he will—if you take my meaning. And what else? You don't want passage for yourself?"

"And leave my family? They're all I have. They couldn't stand to lose both my brother and me."

"Such a caring young man. No thought for himself. And willing to deliver the girl to his brother's bed. You know that's how it would end."

He stifled a cry. "Those are my demands."

She jumped to her feet. "No one *demands* of me! I am the Lady Iltani!"

"And you are Nebuchadrezzar's mother," he shot back, "not the queen who was said to have died giving birth to him. That's why he honors you to this day."

It was a guess, and a wild one at that. Asher wasn't sure where the idea had come from, or the courage to suggest it, but he was gambling for high stakes.

Iltani glared at him. She took her cup, drained it, refilled it herself, and drank again. "You have no proof of such a fanciful accusation," she declared.

"But it *is* true, isn't it?"

"No!"

"You're lying."

"And you, my friend, are pressing your luck."

"Look at me," he told her. "I've enjoyed your favor. You've dressed me in fine clothes, fed me, given me your slave for my pleasure, introduced me to a king, placed me beside you at the New Year Festival—yes, I have lots of luck, and it won't desert me now. Those are my terms: my brother's life, Damkina's freedom, and safe passage for them out of Babylon."

"They'll be caught and dragged back before a day passes," she warned him. "There's no escape from the power of Babylon. You know that."

"I ask only for a chance. Then I trust the rest to my god."

She continued eyeing him with the slightly amused, slightly dismissive expression he'd come to recognize. But he thought he could see something else in her face, too. Not fear—respect.

"Very well," she said. "I agree. But after they're recaptured, I'll be present to witness how a rebel and an escaped slave are punished."

"Then you'll hear me shout to the world that you are the king's mother, you who were born a slave!"

Another guess. But what did he have to lose?

"We'll see who wins," she said. "Now give me my seal."

"I don't have it, and if I did, I'd keep it just in case."

"I could have you searched, but I'll accept your lie. All this is starting to bore me. Tell Ahiyababa to come in."

The steward was right outside the door. He brushed by Asher as if he didn't exist, then bowed before Iltani.

"Shall I call the guards and have him arrested?" he asked.

"Don't pretend you haven't heard every word. Summon my litter. I'm going to the prison."

"No, My Lady!" Ahiyababa cried. "It's not safe."

"Loyal troops will be stationed all around it. I will be perfectly safe."

"I can't allow you to leave the house," he persisted. "I'm sworn to defend your life, something I cannot do if you insist on behaving foolishly."

Asher was astounded to hear the steward address his mistress in such a way.

"Obey me!" she commanded.

The man knelt before her. "No," he replied. "I cannot allow you to endanger yourself."

"Hm! A prisoner in my own home! But very well. I should be grateful, my loyal defender. This isn't the first time you've shown better sense than your mistress."

"Let us agree that it will be the last."

She smiled. "Most likely not. I accept your disobedience, and when I have opportunity, I will reward, not punish you."

"Your safety is reward enough for me," he told her.

The steward was clearly telling the truth. Asher realized then that he himself wasn't the only man who had fallen under this woman's spell. Perhaps she *was* a goddess, after all.

"Listen! Since you won't allow me to do it, you will go to the prison and demand the release of a certain Azarel, a supposed leader in the revolt. Say that there has been a mistake. He was an innocent bystander who was threatened into the rebel force against his will. Say further that I assume responsibility for him, and he's to be brought back here, under your escort. Take two guards with you."

"My Lady, no one will believe such a story!"

She gave him an even look. "Perhaps not, but the name Iltani still has power in this city, unless Nebuchadrezzar has indeed been overthrown."

"His loyal troops are winning the day," Ahihababa assured her. "A slave brought me the message while you were—*bargaining* with this . . ."

"Do you grudge an old woman some amusement?"

"Of course not."

"Well, then. Bring this Azarel back with you. I want to lay eyes on a man who dares challenge the might of Babylon."

"What about me?" Asher asked. "I want to go, too."

"You will stay here," she told him.

"My brother won't trust this man to take him into custody."

"Trust, you say? It seems to me we are all having to trust one another just now."

Asher had no answer for that. It was true, as hateful as it sounded.

Ahiyababa left, promising to return quickly.

That left the lady and her houseboy alone again.

"I'm going to find Damkina and tell her what you've promised."

"As you like. Leave me now. Send another of my girls to me. I'm weary." She dropped into her chair and closed her eyes.

Asher found Damkina and explained to her that she was free—and free to leave Babylon in the morning.

She crushed his spirit by refusing, absolutely, his offer. Nothing he said could change her mind. He told her that he loved her and wanted her to have a different life. She replied that while she liked him very much, she did not love *him*. He promised a future of freedom far away from Babylon. She said it was too dangerous to try and escape. Along with Azarel, she would be caught. He'd be killed on the spot and she branded on the face to destroy her beauty. She preferred the pleasant life in her lady's estate to the hardships of the road. And where would she be going with a strange man? No, her life in Babylon suited her well.

Finally, Damkina kissed him on the mouth, told him that she would remember him and his lovemaking always, but now she had work to do. She prayed the gods would protect him and his brother, then gently pushed him away and disappeared into the slave women's quarters.

Chapter Twenty-Eight

Waiting was torture. Asher sought refuge in the sleeping room where he had made love to Damkina. He lay down, sat up. Stood up. Paced. Lay down again. Repeated his movements. All the while, he prayed: *YAH, free my brother. Spare his life. Hear my prayers.*

It seemed hours before he heard steps approaching the room. Damkina appeared. He wanted to throw himself at her feet, implore her one last time to change her mind, to risk everything and go with Azarel.

"My lady requires your presence," she told him. "Wash your face and straighten your hair. You look terrible." With that, she went away.

Asher made himself presentable. Iltani's rooms were guarded but he was admitted immediately. Inside, he found the woman in her usual seat. She had changed into a robe of shimmering silver.

"My brother?" Asher asked. "He's dead."

"I keep my promises," Iltani said. "Ahiyababa was just in time." She clapped her hands. In a few moments, the door opened and the steward entered, followed by Azarel.

With a cry, Asher flung himself into his brother's arms. Joy turned to horror when he realized how savagely Azarel had been beaten. One eye was swollen shut, his nose smashed, and his face covered with open cuts and blood. His tunic was smeared with more blood and filth. A wracking cough bent him over.

"What have they done to you?" Asher cried.

"Less than they would have if my steward hadn't arrived in time!" Iltani exclaimed. "A little while longer, Nebuchadrezzar's men would have finished him off."

"What did you do to get me free?" Azarel demanded.

His brother's words hurt. "I haven't told them anything if that's what you mean! We made a bargain. I saved her before, and now she's saved you."

"A life for a life!" Iltani exclaimed. She looked at Azarel with scorn. "But your brother asked even more: safe passage away from Babylon for you and the slave girl who's been sharing his bed. She wisely refused, so that leaves you free to go, with my guarantee of safe passage tomorrow at dawn. What do you think of that?"

"I think you're a fool," he muttered. "If you free me, I won't run away on some caravan. I'll stay here and continue fighting—one way or another."

"You don't mean that," Asher cried. "You're going to leave Babylon and not come back. You can't change the terms."

"I didn't agree to anything. That was *your* bargain."

"Please, My Lady. He's out of his head. He'll do what I tell him."

"Stop groveling!" Azarel cried. "You act like a dog begging scraps from its owner's table. You make me sick."

"That's no way to talk, filth!" Ahiyababa shouted. "Not with your life in My Lady's hands."

"My life is in YAH's hands," Azarel replied. "I'm not afraid."

"I keep my promises," Iltani said to Asher. "Your brother can't goad me into breaking them."

"He's been badly hurt," Asher replied. "He's raving."

Azarel grabbed him. "You're wrong, brother! *You're* the one who doesn't know what he's saying. Perhaps one day you will."

"Maybe, but now we have to go!"

"Yes, go!" Iltani cried. "Rejoin the rabble throwing away their lives—or come to your senses and go with that caravan—it doesn't matter. You know there's no escape." The lady clapped her hands and a burly slave appeared through the door. Ahiyababa had not been the only invisible attendant awaiting her orders. "Find Inatu and the two of you hurry to the trader Meri-Ra. The fighting is nearly over, so you will be safe. Take this just in case." She produced one of her seals. "Tell him I no longer require safe passage for anyone tomorrow morning. He will understand. Come back immediately and I'll reward you."

"Stop!" Azarel cried, seizing Asher by the throat.

The slave looked to his mistress for her orders.

"Wait," she told him. He stepped back against the far wall.

"I have a bargain of my own to make," Azarel said.

She laughed. "You have nothing with which to bargain, my friend."

"You're wrong! I have *his* sorry life, for what it may be worth to you."

The woman looked amused. "This becomes more interesting by the moment," she said. "What makes you think he means anything to me now? I've repaid him for saving me. Our business is done."

Asher tried to speak, to plead with Azarel to let him go. Azarel only tightened his hold.

"Let me hear your request," Iltani said.

"It's simple. Let us go, as you've agreed, and promise we won't be followed. Also, keep your first promise of two places in a caravan."

"You don't need them now! You just informed us you're staying in Babylon, and so is my slave."

"What I do with those two places in my business." Iltani said nothing, just looked at the brothers with an appraising eye. "Agree or I swear I'll finish him right now!"

Asher was on the verge of panic. With one mighty effort, he elbowed his brother in the belly. He grunted and released his grip. They stood side by side, gasping.

"I *should* order you both killed here and now," the lady told them. "But I don't like the idea of cleaning up so much blood."

"What about my terms?" Azarel persisted. "If you don't do as I say, my people will find out and your life will be worthless. I have many friends in this city."

"My life *is* worthless," she returned. "You can't frighten me with the prospect of death."

"It's *how* you would die that should concern you," he warned her. "We're experts in causing pain."

"Enough of this!" she cried. "Here's my answer: Despites your insults, I will let you go, as I've promised. You'll have your two places in the caravan. But it won't matter—two or twenty. Before you get far from the city, you'll be detained and thrown back into prison. Maybe your god can prevent that, but I doubt it. Be at the west gate of your village before sunup. Meri-Ra leads the caravan. He's promised safety for two days, but after that? Nebuchadrezzar's chariots are swift. Besides, who knows if Meri-Ra can be trusted? Egyptians have no honor!"

"Are we done?" Azarel asked.

"Let them go," Iltani told Ahiyababa. Just then, someone knocked. Invited to enter, another slave went to Iltani and spoke to her softly. She nodded and dismissed him.

"We've had a slight change of terms," she announced. "I've gotten word that Meri-Ra has room for only *one* extra person tomorrow. Do you still want that place?"

Azarel didn't hesitate. "We have no choice," he said. "We agree."

"A wise decision. Now get out, the two of you. I'm weary of your faces."

With that, they were escorted to the back gate. There Ahiyababa cursed them and spat at their feet. "May you both die quickly," he told them. "If I'd had my way, the dogs would already be gnawing your bones."

He disappeared behind the gate. They heard it lock, and that was the end.

* * *

Asher and Azarel came to the corner and found the alleyway deserted.

"Go home," Azarel told him. "Use the way I showed you. I'll come over the back wall tonight. Not a word except to the family. Let everyone else think I'm still in prison. Understand?"

Asher nodded. "But where are you going?"

"Where do you think? To rejoin the fight. We have to win!"

"No! Come home. We can hide you until tomorrow morning. Then you can join the caravan."

"I've already told you I'm staying here."

"You meant that? It wasn't just a threat?"

"Do you really think I'll give up and run away?"

"No, but I wish you would."

Azarel smiled. "Maybe you like me, after all!"

"I love you."

"And I love you, but I love our people's freedom. That's worth fighting for."

And dying for, Asher realized, but he couldn't say so.

"Then who *is* going tomorrow morning?" he asked.

Azarel gave him the "I can't believe you're so dimwitted" look that Asher had seen so often.

"Not me!" Asher exclaimed.

"Of course, you. Who else?"

"I can't leave the family. No!

"We'll figure it out later."

Asher felt his throat. It ached. "Would you really have strangled me?"

"I don't know."

"That means you would!"

"No one can tell what he might do. That's another thing we can talk about someday, sitting under our grapevines and watching our grandchildren play."

Asher couldn't imagine such a thing.

"Go now!" Azarel ordered him. "I'll see you tonight."

"What if something happens to you?"

"It won't! We're both lucky fellows, right?"

"I'll never see you again."

"Stop with that kind of nonsense. You'll see me in a few hours. I promise." Azarel tousled his hair. "You need a haircut."

"Now you tell me."

"One other thing, Asher. Thanks for saving my life. I owe you mine."

"No, you don't. Brothers don't carry that kind of debt."

Azarel grinned. "Maybe you're right."

He made his way down the alley, keeping to the near wall. At the corner, he peered around, saw it was safe, and disappeared.

Chapter Twenty-Nine

Asher sneaked his way through the city, frightened of being stopped and questioned. He felt Iltani's seal in his pocket, grateful he still had it and hopeful he wouldn't have to use it. At the garden he slipped into the pipe and crawled his way to the canal. People were up and about, and he had to wait, hidden among the reeds, until there was no one to see him paddle across. His village was mostly deserted, but at a corner he encountered two Babylonian soldiers.

"What are you doing out?" one challenged. "Don't you know that all you dogs are under orders to get to your kennels and stay there? What have you been up to—swimming?"

They both laughed. Asher made a feeble excuse, something about enjoying too much wine and falling into the canal. The guards let him go with a stiff warning about what would happen if he were caught again. Asher ran to his street, stopped at the corner, glanced both ways for more soldiers on patrol, and went to his house when he saw that the street was empty.

Inside, he delivered the news that Azarel was safe. His father insisted the entire family go into the courtyard so that Asher could share his story. He made an effort to tell everything, but he had to fight to keep from breaking down. He did, finally, when Elisheva asked him how he'd gotten the bruises on his neck.

Asher came to the end of his account, explaining the bargain he'd made with Iltani, and how she'd arranged safe passage for one person—Azarel, of course--the next morning. He didn't say anything about Azarel's vow to stay in Babylon or to send himself in his place. When he came home, the family would persuade him to change his mind.

So Asher hoped.

Benaiah did not speak right away when Asher finished his story. Then he addressed himself to his brother. "Do you believe the woman was telling the truth—about safe passage for Azarel?"

"Who can tell?"

"You're a prophet!" Benaiah exclaimed. "Ask YAH for an answer."

"I'm not a fortune teller," Ezekiel replied.

"Can't you at least ask? The priests used to consult YAH about what was going to happen, and then they'd cast lots for an answer."

"All that happened long ago."

"You won't do me this one thing," Benaiah said bitterly. "I need to know my son will be safe."

"None of us are safe," Ezekiel reminded him.

"All we can do is wait," Asher said. "At least we can be prepared. We should gather up his clothes, food—everything he'll need."

"Asher's right," Elisheva added. "We have to do what we can and pray that woman told the truth."

Benaiah sighed. "Very well. If he makes it home tonight, we'll be ready. But right now, Asher, you need to get washed up. This is the second time today you've come home covered in green slime!"

* * *

As it turned out, there wasn't much to get ready—a cloak, a blanket. Like the rest of them, Azarel owned few clothes. What food they had in the house, they packed. The market was closed, and they weren't supposed to be on the streets at all, but Benaiah made stealthy visits to neighbors and returned with dates, rounds of bread, and three small jars of cooked millet. He produced some coins as well, but he refused to say what he had sold in exchange. Nor would he share what lies he'd invented to explain what he was doing.

Asher spent the afternoon tortured by his thoughts and feelings. One moment he was overcome with grief. That gave way to rage. That, to worry. Then he wallowed in guilt. Much of what had happened *was* his fault, and his alone. He tried to pray, imploring YAH for forgiveness, but as usual, there was no response.

Until . . .

At dusk, Elisheva and Tirzah called the men for supper. Asher left his room and started for the courtyard, but suddenly bursts of shimmering light circled the edges of his eyesight. "Uncle Ezekiel!" he cried. "It's happening."

His uncle appeared. "What is it?" he asked. Then, "Oh, Asher! Now, of all times?"

"We have to go to the place of seeing," Asher urged.

"How can we? No one is supposed to be on the streets."

"YAH will guide us. We have to go. *I* must."

Ezekiel disappeared but returned in a moment. "Your father forbids you to leave the house."

"Then my father is against YAH. Please, come with me!" The ring of radiant light grew stronger.

"All right," Ezekiel agreed.

Benaiah met them at the door. "You're not leaving," he informed them. "I forbid it."

"That doesn't matter," Asher told him.

"Now I have no authority in my own house? Over my own son? I'm just trying to protect you! You'll be caught and taken to prison."

"We won't. YAH will keep us safe. We'll be back before Azarel gets here."

"And how do you know that?"

"Father, I *have* to go. Please don't try and stop me. I saved Azarel's life today. You owe me this."

"Owe you? After all the harm you've done?"

"Move aside, brother," Ezekiel said. Still, Benaiah didn't budge. "*Now!*"

Benaiah glared at them, then gave it up.

The street was deserted, as was the path along the canal.

"Hurry," Asher said. "It's coming closer and closer."

"The throne of YAH?" Ezekiel asked.

"Hurry," is all Asher could manage.

They ran through the grove of Ishtar. Asher would never forget the first time he and Ezekiel went through it together. That seemed a long time ago. Then, he was still a child. Not anymore.

At the place of seeing, Asher crashed into some kind of invisible wall. The force knocked him backwards onto the ground. Next to him, his uncle fell down, too.

"Take my hand!" he shouted at Ezekiel. He did, and then the glory of YAH, a blaze of fire, encircled them.

They were snatched from the ground and carried, as on eagles' wings, north along the river. On both sides, desert. The only green, living things clung to the banks of the Euphrates, bringer of the water of life. Then the Spirit of YAH swooped west over the desert. Down it hurtled, so fast that Asher feared he and Ezekiel would be dashed to pieces when they struck the earth. But the Spirit slowed its descent and set them down so gently that they landed on their feet.

All around them the land was barren. Rocky outcroppings broke through the sand. Above, the sky was as gray as the dust under their feet. As Asher stepped forward, he realized his uncle still had his hand.

They trudged through this dead land, void of any sign of life. Not a bird in the sky, not a leaf of grass, not a lizard scurrying along the sand, not a grasshopper on the wing.

Then it appeared—a valley so wide and long that it seemed to have no boundaries. They stood at the top of a sheer cliff; another step forward would plunge them to their deaths on jagged boulders far below.

Asher gasped when he realized what he and Ezekiel were looking at: the valley was overflowing with bones--the bones of human beings like themselves.

Piles of bones.

Hills of bones.

Mountains of bones.

The bones, perhaps, of all Israelites who had ever lived.

And they were very dry. Not a scrap of flesh clung to any of them. Not a wisp of hair remained on a weathered skull. Not a sinew nor a tendon or a bit of skin.

Asher felt the vomit rise in his throat, and his stomach heaved, eager to empty itself. All that came up was a mouthful of bile.

He looked at his uncle and saw scrawled on his face the same bewildered horror he himself was feeling. "Uncle?" he managed to whisper, "where are we?"

Ezekiel tried to form words, but there was no sound.

Then the Spirit of YAH took them by their hands and carried them down the cliff face and dropped them in among the bones. Skeletons of warriors and of poets. Skeletons of mothers and small children. Of aged grandparents and babes newly thrust from the womb.

The Spirit stopped them and showed them three skeletons lying together. Two were locked in embrace; the third, nearby, still raised bony hands up in front of her, as if to ward off attack.

Asher's grandmother and grandfather.

His mother.

Then the Spirit led them to another skeleton, this one lying alone, the skull facing up into the sky, grinning.

Josiah.

Asher fell to his knees, overcome. Why had YAH brought him to this valley of death?

Then from somewhere high above came the voice, the one Asher recognized as the voice of YAH, the voice containing within it all life, all animal sounds, all human speech, all the tongues of the living and the dead: "Son of man," it demanded. "Can these bones live?"

Asher looked to Ezekiel to see what he would reply. But his uncle seemed not to have heard anything.

Then he realized the truth of the unthinkable: YAH was addressing *him*, and him alone.

"Can these bones live?"

"Ask my uncle."

His words sounded small and foolish even as he uttered them.

"Can these bones live?" the voice repeated.

There was nothing for it: he had to answer. "O Lord YAH, you know."

"Prophesy over these bones, and say to them, 'This is what the Lord YAH says: Look and see! I will breathe my breath into you, and you will live. I will put sinews on you, and muscles shall again cover your bones, and skin cover your muscles. I will put hairs onto your heads, and eyes in their sockets, and lips over your teeth. I will put my Spirit into you, and you shall live.'"

Ezekiel knelt beside him, then seized a bleached thigh bone. He cradled it close to his chest, crooning a broken lullaby.

Asher ignored the chaos of clamoring voices in his head and did as he was commanded: "O bones, hear the word of YAH. He will put his Spirit into you, and you shall live. Rise up! Live! O dry bones, hear the word of YAH!"

At first, nothing. Then a sigh. A whisper. A knocking. A clicking like that of dice against a wall. Whirring like that of summer locusts in swarm.

Then a rattling like that of seeds shaken in dried gourds, drumming the beat to dances at wedding feasts.

The bones began to move, prodded by invisible hands.

They knit together. Inner organs appeared, then the attaching sinews. Then muscles, then skin. Hair, eyes, tongues, fingernails.

They rose up, a mighty army of the slain. But there was yet no life in them, no breath.

"Prophesy to the breath," the Spirit commanded Asher. "Prophesy and say to it: 'Thus says the Lord YAH: Come from the four winds, O breath, and breathe on these slain that they may live.'"

Asher obeyed. "Come forth, O breath, and breathe life into these dry bones, that they may live."

The bone heard. Asher and Ezekiel watched, astounded, as the dead came to life. They stretched their arms, raised their faces to the sky. Naked, they rose up, unashamed. Asher could see no sign of old age among them. None was crippled. None had lost a leg or an arm. None was blind. All were full of youth, of strength, of life beyond anything Asher had ever imagined.

They stood all around him and Ezekiel, an exceedingly great army.

Then the Spirit spoke to Asher again. The moment it began, he glanced toward his uncle, and he realized immediately that Ezekiel now heard the same voice and would receive the same message:

"Sons of man, these bones are the whole house of Israel. Behold, they say 'Our bones are dried up, and our hope is lost, we are indeed cut off.' Therefore, prophesy and say to them, 'Thus says the Lord YAH: 'Behold, I will open your graves and raise you from your graves, O my people. And I will bring you into the land of Israel. And you shall know that I am the Lord, when I open your graves and raise you from your graves, O my people. And I will put my Spirit within you, and you shall live, and I will place you in your own land. Then you shall know that I am the Lord; I have spoken, and I will do it, declares the Lord.'"

Asher bowed his head to the earth. His heart jumped within him. Astonishment, delight, awe—these filled him. He looked toward his uncle, who stood gazing into the sky, an expression of bliss on his face unlike anything Asher had ever seen on another human being.

Asher stood. He threw himself into Ezekiel's arms, and the two men clung to each other, sobbing for joy.

They held one other a long time. Then they felt themselves snatched up from the ground. Looking down, they were granted a vision of the armies of YAH, his people returned to life from the valley of hopeless despair.

One thing was certain: despite whatever awaited them back in their village on the outskirts of Babylon, there was hope.

* * *

The next thing Asher knew, he and Ezekiel were sitting on the ground in the field next to their place of seeing. Without a word, they turned their steps toward home. There, things were the same as before. Benaiah paced like a caged lion. The women put finishing touches on the pack they had prepared for Azarel. Now there was nothing more to do except wait. As they did, their evening meal grew cold.

They kept vigil in the courtyard. Long after it was dark, they heard something above them, and Azarel came down the steps from the roof terrace. He shushed their cries of joy and urged them to go indoors. Then he was greeted properly, with hugs, tears, and prayers of thanks for his safety. He accepted them all.

"I have news," he began. "Bad news. Our forces are defeated and Nebuchadrezzar still sits on his throne. Many of my friends are dead, and many sit in prison, scheduled to be executed tomorrow. King Jeconiah himself has been arrested, accused of being part of the plot."

He sighed. "There is some good news, though. Our queen has given birth—to a son! The rightful line of David has an heir!"

"Who cares now?" Benaiah said. "It's you I'm worried about. You can't wait until morning to try and escape. They'll start searching the village at dawn. I don't trust a thing that woman promised you. Who knows if there even is a caravan? My guess is that she lied to you, hoping to catch you in a trap."

"We've prepared everything," Elisheva added. "Food, clothes, water, even some money."

He smiled at her. "Thank you, but I'm staying. I already told you that, Asher."

"I know you did, but I thought you just said it because you were so angry."

"Asher's right," Benaiah added. "I'm telling you, son, you have to leave. They'll find you and kill you!"

"No, they won't. My place is here, among our people."

"Where will you hide?" Tirzah asked. "The village is small."

He smiled again. "You didn't hear me coming just now, did you?"

"Not until there was a noise on the stairs."

"I made it on purpose so I wouldn't startle you. I could have dropped into the courtyard and robbed you all before you ever knew what was happening. Yes, the village is small, but there are hiding places, secret passages, safe houses that you don't know about. Few people do, and they are all sworn to secrecy."

"You're not thinking straight," Benaiah insisted. "It's noble to want to stay, but the revolt failed. Now Nebuchadrezzar will take his revenge."

"He can do what he likes. My place is here."

No one had another argument. Azarel meant what he said.

Benaiah sighed. "You always were stubborn."

"I learned it from you."

"Probably so. But this is one time I'm proud you are."

"So do we abandon the chance of a safe place in that caravan, assuming the lady's promises are good?" Benaiah asked. "Shouldn't one of us take it?"

"We don't even know where it's going," Azarel pointed out. "What did you have in mind, Asher?"

"I didn't think about it much. I just told Iltani to the north."

"Haran?"

"Anywhere far from here."

"*I* can't go," Benaiah began. "Who would run the shop? What about you, Ezekiel?"

"And leave Elisheva? Why would you suggest that? Besides, even if I were unmarried, YAH has shown me that my place is here, too."

"I'll go," Tirzah volunteered.

Ezekiel looked at her lovingly. "You would, wouldn't you?"

"I hate it here," she said.

"Do you know what could happen to you on a caravan without someone to protect you?" Azarel asked her.

"I'd be on the lead camel before the first day was done," she replied confidently. "No man is going to mess with me."

"We believe you," her father said. "But it's too risky. You must realize that."

Tirzah looked disappointed, but she nodded.

"I guess that leaves me," Asher said quietly. He'd known from the beginning how it would be, and why it had to be that way.

"Alone?" Benaiah asked.

"I can take care of myself."

"He's right," Ezekiel added. "He's as much a man as you are, Benaiah. Or you, Azarel. Or—myself. Trust me, I know."

"I won't have it!" Benaiah cried. "I can't stand any more losses."

"He *has* to go," Ezekiel said. "He's received a vision from YAH—one that he's been commanded to proclaim to our people."

"In Haran?" Benaiah asked.

"No, Father," Asher said softly. "You know where."

"In Jerusalem."

"YAH has commanded me to speak to our people here," Ezekiel said. "Now I see that Asher has the same charge to our sisters and brothers back home. Perhaps it's still not too late for them to repent."

Elisheva began to weep.

Asher took her hand. "You've always been good to me. Pray to YAH, but don't worry about me. We'll see each other again one day."

Now Tirzah was crying, too, and so was Benaiah, and even Azarel. Asher was given the chance to do something he'd never done before: comfort everyone in his family.

Azarel told them he had to leave in case enemy soldiers came looking for him but would keep in touch when he was able. Then he embraced Asher, tore himself away, climbed back onto the roof and jumped down. Then he was gone.

For a while, the family sat in the darkness, too overcome to speak. Finally, Elisheva said they had to get Asher ready to leave, so they gathered his clothing and the supplies they had intended for Azarel. Then they tried to sleep, but it was no good. Asher lay in darkness, missing the sounds of his brother's snoring, something he thought could never happen. He could hear the rest of the family turning on their beds.

The night dragged to its end.

At dawn, Asher dressed, shouldered his pack, and said his farewells. He insisted on going by himself, a decision that had tormented him for hours. He longed to have everyone with him, but it was too risky. His father and uncle blessed him. Everyone cried again, Benaiah more bitterly than anyone else.

He opened the door—perhaps for the last time—and peered into the darkness. Not a sound, not a movement anywhere.

Then he was off. Side streets and alleys led him toward the gate. Then a terrible thought struck him: what if it were guarded? Why had no one thought of that? The Babylonian soldier had told him the village was locked down tight, no one to go in or out. In the confusion since yesterday, he'd forgotten that. If there were guards, they would not let him through. Then he remembered Iltani's seal. Did he still have it? Yes, in the pocket of his other tunic. He found it and eased his way to the gate.

No guards.

And the gate was open.

Iltani had kept her word.

The eastern sky was just getting light. No one appeared to question or stop him as he walked through the gate. Sure enough, on the other side, a caravan had formed: camels and donkeys loaded with trade goods. There were men and women, too, each carrying a pack.

He found Meri-Ra, the leader, who demanded that he prove his identity. One look at Iltani's seal satisfied the Egyptian. "You have a powerful friend," the man told Asher. "And a rich one."

"She was always generous with me." As he spoke those words, he realized that in some ways, they were true.

"It's time to leave," Meri-Ra told him. "Follow me."

When Meri-ra turned away, Asher dropped the Babylonian seal in the dirt and crushed it to powder. He wouldn't need it anymore.

The Egyptian must have heard something. "Hey, you," he called to Asher. "Look behind you. I think you've got a farewell party."

Sure enough, his father and uncle were coming toward him. He tried to hold back the sob rising from his belly, but nothing could keep it down.

"We had to bless him one more time," Ezekiel explained to Meri-ra.

They prayed the protection of YAH over him. Promised they'd see him again. Made him promise to send word when he could. Smiled through tears.

"We're leaving," Meri-Ra said impatiently.

"Shalom," Ezekiel said. "Until we meet again."

"Shalom. Blessing and peace to you."

"Shalom, my son," Benaiah said.

"And to you, Father."

"I love you, Asher, and I am proud of you. Go now. We will see you again one day. I promise."

"I know. Goodbye."

He walked to the end of the caravan. From his place by the lead camel, Meri-ra looked back to see that all was in order. Then they started: camels, donkeys, men, women, children--about thirty people in all. When Asher turned around, his father and uncle waved. The next time, they were gone.

Asher set his face toward the north; he would not look back again. Just ahead of him walked a young man who seemed to be about his age, but it was hard to tell in the half-light of dawn. Asher came up beside him. "I'm Asher," he said.

"Jonathan," the other replied, giving him a friendly smile. Then he glanced away.

Asher knew that reaction well. "My eyes, right?"

"I'm sorry. It's a surprise, that's all."

"It's all right," Asher assured him. "I'm used to it. Once, it bothered me, but now—I'm proud to look this way."

"That's good," Jonathan said. "You're an Israelite? Your accent—"

"Yes. And you?"

"The same."

"How are you in the caravan?" Asher asked. "We Israelites need special permission to leave Babylon. Especially now, since the fighting . . ."

"Money makes anything possible," Jonathan declared.

Asher knew that well.

"What about you? How did *you* get here? Jonathan asked.

"It's a long story," Asher assured him.

"Then we'll have something to talk about! I like hearing people's stories. Where are you headed?"

"Haran."

"No further?"

"Then Jerusalem."

"Jerusalem? Why go there?"

Asher stood taller despite the weight of all he carried. He fixed his eyes—one brown, one blue—on the road ahead.

"Because I am a prophet of YAH."

Afterword

598/7 BCE In December, 598, Babylon marches on Jerusalem. The king, Jehoiakim, dies that same month, perhaps by assassination. When the Babylonians take the city three months later, Jehoiakim's eighteen-year-old brother, Jehoiachin (also known as Jeconiah), becomes king. He is exiled to Babylon, along with his mother Queen Nehushta, high court officials, priests, other leading citizens, and their families—a possible total of somewhere between 8 and 10,000 people. Jehoiachin's uncle, Zedekiah, is appointed king in Jerusalem by the conquering Babylonians.

595/4 A rebellion flares in Babylon, apparently involving elements of the army and some disaffected Jews. It is soon put down. Suspected of assisting in the rebellion, Jehoiachin is imprisoned and remains incarcerated until the end of Nebuchadrezzar's reign. He probably dies in Babylon.

587/6 In January 588, Babylon again marches against Jerusalem. The city falls in July 586. Its walls are destroyed and the temple is burned. King Zedekiah is forced to witness the execution of his sons before being blinded and taken in chains to Babylon. More citizens accompany him. The state of Judah is ended forever.

571 Last recorded prophecy of Ezekiel.

c. 570 Death of Ezekiel in Babylon.

562 In October, Nebuchadrezzar II dies, age 80. He is Babylon's greatest king and one of the foremost monarchs of the Ancient Near East.

539 In October, Cobryas, a general of Cyrus, King of Persia, takes Babylon without a fight. The neo-Babylonian empires collapses. Power in the region shifts to the Persians.

538 Cyrus of Persia issues his famous edict allowing Jews to return to Palestine and re-establish their traditional worship.

c. 515 The rebuilt temple in Jerusalem is dedicated.

Asher's Eye is a work of imagination, but it is grounded in knowledge of the Ancient Near East and of the Hebrew Bible. Among its characters the following are historical figures: Jehoiakim, Jehoiachin, Queen Nehushta, Zedekiah, Jeremiah, and Ezekiel. All the others, including Asher, Benaiah, Azarel, Tirzah, Elisheva, Josiah, and the Lady Iltani, are fictional.

The visions and prophetic actions of Ezekiel dramatized in this novel are all recorded in the Book of Ezekiel in the Hebrew Bible.

www.ingramcontent.com/pod-product-compliance
Lightning Source LLC
Chambersburg PA
CBHW051816020726
47502CB00005B/1487

* 9 7 8 1 6 6 6 7 3 7 1 2 7 *